THE DECISION THEY MADE

MARIA P FRINO

Maria P Frino

This is a work of fiction.

Title: The Decision They Made – a novel

Author: Maria P. Frino

Cover Design: Mark Drolc - http://onthemarkdesign.com.au/

Print Cover Design: Andrè Frino

Visit the author's website at https://mariapfrino.wixsite.com/authorwebsite

All inquiries should be made to the author - mariapfrino@gmail.com

❀ Created with Vellum

For my parents
You taught me to dream big

I have just finished your book and wanted to let you know that I loved it. The characters and story were well written and made me really feel for all they were going through. Although the subjects tackled in the book were hard, it was still an enjoyable read, with me staying up way too late to read just another chapter!

Well done on a fantastic debut novel and I look forward to reading more of your work.

I have tried to add a review on Amazon but it won't let me?

Regards Alison White,

voraciousreadersonly.com

Review - The Decision they Made, by Maria P Frino

War is terrible; so is abuse within a family. Decisions taken under the duress of such circumstances can be regretted for generations.

Frino examines the original crucial decision made by two sisters and explores the resulting torment that thereafter occupies the centre of their lives. They have moved on, lived lives and raised families; but in so doing, they have created new barriers between them. Can they protect those they love and still be reunited?

The writer explores the basis of the original decisions and the intense loyalty to family that both separates the sisters and gravitationally pulls them together.

The Decision They Made, is far more than a romance It is an examination of a very different kind of courage.

Ross Venner via email

Dear Maria Frino,

Thank you for letting me review your wonderful book. I love the twist and turns of the story of two people come together though familial connections and the dark secret that is revealed. The story will hold your attention to the very end.

Sincerely yours Tabitha Liston

via email

Hi Maria

I have nearly finished reading the book and all i can say is wow!!

What an incredible piece of writing, i really am enjoying your writing style, the characters are ablaze with personality and as a reader I can wholly relate to their predicament.

Please keep writing and I look forward to reading more.
Kind Regards Kim Dowman
via email

Hi Maria,

I finished your book. It was good, I couldn't put it away wanting to know what was happening next.

Regards Maria Antunez
via text message

The Decision They Made

Hi Maria,

The times in which the events in the book took place, makes the story quite plausible. The research, the sequence of interspersing the various events, both cleverly executed. The story captivated the imagination and was difficult to put down.

Once again, well done,
Aldo Barnaba
via email

Hi Maria,

Loving your book Maria P Frino. Half way through it. I enjoy your writing style, easy to read and very relatable. Looking forward to reading more.

Keep writing,
Maria Dal Cin
via text message

Prologue

Naples

1935

Amelia covers her sister's mouth with one hand. She presses her other index finger to her own lips. Quiet. They must stay quiet. Simona's eyes widen, the whites shining in the dim light. Amelia squeezes her tighter. If they can just hold on a little longer everything will be alright.

Stifling dampness envelopes them, the air is limp with it. The smell of stale wine and old cheese makes Amelia want to heave every time they escape to hide down here. Something tells her this smell will stay with her for the rest of her life.

It is pitch black with only the light of the small torch she always has handy dimly piercing the stillness. Be still, we have to be still. Her heart pounds, her face wet with sweat. Perspiration drips from her armpits. Her limbs stiffen.

Simona whimpers. Amelia whispers, "Be quiet, be still. I'm here with you." Simona listens. She always does. Adrenaline pumps through Amelia's veins, she is determined to keep them both safe.

They stay hunched on the cold cobbled stones for what seems like hours. Simona has fallen asleep in Amelia's arms. Her lithe little body is now a dead weight, but it does not bother her. She is strong. She has to be for the two of them to be safe. She allows her shoulders to droop, relaxing a little. She has to focus and stay calm.

Soon her arms ache with Simona's weight, so she rests her on the old blanket. There is many a time they have both slept down here, but not today. Amelia needs to check. She unfurls her cramped limbs and rises from where they are hiding. Walking tentatively up the two worn steps, she pushes the basement door ajar. There is hushed silence. Only the echo of the empty laneway.

She needs to be sure. She steps out of the basement leaving Simona. She has to hurry; her sister may wake before she returns. Reaching their front door, her palm is clammy against the doorknob. She draws in a ragged breath. Swallowing her nerves, she inches the door open and peers through the crack. The kitchen sink is cluttered with dirty dishes. The only sound is water dripping to the floor. Her heart thumps against her ribs as she strains to listen. Nothing. No other sound. He has gone.

She turns and rushes back down to the basement. Simona is still asleep where she left her. Asleep and peaceful. She wakes her and immediately she starts crying. Amelia wraps her arms around her, cradles her. Everything is fine for now. He has gone. She pushes Simona's fringe out of her eyes, gently stroking her face. Waiting for her to calm.

Eventually her body softens. The sobs subside. She angles her pale face up towards Amelia. They both nod, placing their foreheads together. Simona's smile is melancholy. They are ready to leave once more.

She checks. There is no one in the lane. No one to ask questions and pry into their business.

Hand-in-hand they walk up the stairs into their home. Scraps of food litter the bench. He has eaten most of the food Amelia prepared earlier. But it doesn't matter, they are safe. She will scramble something together for them with what he left. Keeping them safe is her priority and once again she has managed to protect her little sister.

Chapter One

LARISSA

1980

She is poised on the sandstone stoop. Her clasped hand is about to knock when she hears it. Her grandmother is screaming at someone. But who? She lives alone.

"No, I told you before and I am telling you again. Leave things as they are, no good will come out of this if we speak up now."

The collision of a stamping foot and glass shattering hits her ears. Panicked Larissa knocks hard on the front door. Has her grandmother hurt herself? Is someone attacking her? Her knuckles hurt as she knocks harder.

Finally, her grandmother opens the door, her face flushed. "Bella mia. What a surprise, why didn't you tell me you were coming to Naples? Come in, come in, it's cold out there." Simona places her hand on Larissa's shoulder as she bends to kiss her grandmother's cheeks.

The apartment is just as chilled as outside, so she leaves her coat on. "Nonna, are you alright? I heard you screaming and then did something break? There was a loud crash."

"Oh, that was the television you heard. I was watching a movie and when I got out of my chair, I knocked my water glass on the floor."

Simona blurts this out a little too quickly. Larissa is uneasy while she takes in the scene, which right now is silent. The television sits mute in the corner and there are large shards of glass near the fireplace. Larissa is not convinced, but what reason does Simona have to lie? Watching her grandmother heading back to her chair, Larissa sees she hasn't injured herself. Thankfully.

"Nonna, sit down before you step on any of the glass. Let me clean this up." She hands her grandmother the cane resting against the lounge. Simona eases herself into the heirloom rocking chair, taking care not to aggravate her recent injuries.

The small antique coffee table next to her chair has her reading glasses, a book and a glass of water on it. Whatever had shattered on the floor was not a drinking glass. "You rest here while I get the dustpan. With your arm in a sling and your injured knee, you have to be more careful."

Larissa opens the laundry cupboard, collecting the things she needs. The fireplace has no ash, the timbers are dry and ready to be lit. She shivers as she bends down to light the firelighters. They crackle once the timbers redden with flame. The curtains are drawn, making the room dark. She pulls them back to allow the sun to stream in, which makes the shattered glass on the floor shimmer with light and colour.

"How pretty," says Simona, "it looks like a rainbow."

Larissa doesn't speak, she concentrates on cleaning before anything else can harm her grandmother. Going by the thickness of the glass makes it obvious it was a vase that had broken. The one that was always on the mantle.

Once the floor is free of glass, she takes off her coat and makes herself comfortable next to Simona, taking her grandmother's right hand in her own. She strokes it wondering why she refuses to have someone come and help. After she fell breaking her left arm and injuring her left knee a few weeks ago, Larissa's mother, Gee, came to stay. She wanted to help her mother, but Simona sent her back to Rome after only three days.

"We worry about you living here all by yourself, Nonna. Gee wanted to stay longer so she could help but you sent her home."

"I'm fine. I've looked after myself all these years since your grandfather died. Tell your mother to stop worrying. She sent you here, didn't she?" Simona's finger is wagging menacingly towards her.

Does her grandmother really think Gee put her up to this? The way Larissa sees things, a granddaughter visiting her grandmother is not an unusual event. "No, she only told me of your accident yesterday. I'm here doing a story for the show. My crew and I are staying at the Best Western in Pozzuoli for the next week. Now, will I make us some coffee?" she asks, heading to the kitchen without waiting for an answer.

Her grandmother seems out of sorts. Uncomfortable shudders rip through her. Simona has never made her feel unwelcome, but right now she is feeling some strange vibes. It's almost as if Larissa visiting has unsettled her. This is strange behaviour from her loving grandmother.

What would have happened if she had not made this impromptu visit? Her grandmother would have sat here on her own in this dark, cold apartment. This is just not good enough; she has to accept help whether she likes it or not. At least while her arm and knee heal.

Larissa arranges coffee and biscuits onto the smaller coffee table, which she had placed in front of Simona. Adding three heaped teaspoons of sugar into her grandmother's cup, she hands it to her.

"Now tell me, what's going on in your life?" she says savouring her coffee from her favourite cup, an heirloom from her own mother.

There are many heirlooms in this apartment. This porcelain china espresso set with gold etched leaves and trims is so precious, only two cups have been used. The one Simona is holding and another locked behind a glass cabinet. The cup Larissa's great-grandmother used takes pride of place in the cabinet, as will Simona's. The set is to be handed down again one day. This is her grandmother's wish; a wish Larissa has known since she was a child.

The strange vibes Simona was giving out have disappeared, this is the grandmother she knows. Before her fall, she was driving and capable of looking after herself. The fall, as she attempted to walk up her ancient sandstone basement steps holding firewood, left her bruised and disorientated. And with an arm broken in two places and a swollen, bruised knee. It will be some time before she is her independent self again.

Simona has been widowed since the late 1960s. Her husband, Marco, died of a brain aneurysm on their twenty-fourth wedding anniversary. She has lived alone since. Always maintaining she is never lonely, her face beams with a smile whenever someone visits. Larissa remembers little of her grandfather, he was away working in Germany most of the time.

Now, as Simona sits in her chair with the walking stick leaning next to her, she seems older. At the time of this accident a neighbour was around to help when she fell. What if something happens again and no one is around to help?

Shivers run down Larissa's spine. Not wanting to think about this right now, she puts these awful thoughts aside. Brightening up, she adopts her best chatty voice to speak with her grandmother. There is no point her knowing how worried Larissa is about her. It won't change the situation.

Telling her how work is keeping her busy, she knows her grandmother is not interested in her day-to-day stuff. All she wants to know is whether she is dating. Especially if a serious relationship is on the horizon.

Averting their conversation away from this question in particular, she talks about her friends and what is happening with everyone at the office. Simona cocks her head towards her. She is genuinely interested. It is not often they are together, just the two of them. She is now animated, asking more questions. Larissa sighs, just as she was relaxing into their conversation, a slight pang of guilt rears its head. She can go months without even calling her grandmother. Despite the mood Simona was in when she first arrived, she should make more of an effort. Gee worries about Simona spending too much time alone, and seeing her injured like this, Larissa knows why Gee is concerned.

"You must tell Gee to stop worrying. I'm happy being on my

own. I adore your mother, but there are times when she refuses to see my point of view. We're better seeing each other in small doses."

Larissa doesn't answer because she is stuck in the middle. Loving her mother and grandmother equally, they are both very different people. She always treads carefully when they complain about each other.

Simona yawns, and Larissa. is surprised to see they have been talking for three hours. "I'll get going, Nonna," she says as Simona nods.

She yawns involuntarily. "Oh, excuse me. These painkillers take their toll. Must you go already?"

"Unfortunately, yes. My crew will have set up by now, I'm meeting them in an hour. I'll come over again before I leave Naples."

Her grandmother nods graciously, "I'll look forward to you visiting again."

After kissing her goodbye, Larissa checks the windows and the front door, making sure they are locked as she leaves. Then she knocks on the door of her grandmother's neighbour, "Sorry to bother you, Laura."

"It's not a bother at all, you know I'm here to help. I was away when Gee was here, so I didn't have a chance to discuss Simona's attitude with her."

Laura invites her into the kitchen, and she takes a seat at the bench. Larissa listens as Laura tells her how she has heard her grandmother screaming at different times of the day and night.

"Oh really? I heard her screaming when I arrived today. She said what I heard was a movie she was watching on TV."

"Hmm, she told me the same thing. Someone is phoning her. I think she's screaming at whoever it is calling."

"When I arrived, she was cagey and dismissed my questions. I was the butt of that attitude you mentioned. We'll have to be careful. Whatever is going on, she wants us all to butt out."

Laura nods in agreement saying, "I'll keep an eye on her and let you know if I hear her screaming again."

"I'd appreciate that, thanks," Larissa says as she stands to leave, "Gee and I are glad you're here to help, it certainly eases our minds."

"Don't mention it," Laura says as she sees her to the door.

Larissa returns to the hotel and heads straight for the mini bar. Unscrewing the cap on one of the bottles, she gulps the scotch. Holding the bottle with two fingers, she thinks how these tiny bottles are so unsatisfying.

Collapsing on the bed, she places a call to her mother. Whilst fiddling with the phone cord, she tells Gee how Laura has heard Simona screaming as well, "She was screaming at the top of her lungs! It was something about not saying anything to anyone. I've never heard her scream like a banshee. She's raised her voice occasionally but not to this extent."

Gee answers in a distressed tone; she too has been worried.

Larissa stops fiddling with the phone cord, sitting upright, "So, you've heard her this angry recently too? Do you have any idea who she's arguing with?"

"I know as much as you do." Her mother's tone is mournful.

"I'm worried for her, Gee. She's all alone. And now with the broken arm and sore knee, she really needs someone there every day. The place was dark and damp when I walked in. It was lucky I dropped in to visit and warmed the place for her. Late November and no fire lit yet?"

Gee explains Simona has a habit of not warming the apartment. The thought of carrying firewood from the basement annoys her. Especially more so now after the accident.

"Well, I'm sure there's someone local who can help her with chores like that? Laura's husband for instance? Oh, and the broken glass was the vase. You know the one? The green-speckled Murano glass one on the mantle. Doesn't it have something to do with her sister, Amelia? I'm telling you something isn't right. Why would she break something so precious to her?"

Gee is surprised to hear about the vase. Her mother's heirlooms are her favourite things, and this vase was a memory of her older sister, someone she has never stopped loving even though she passed years ago.

Larissa cautions her mother to be careful when questioning Simona. Their relationship is already volatile. They can go for weeks without talking to each other. These are the times Larissa has to step in to calm them both. It isn't easy trying to get them to reconcile because each believes they are right.

"She told me she broke a glass. Why did she lie? I knew instantly when I saw the thick shards it wasn't a glass that had broken. I don't understand, she loved that vase." They continue talking and Larissa listens to her mother's frustrations with trying to help. Laura is a good neighbour and helps out when she can, but Simona does not want her help either. Always a strong, independent woman, she is used to fending for herself. This Larissa already knows. But something about Simona's shrill scream this morning keeps troubling her.

"Gee, I have to go. We're having a meeting about tomorrow's filming. I know you're worried, I am too. Between us we'll resolve this. I'll call you when I'm back home in Rome." Replacing the receiver, she pushes herself off the bed with a groan. There is something behind Simona's unusual behaviour and she is determined to find out what it is. For now, it's time to go to meet with her crew.

In the bathroom she turns on the shower taps. No hot water! Another cold shower in another crap business hotel.

Chapter Two

ALEXEY

1980

Alexey is watching out the open window, waiting for him. A musty smell wafts in from the surrounding damp forest. His grandfather is struggling to get out of the car. He knows not to go and offer help. He looks away.

The room is devoid of furniture except for two wooden chairs that are older than Vladimir. He had been summoned here, asked to be on time and to make sure he came alone. He had arrived early on this crisp, autumn morning knowing his grandfather doesn't respect tardiness.

His ailing grandfather hobbles into the room. With his walking stick wobbling in front of him, each step is carefully placed. Staunch and proud Vladimir never accepts help no matter how much he is suffering. He wants his dignity intact. In fact, he demands it. The Dubrovnik family is known for their strength, no matter what life throws at them. Alexey watches as he falters trying to make himself comfortable. He is in pain but doesn't complain. His drooped posture is enough for Alexey to know.

Vladimir opens his mouth about to speak but a cough wracks his chest. The acrid smell of smoker's breath attacks Alexey's nose. His grandfather still has not given up smoking. He remembers the many stories Vladimir has regaled of his misspent youth stealing cigarettes. He was ten years old when he started, the youngest of four siblings. Only he and one brother remain alive. Now the toxins, nicotine and tar have taken their toll on his health. His doctors had warned if he did not stop smoking, he will die. He has obviously taken no notice of this advice. Privileges for Russian citizens can be few but purchasing cigarettes had never been a problem for Vladimir. He had always had contacts.

"It is good to see you after such a long time, my grandson," drawls Vladimir, his voice as gruff as a bear's growl. Alexey is still standing near the window. "Yes grandfather. My apologies for not seeing you sooner…" Alexey stops, knowing he is talking out of turn. One look at Vladimir's face is enough. Vladimir commands authority. No one, not even a family member, is allowed to break protocol.

"The reason I have summoned you to my remote cabin is so I may tell you a story, something no one else must know," cautions Vladimir.

Alexey knows a little of his grandfather's checkered career as an agent. There are rumours he spied for the West during WWII. However, these are unsubstantiated claims and the Soviet Government had bestowed Vladimir with high honours of merit. He senses his grandfather's ailing health is the reason he has been summoned, but why here and why all this secrecy?

Grabbing the other chair, he flips it backwards and moves it closer to Vladimir. Sitting opposite his grandfather, he is ready to listen. Smoke filled breath attacks his nose again as he notices Vladimir's nicotine stained teeth. He looks his grandfather directly in the eye.

"This is a story from my youth. Please listen and do not interrupt, you may ask questions later. During the early part of the war I was sent to different areas of Europe and worked on many missions. The things I and my comrades endured you cannot imagine. We became disenchanted, the barbarities of the war grated on all of us. Prior to the siege of Leningrad, my office was informed of an initiative to remove a collection of precious art and jewellery from the Hermitage Museum. Along with four of my fellow comrades we assisted in this operation. With utmost secrecy we managed to transport these historical items to a location in Sverdlovsk. Before we were able to transport more, the Germans bombed the museum. This was abhorrent to us. How dare they ruin items of such cultural and historic value. So, with the acceptance of the museum directors, we devised a plan to protect surviving pieces. It was agreed not to take these to Sverdlovsk but to locations of our choosing with no discussion as to where. Each of us was to protect our items in our own way, promising to return them after the war. It was my intention to hide the items I saved here in Oblast. This cabin was to be my safe house. Unfortunately, one of my colleagues barged into my office as I was bundling them away. He insisted on knowing how I had come across such items of value. He wanted me to share them with him or he was going to our superiors. This was a top-secret mission; I could not allow anyone to find out what we were doing. A fight ensued and I left him unconscious on the floor. He probably died before someone found him because no one came looking for me as I escaped heading to this cabin. But I never made it here because the Germans were bombing this area. It was then that I found myself on a train heading to Moscow, where I enlisted into the army. My grandson, once Hitler broke the pact between Germany and Russia, I had no choice but to join. As much as it pains me now having seen much suffering, at the time it was the only choice I had. Eventually I ended up in Naples. It is here I befriended persons who, like me, wanted an end to the bloodshed. Together we kept preserving history, everyone's history. I, along with my four comrades and others saved artefacts so future generations would still enjoy their beauty. As well as saving these treasures, we also assisted innocent casualties. It was dangerous work. Caution was required at all times because the war was intensifying. I befriended a woman and we became lovers. Too many people had lost so much, and we had no idea how much worse was to come. Enlisting my Italian lover's help, she hid some treasures in her basement. She was never to mention this to anyone."

He takes a large iron key from his coat pocket and rests it on the table. He explains how fortunate he was to have met someone who owned a place to store things away, apartments in the inner suburbs of Naples are small and basements are not common.

Alexey takes the key and feels its weight in his hand. It is solid iron, an old-fashioned rusty key that would likely injure someone if it were thrown towards them. Holding the key, he bends forward towards his grandfather, about to speak. Before he can say anything, Vladimir raises his hand, indicating he wait his turn.

"Let me continue," he says clearing his throat. "She gave me that key, keeping one for herself. It opens the basement. Not being used by anyone other than Amelia, it was a safe place for both the artefacts and for me to hide after I became part of the Italian Partisan Army. Yes, I was a deserter and it was here our love grew." He stops, catching his breath.

Alexey's face twitches at learning this fact even though he tries not to show any emotion. How did he make it back to the Soviet Union? How did he achieve the high position within his agency if he deserted?

"You can judge me if you wish, but it will not change what has been done. So, I ask you to find these treasures and return them to our country. To where they belong. Technically, I stole those treasures so I would have been punished had they found me with them. As for my comrades, we each found our way to Naples, but we never revealed where we had hidden our pieces. It was my dream to return to Naples to retrieve them. So, now I am asking you to find these treasures and return them to where they belong. I also ask you to take care not to let anyone know about these treasures until you are ready to return them." Anguish floods his face as he speaks. Vladimir is a proud man who would never consider doing anything against his beloved country. Alexey is sure Vladimir had not considered saving these artefacts as an act of thievery. However, he took them out of the country. In the eyes of the authorities, this is stealing. Of all the war stories Vladimir has relayed, this one seems to have profoundly affected him.

Vladimir coughs, this time covering his mouth with a handkerchief. He takes more deep, fragile breaths. He indicates by pointing his index finger towards him that he may now ask questions.

Giving him time to recover from the coughing fit, Alexey respectfully asks, "Did anyone know of this affair?"

"No, your grandmother would have been devastated. But being without her for so long… I was a young man with needs." Vladimir drops his gaze.

Is his grandfather embarrassed? This secret has definitely affected Vladimir. Shifting in his chair, Alexey feels uncomfortable for him. Vladimir is showing a vulnerability he has never witnessed. "The museum directors agreed to your plan, surely you could have contacted them before trying to come to the cabin. Would they not have helped you?"

"Working for the NKVD, the People's Commissariat for Internal Affairs, allowed me certain privileges. During this time however, the directors had their hands full protecting what they could, they had no time to help me."

"The NKVD? The agency now known as the KGB?"

Vladimir simply nods.

"Grandfather I can see you are tiring. I have two more questions. What made you join the Italian Partisan Army and what happened to your comrades?"

Vladimir's coughs almost drown out Alexey's voice. When he does answer his voice is full of raw emotion.

Sweat beads appear on Alexey's lip. He shifts in his chair as his grandfather's vulnerability makes him uncomfortable again.

"You are young, you cannot know the barbarity of war. And I hope you never will. By the time I reached Naples I had had enough. The bloodshed, the innocent lives lost and the destruction of human history. All I wanted was peace. Unfortunately, many of the partisan army members were caught by the Germans, they headed north to Milan. Their safe house was raided, and I did not see them again. I would have been one of them too had it not been for an incident in Naples that meant I had to run for my life. I returned to our homeland without anyone knowing I had deserted. There was no one left to report my indiscretion."

Alexey is quiet for some time. He walks over to the window, opens it and breathes in the cool air. His grandfather is blaming himself for their deaths and the guilt is still tormenting him.

"I take it my job will be the means to get me to Italy?"

Vladimir nods, "There is an awards ceremony next month. Amelia's granddaughter has been nominated." He instructs Alexey to go to his car and retrieve a folder on the front passenger seat. Alexey enters the cabin holding the folder. He hands it to his grandfather. "All the details you will need are here. Read them carefully then destroy them. You will act as a photo-journalist for a magazine doing a story on the awards."

"This is not a legitimate assignment. The authorities won't allow me to leave without clearance from my agency."

"This has already been cleared. I still have contacts who will circulate a copy of the magazine throughout NKVD offices. It will look like a legitimate assignment for the interest of members and their partners."

He decides not to correct his grandfather, it doesn't matter what the agency is called. It is still the secret service. Alexey's admiration for his grandfather grows, even in his state of ill-health he had thought of everything. He knew his grandfather's life had been rather unorthodox but being part of the secret police and stealing historic treasures was beyond even his imagination. To think the *agency* his grandfather had mentioned all these years was the KGB.

"I have not heard from Amelia since the war ended but her granddaughter is a journalist working on a television news show. Befriend her and she will help you to return these treasures," he concludes.

"Grandfather, how can you be sure she will help me?"

"All you have to convince her to do is show you to the basement. You have the key. I have a vague memory of where it is but no address." Vladimir sighs as he rises from his chair, "I will leave the finer details to you. I must leave you now as it is time for me to take my many pills and rest. Please read everything and familiarise your-self with the photos. Leave before dark, destroying everything contained within the folder. I want my memories of my youth to remain with me and I trust you will respect my privacy. Please keep certain facts I have highlighted secret. Just start the process of bringing the treasures back to where they belong."

Alexey follows Vladimir onto the porch. He places his hand on Vladimir's elbow to help him down the stairs. Vladimir stops, breathing in the dampness surrounding them. He turns to Alexey telling him it would be best not to chance being seen together here in the woods. Dropping his hand, Alexey walks back onto the porch acknowledging his grandfather's wishes. He watches as Vladimir struggles towards his car. His knees bent, the walking stick wobbling once again on the cobbled path. As he stands on the porch his eyes glisten with tears. He remembers his many trips to this cabin with a more youthful and adventurous man. Lingering there long after the roar of the car subsides in the distance, he breathes in the smell of the fresh pines and spruce. He thinks about this cabin. Vladimir had built it when Alexey was a child. There are many memories here, they shared great times together here in the woods. Vladimir taught Alexey survival skills; how to hunt, how to plant food and cook his own meals. This cabin has a special place in Alexey's heart.

He turns to go back inside. The folder is still on the chair where Vladimir had sat. Alexey sits reading the contents. If what his grandfather had just told him is true, and there seemed no reason to doubt him, then it is an amazing true story of war heroics. Also, a story of a forbidden love lost. Vladimir's eyes sparkled whenever he mentioned Amelia. Once these artefacts are found and returned to the Soviet Union, Alexey is sure the Russian people will see what happened as a story of heroism. The danger Vladimir endured to protect the treasured pieces is enough, he hopes. And it is the people who will be the beneficiaries.

Looking at the photo of the television journalist he sees a woman who knows who she is. Her face glows with confidence. This is a woman he wants to get to know. All he has to do is convince her to help him find the artefacts in the basement Vladimir mentioned. She is a journalist and they are a curious bunch who are always looking for a good story. This one is a true story with historical significance, but he must remember to keep things quiet out of respect for

Vladimir's wishes. This will not be easy. Whatever does eventuate his grandfather's name must not be connected. Not until Alexey is sure the Soviet government does see the return of the artefacts as an act of heroism. He will contact his own comrades in Moscow to ensure his grandfather's good name is not tarnished. Nor those of the people who helped him protect the treasures.

Gazing out the window to see the last shadows of afternoon sun spray through the spruce, he ponders his next move. Tapping his left coat pocket, he checks the flight ticket is safe. Alexey torches the remains of the folder in the fireplace. He leaves the cabin with details and faces imprinted in his mind.

Chapter Three

The gates of the independent television station 7Oro open automatically as she drives towards them. Looking in the rear-view mirror, her tired eyes stare back at her. Simona is still on her mind. After discussing the problem with Gee for much of the past week, they have agreed to find out what is upsetting her and why she is being so secretive.

"Good morning Larissa, you're bright and early," greets the portly security guard with a smile.

"Good morning," she replies stifling a yawn, "I have heaps of work to do. And with your lovely greeting, I'm sure I'll breeze through it all today."

"Glad to be of assistance," he laughs, "enjoy your day Larissa."

Nodding her head in thanks, she knows she is one of the few who actually acknowledges the guys in the booth. The security guards do a great job of keeping everyone who works at the studio safe. They are needed and this morning she is happy to have been put into a better mood.

Walking into her small corner office she frowns at the mess on her desk. "Oh, wouldn't it be good to have some filing space!" In the rush to be in Naples with the crew, there had been no time to sort the stories already on her desk. Flicking through some of the previous day's messages, Gee had called. She places this message in her diary as a reminder to call her later.

The scripts from the Naples' shoot are her next priority. These are needed for the production meeting this afternoon.

They are all seated. Journalists, researchers, production crew and administration. As an independent television station, the main focus is news and current affairs. The station's Board likes to nurture young talent. Larissa sits with her colleagues as they listen to their producer, James. Including him, the average age in this meeting room is thirty. They are a young team by the national network standards, but this doesn't mean their work is inferior. 7Oro is beginning to make some national stations take notice. Viewers are tuning in and the television ratings war now has another contender.

James is discussing the agenda for the next week. It is he who has had a lot to do with the success. Their show, Roma Tonight, is in the forefront of investigative journalism. Everyone in this room is a part of this success, and proud to be a part of it. James took a chance when he hired her as the anchor. If she is being honest, she was sceptical at first too. So was most of the national media. They bagged the idea. As it turns out, viewers are responding to her and tuning in every night.

"Larissa, do you have the scripts from the Naples shoot?" asks James.

She hands them over to him and he continues briefing the editors. Her grandmother comes to mind. She had visited her once more while she was in Naples and still her demeanour was chilly. When she calls Gee later, they will certainly discuss Simona's unusual attitude towards them again. It seems to be the only topic they talk about now.

"Ok everyone, thanks for your time. I'll pass you over to Larissa."

"Thanks James," she replies as half of the team leave. The meeting is over for them. She now has the attention of her two researchers, editing team and her production assistant. As she briefs them on the stories for tonight's show, she is glad to forget her family issues, at least until she phones Gee later. For now, she concentrates on her work.

Chapter Four

Back in her office, she is sorting through her notes when she is startled by Brigite pouncing into her office.

"Congratulations!" she screeches.

Larissa smiles taking in her enthusiasm. Brigite's bubbly personality is infectious.

"Umm, ok thanks but what for?"

"Haven't you seen your invitation to the awards? You've been nominated for 'Best News/Current Affairs Personality 1980," she announces.

"What! You're joking?" She shuffles through her in-tray looking for the invitation. Her hands seem not to be moving fast enough. How is this happening? She's only been an anchor for a short time. Finding it she reads …

TAI JOURNALIST AWARDS 1980
"TELIVISO AUDIOVISIONE ITALIANA"
cordially invites
Ms Larissa Mina & friend
to an awards function
on Friday 9th September at 8pm.

Venue: HILTON HOTEL, ROME
RSVP: Mary Fraginare, 01 – 234 8961

There is a separate sheet with the invitation announcing her nomination. She is one of four television journalists nominated. "Oh my, wow! Brigite, how did you know before I did?" "One of the secretaries who opens the mail told me. Sorry, I thought you would have sorted through your mail by now. Me and my big mouth… but how exciting for you?"

"Yes, of course it is. Thanks for your congratulations. It's a little presumptuous though, look who I'm up against. They are all old hands at this game compared to me."

"Ah you'll blow those guys out of the water," says Brigite with a swish of her hand as she exists the office.

Larissa grins as she watches Brigite, with her blonde curls and musky perfume, leave. She may be little in stature, but she makes up for it in her work attitude. Brigite started as a junior in the sales department. She has been working with the team on Roma Tonight as a production assistant since Larissa became anchor. Two young women in a sea of men. Together they keep the crew in line and Brigite is savvy about keeping things running on time.

Looking at the invitation in her hand Larissa ponders this honour being bestowed on her. Excitement floods her senses, what a thrill it is to be honoured with an industry award. Her mind races as she comprehends what she's reading. What a shock! Other journalists who are her peers nominate colleagues for such awards.

"I already know what you're thinking," James says as he walks into her office, "you're not worthy of the nomination."

"You know me too well, James. Brigite roared into my office screaming her congratulations only a few minutes ago."

"I know. The whole building heard," laughs James. "I wanted to be the first to congratulate you but… never mind. We all know when Brigite is around, secrets can't be kept."

"It's not her fault, a secretary told her. No one in this place can keep secrets," she grins.

James kisses her on both cheeks. "Congratulations. You deserve this. The show's ratings prove you're doing things well."

Larissa is humbled by his words, "Thanks James but you deserve this too. It's a team effort. A show like this doesn't just happen. It's not all about the anchor."

He acknowledges putting together a current affairs show five nights a week is a team effort but without an anchor the audience can relate to, there is no show. She is the face of the show.

"Anyway, I'll leave you to it and let it all sink in."

As he leaves, she thinks about her talented producer. James Smythe is a colleague as well as one of her best friends. He came to the show five years ago from a local station in England. His English father is an ex-Olympic athlete, a rower. His mother a model born in Southern Italy. He has inherited his father's athletic body and his mother's European features. Women whom she has introduced him too always comment on his broad shoulders, high cheekbones and long lashes. "That face is wasted behind the cameras," they say. "And, those long, curly lashes!"

He was 28 years old when he joined the show and quickly became one of Italy's most respected current affairs producers. Under his guidance the show has won awards, top politicians and celebrities clamber to be interviewed and the 7Oro Board is kept happy with its success. James' insight into what makes people tick has kept the show from being axed. He convinced the Board not everyone wants to watch mind-numbing game shows and that there are people out there who care about what is happening in the world.

With scripts ready for yet another production meeting she stretches in her well-used but oh-so-comfortable executive chair and allows herself time to ponder the nomination. Slowly coming to terms with being nominated she contemplates how far she has come in the last few years. As an intern for a local paper whilst still at university she honed the skills needed to become a well-rounded reporter. No story was too small for her to cover because she knew the big ones would follow. The road to reporting the bigger stories had not been easy but here she is looking at an award invitation with her name on it. She feels encouraged and allows herself a moment to bask in some glory. Being nominated is already a win.

Chapter Five

Larissa is checking her make-up one last time. She adds more blush under her cheekbones and around her temples. With some liquid eyeliner she lengthens her eyes. She becomes jittery and her hand slips smudging the liner onto her cheek. She swears as she grabs a cotton bud to remove it before it dries. Patting the area with extra powder fixes her mistake. "It's ok, if you are up on stage, just pretend you're staring through the camera lens," she says out loud with a sigh. Taking a few deep breaths, she walks out of the bathroom.

James will be here in the limousine in half an hour. There is still time to calm herself and make sure everything is right. Her wardrobe seamstress had designed a full-length evening gown in violet taffeta and velvet with an elegant shawl collar. The richness of the fabric falls graciously over her body. The luxurious velvet bodice hugs her breasts. Her right leg peaks through the split in the skirt as she walks. Dabbing her favourite perfume onto her wrists, she feels wonderfully feminine for the first time in a long time. Tonight, she is a woman with a purpose. One who embraces everything about being a modern, professional woman.

Walking into her bedroom, she picks up her grandmother's antique gold necklace. Simona had given it to her to wear tonight.

Placing it around her neck she checks herself in the mirror. Bending forward, she makes sure the necklace doesn't fall. She has secured the latch well. This is important as it's a family heirloom passed down from mother to daughter since the early 19th Century. This is the only jewellery she's wearing. The rich fabric of the dress is dazzling enough.

Her long brunette curls are up in a low bun, with some curls allowed to fall strategically around the collar. She decides to check her make-up again. Just one last time. As her amber eyes look back at her in the mirror, the doorbell chimes. James is here. "Just a minute." Collecting her shoes and evening bag from the bedroom, she walks barefoot towards her front door. As she opens the door it is not James she sees.

"Miss Larissa Mina?" says a delivery man standing in front of her.

"Umm, who wants to know?" She looks behind the man for signs of James. How the hell did this man get into the building without being announced! She will have to have a word with their doorman.

"These are for Miss Mina," he says handing her long-stemmed rose buds wrapped in red cellophane with a red sateen ribbon.

"Ok, umm thanks," says Larissa hesitantly taking the beautiful bouquet, "who are they from?"

"I don't know, I just deliver them," he says turning towards the elevator.

"But…" she calls after him. He doesn't bother answering.

The scent of the roses wafts through the apartment as she takes them into the kitchen and begins arranging them in a vase. There was no card attached so she has no clue who sent them.

As she is placing the vase on the sideboard her doorbell buzzes again. Holding the buzzer button, she hears James' voice.

"I'm downstairs, are you ready?"

"Yes, I'm coming." Slipping on her shoes, clasping her bag and sucking in a huge breath, she is ready.

Walking out of the front gate, James whistles from inside the car.

"Thanks. You brush up well in your black tux too."

Their driver waits for her to be seated before closing the door. As the limousine edges off into the traffic, she thanks James for the roses.

"What roses?"

"Come on James don't play games tonight, I'm already nervous as it is. I just received twelve gorgeous long-stemmed rose buds. You organised them, right?"

James looks at her with a blank expression.

"Oh please, if you didn't send them who did?"

He shrugs. "Wasn't there a card with them?"

"No nothing. That's why I assumed you had organised them to be delivered."

"Really? Why would I organise good luck flowers when Brigite already did all that at the studio," says James, "but I guess it is strange. Maybe it's just another secret admirer. You have many fans remember?"

"Terrific! As if I'm not nervous enough tonight. And please don't joke about admirers James. You know the last crazy idiot scared the hell out of me." Her hands begin to shake. She needs a drink.

"Larissa that was a year ago and you know the stalker is safely away where he can't bother you. But sorry I did blurt it out, I wasn't thinking," James apologises, "come on let's have some champagne."

Larissa accepts the glass of Moet and takes a large gulp. The bubbles tickle her throat as she downs the rest of the glass. Handing the flute back to James she asks for a refill.

James looks at her sternly, "No."

Concern is etched on her good friend's face. She knows he worries about her drinking, he has commented a few times when she has had too many. One will have to be enough for now. She remains quiet for the rest of the ride to the hotel. Staring out the window she remembers the horrible time when she was stalked...

It started innocently enough. She received a fan letter. There is nothing unusual about that except they kept coming, and each one was darker and more crazed than the last.

"Outside my window a sliver of the moon lights the dark side revealing ever

so slightly the moon itself. This sliver of light lights my way to you, and I will always find you. There is nowhere to hide anymore. I always know where you are."

She shudders at the thought of him ever being released. Her mood changes as the hotel comes into view. Now is not the time to think about stalkers and the dark side of being in the public eye. They have arrived and tonight is a night to celebrate.

James offers his arm to her as she exits the car. She threads her arm through his, as he looks down towards her, smiling. He is a head taller than her even though she is in heels, "Come on, let's go get them."

As they enter the Grand Ballroom, the glistening chrome chandeliers cascade in a waterfall shape. She sees colleagues who wave to them. Men looking smart in their tuxedos and women wearing gowns adorned by jewels that sparkle as bright as the chandeliers. The vast mahogany room is filled with Europe's best and brightest journalists. To their left, elegant waiters offer canapes and alcohol. Larissa picks up two champagne flutes offering one to James. As they head further into the room, they mingle with fellow nominees and other guests.

Tables, resplendent in white with gold trimmings, are beginning to fill with people. James tells Larissa they are seated at table number three, right near the stage.

"I'm heading over to our table, I can see Brigite and the others already seated. Are you coming Larissa?"

Grabbing another champagne, giving her regards to a colleague who wishes her luck, she says, "Coming James, I'm right behind you."

"Here's to our star," announces one of her cameramen raising his glass after she and James are seated.

"Thank you, umm this is all very moving." She feels the heat of embarrassment as her face reddens. Her heart beats faster. This is actually happening. Colleagues from other shows, newspapers and magazines pass by the table wishing her luck. Larissa is used to attention, but this is overwhelming. She takes another gulp of champagne.

A tall, blonde man she doesn't recognise is heading her way. His magnitude fills her eyes. His presence overpowers her senses.

"Good evening, my name is Alexey, I'm the photographer for tonight," he greets the table, "would you mind if I take some photos?"

"No, go right ahead," answers Larissa emphatically, the champagne working its magic. He has an accent and a deep, sonorous voice. How sexy is this man? I'm going to find out more about who he is later.

She watches him as he clicks, the shutter clacking and the flash blinding her momentarily. She knows most of the photojournalists who work the European circuit, but this is the first time she has come across Alexey. He is dressed in a tight-fitting black tuxedo. His buff arms strain against the fabric as he points his camera. He is at ease with himself and she smiles as she notes his white sneakers. He likes going against convention, which is another plus. She likes this nice casual touch of fashion at a stuffy awards ceremony. Fantasising about this gorgeous blue-eyed man, he is a good distraction. Her heart skips a beat. It's the first time in months she has even thought about being with a man.

The ceremony is no different to any other awards night she has attended. The exception this time is her nomination. Too nervous to eat she keeps sipping more and more champagne. Her nerves are sent into overdrive with the next announcement. She gulps down what is left of her drink.

"Ladies and gentlemen, our next award is for 'Best news/current affairs personality 1980'" comes the announcement, "the nominees are; Joseph Pennuci, GianFranco Ferris, Larissa Mina and Paulo Menozzoti. And the winner is… Larissa doesn't hear the name, or does she? This is surreal. All she can hear is thunderous applause and cameras clicking left, right and centre. James and the others are congratulating and kissing her. He pushes her chair out and guides her to the stage. Tears are streaming down her face unchecked. The next minute she is on stage. Then the gold award is in her shaking hands. She almost drops it. Now, the microphone is in front of her. Clearing her throat and wiping her eyes, "I must look a mess," she stammers looking at her friends. Brigite smiles mouthing, "You look amazing."

Looking out to her peers she composes herself. "Thank you so much. This is a great honour. Thanks to everyone who voted. Oh my…" Looking down at the award, she pauses not wanting to gush. "This award is not just for me, it's for an amazing bunch of talented people. From my producer, James Smythe, through to everyone in my crew. Come on up, this is for all of us." Waiting until they are all with her on stage, she hands the award to James. Then she names each of her crew thanking them for being part of Roma Tonight team. "Thanks to my parents for pushing me to stay at university when all I wanted to do was quit and just party my way through life." She pauses again because there is laughter throughout the audience as well as a few "whoop whoops". "Thank you everyone who voted for me. Most of all thanks to the people who watch our show, we're very proud to bring it into your homes five nights a week."

More applause follows as they head backstage. James is handing her award back to her when she catches a glimpse of the young photojournalist aiming his camera at her. Her body tingles with anticipation of becoming more acquainted with him at the after party.

"Congratulations, we knew you would win," come more greetings as they walk off stage. "Thanks, and I meant what I said, this is for all of us."

"You deserve it kid," says James giving her one of his huge bear hugs. They are all seated again when James gives his own speech to everyone about how hard work and professionalism does pay off. Larissa is only half-listening to him. She is too interested in watching Alexey. She doesn't focus until he mentions her name.

"Larissa was right," he tells them, "this award reflects all our hard work." Then she loses focus again as he drones on about getting to the top of their game is one thing but staying there takes hard work.

He completes his little speech by saying, "…now, let's go and party."

With the official ceremony over, nominees and winners mingle congratulating (or commiserating) each other as the after party begins. Revellers move to a smaller part of the ballroom. This is an intimate room with the mahogany grandeur still apparent, especially at the bar area. There are tables, chairs, comfortable lounges, and the lacquered stools upholstered in burgundy leather at the bar are already popular.

They squeeze past people waiting for drinks. Larissa holds her award, smiling and accepting more congratulations. A DJ spins dance hits as a disco ball turns throwing glittering coloured lights around the darkened dance floor, which is soon full.

"I don't suppose the best news personality of 1980 would like to dance?"

Larissa looks up to see Alexey. With her face beaming, she asks, "James, would you please look after this for me?"

She hands over her award as Alexey leads her onto the dance floor. She notices the look on James's face. She knows this look; he is worried she will be hurt again. James is her protector, her second brother when it comes to needing a shoulder to cry on. She has made good use of his shoulder many times.

"And he can dance as well as take photos," slurs Larissa as she sways. She is drunk but doesn't care. Tonight, is her night.

"I get by," answers Alexey, "but then with such a beautiful partner how can I go wrong."

"Thank you, the feeling is mutual. How long are you in Italy?"

"Six weeks. Just until the award ceremonies for TV and film are over. I'm doing a cover story, 'Awards – Reflection of Talent or Egos'".

"I look forward to reading the story and seeing your photos. I do hope the writer won't bruise my ego too much." Staring at his lips she wants to kiss him right now in front of everyone. Too much alcohol?

Yes. Or maybe it's about time she let loose and had a good time? Oh, who cares? Stop trying to over-think things like you always do.

She decides to enjoy the night for what it is, an after party with her peers and this beautiful man who is giving her the right kind of attention.

Alexey pulls her closer as the rise and fall of a slow song clears most of the dance floor. His aftershave wafts through her senses. She knows this smell well; her ex-boyfriend wore the same one. Kicking herself for thinking of him she looks into those piercing blue eyes. Tonight, is all about getting to know Alexey. She will let her inhibitions go and enjoy his company.

As they head off the dance floor, she sees James walking over to the bar where other winners are cheering each other's success.

"I thought you two would never get off the dance floor. Hi, I'm James," he introduces himself to Alexey presenting his hand to be shaken.

"Pleased to meet you James, I'm Alexey Dubrovsky." He grabs James' hand firmly and looks him straight in the eye.

James is very protective of her, and in turn, their show. Larissa knows what he is thinking. He hands the award back to Larissa. The three of them exchange general chitchat. As their conversation continues, James becomes heavy-handed when speaking to Alexey. She senses tension between the two of them. Excusing herself and James, she asks Alexey if he would mind waiting at the bar. She knows what James is doing and takes him for a little walk out of earshot.

"How about you lay off. We have only just met Alexey and you're treating him like he has hurt me already."

"Larissa, I picked up the pieces after your last two relationships, I'm just worried you're going to make another bad decision."

"James, I appreciate you caring about me, you are my best friend after all. Yes, you were there for me when my ex-boyfriend told me he was married, but it's been months since I broke up with him. I'm ok now and need to get out there dating again."

"With someone who doesn't even live in a free country?"

"Let it be whatever it's going to be James. He's here for a few weeks, let me enjoy a fling. If there is going to be one at all."

"I guess it's your choice Larissa," he hugs her telling her he will always worry about her and her reputation, but she can rely on him for help. Anytime. Asking her whether she wants him to stay, she tells him to go home. He agrees, with some reluctance, but then heads towards the exit as she returns to Alexey and the others at the bar.

Alexey is chatting amicably with members of her crew and they are fascinated to hear what it is like living in the Soviet Union. She grabs herself another drink along with a bowl of nuts and joins them listening in on the conversation. As she listens, she reflects on James. When she was dating her ex-boyfriend, James had warned her there was something not right about him. He felt he was not to be trusted. It was something about his weird, beady eyes that made him feel uncomfortable.

"He never looks you straight in the eye. What is he hiding?" he had told her.

As it turned out, he was hiding something… his marriage. James had been right about him from the beginning.

Alexey will be a distraction. A bit of fun. This time she will keep things light and lead with her head not her heart. She sidles closer to him. He is talking about how his work takes him to places not many Russians will ever be allowed to see. Someone asks him about the government. Larissa shudders. Imagine not being free to have a say on how your country is run? Or even just to travel if you want to?

As he finishes talking, he places his hand on her arm and whispers, "Everything ok?"

She feels his breath on her neck. Her skin prickles with excitement. "Yes, fine."

Brigite weaves her way up to them. Wafts of alcohol and stale cigarettes come from her and other members of the crew. "We're going to keep this party going at Juliana's. Who's coming disco dancing with us?" Her enthusiastic voice has risen a few octaves fuelled by the alcohol.

Larissa declines and to her delight, so does Alexey. Brigite gives

Larissa a wink then a boozy "good luck" whisper. She smiles as Brigite and the rest of her crew head out waving them all goodbye. "See you all bright and early on Monday." They leave with back-handed waves and in unison they murmur, "yeah, yeah."

Still feeling exhilarated she suggests to Alexey they go to a local bar she knows where they can sit and talk rather than dance.

"Sounds good to me. Let me organise my equipment to be dropped off at the hotel where I'm staying. I'll be right back."

Other journalists are mingling around. Some of them congratulate her. Paulo, another nominee comes towards her placing a kiss on her cheek. He tells her she deserves the award. Again, Larissa feels humbled. Paulo is a good journalist and she lets him know this.

He looks at the award sitting on the bar. "Do you mind?" She nods ok and he picks it up. "Oh, it's not as heavy as it looks."

"I know, I thought the same thing when they handed it to me. It must be hollow."

Paulo places it back on the bar and they keep chatting. Other colleagues come to join them. More congratulations and kisses come her way. Larissa's smile hasn't waned all night. She has known most of the people in this room for years, some of whom are more competitive than others. When she sees Alexey heading back towards the bar, she says her goodbyes and wishes them all well.

She picks up the award as Alexey places her wrap around her. He holds her shoulders for longer than he needs to. Larissa feels the warmth of his hands. Holding her award in one hand, her other hand brushes Alexey's hand. He winds his fingers through hers and smiles.

"Here let me hold that for you," he offers taking the award as they walk down the stairs onto Via Alberto Cadlolo. There are others still mingling on the street, Larissa waves as they walk by.

Larissa's happiness bubbles over, "What a night. I feel like I'm walking on air. Did it really happen?"

Alexey lifts the award up to her face, "If it didn't happen then what is this I'm holding?"

. . .

They arrive at Bar Necci. It takes a minute for their eyes to adjust to the dim light when they walk in. There are three people sitting on black bar stools. They have beers with whisky chasers lined up in front of them.

One, an immense specimen of a man, recognises her, "Oh hey, I watch your show. Look guys, do you recognise her?" They ignore him and concentrate on their own conversation. Larissa gives him a quick nod, but she is grateful his friends don't acknowledge his question. Having fans can be great, but she doesn't want to deal with any right now. Other than these three, the bar is empty. This is perfect, they won't be bothered here.

Charlie the bartender, who knows Larissa, points them both to one of the wooden booths at the back corner. A waiter walks over and tells them what is left on the menu. The kitchen is closing soon. Alexey orders for them and then turns his attention to Larissa. "So how are you feeling? Forgive me if I'm talking out of turn but you seemed a little overwhelmed on stage?"

"That's because I was. Being on stage is very different to having a script and a teleprompter in front of you. I look down the lens of a TV camera and talk. On stage you look out to a sea of people. I'll admit I'm glad it's over. Now, enough about me, tell me more about yourself, more than just the fact you are a photographer."

He smiles. His eyes brighten as he looks at her. Or is that her imagination?

"There is not much to tell. I'm an only child and an orphan as of ten years ago. My parents..." He stops clearing his throat, "were killed in a car accident."

"Oh, I'm so sorry. How awful." She places her hand lightly on his.

As the food is being laid out in front of them, Alexey also tells her about his grandfather and of his illness. Worry creeps over his face as he speaks. "I have an uncle, but he and Vladimir have not spoken in many years. It's just grandfather and myself. We look after each other. I do become concerned when I'm away from him for long periods of time with my assignments."

With one hand still on his, she pushes her plate aside with her other hand. She doesn't feel like eating. She sips her wine, "It is nice to see how much you care for your grandfather." Larissa begins telling him about her parents who live in Cerveteri, about an hour's drive away. She has a brother Philip, who is a wildlife photographer living in South Africa. "You and Philip have photography in common. Me, I'm hardly even able to hold a camera correctly. I have a habit of cutting everyone's head off," she laughs.

He proceeds to tell her he'll be happy to teach her some tricks of the trade.

Alexey teaching her photography tips, now she would like that. She feels herself warming to this gorgeous man. "I've got an idea," says Larissa, "let's go back to my place. I have a cognac I want to share with you." Oh my, I'm inviting someone I have only met tonight to my place? James would certainly have something to say about this spontaneity.

But there is something about Alexey. She's not sure what this something is yet, but she feels giddy. Is this giddiness coming from the alcohol? Whether it is or not, she feels gloriously happy. Asking a man to her place is something she has never done before. Not on the first date; and this isn't even a date. Also, she has been cautious about dating for some time now. Between the stalker and her ex, she has not been very trusting of men. Maybe it's the euphoria of the awards, maybe it's the alcohol? But it doesn't matter because somehow this feels right. Alexey is only in the country for a short time, she decides she is going to make the most of the time they have together.

Outside Bar Necci she hails a cab to take them to her apartment in Prati.

It's three in the morning and she is holding the bottle of cognac, "Would you like a shot of this?"

"Of course, thanks. Nice place," comments Alexey. She sees he is taking in the ambience of the apartment, which she furnished in light timber and decorated in muted peach tones with teal accents.

"It's comfortable, I love it here. A designer friend of mine helped me decorate." She hands him a snifter and places the bottle on the coffee table.

"Mmm, Paradis cognac. This is a nice drop."

"It is isn't it? I love the way it glides down my throat, it's so smooth." They are sitting together on her teal lounge, both have their shoes off, and Alexey tells her he is enjoying the softness of the peach woollen shag rug.

"Your designer friend has good taste. My feet feel like they are on a cloud."

"This lounge and rug were worth the price. I probably would not have spent as much without her recommendation. I'm glad I listened; the comfort is worth the cost." She looks at the statue on the mantel. It still feels surreal but there it is, she won. The euphoria is starting to subside, more because of fatigue than anything else. She cuddles further into Alexey's body asking him what he likes about living in the Soviet Union.

He is playing with her hair taking a moment to answer, "Where do I start. There is so much history to learn and enjoy. The rich Byzantine architecture, especially the churches, museums and our arts. You know of the Soviet Ballet, right? It is such a spectacle. I went with my grandfather as a teenager and was mesmerised. Then there are the magnificent forests and wide-open spaces. And, of course, my grandfather is there. He needs me now more than ever." Wiping a tear from his eye he continues, "He has done so much for me. It is now my turn to repay him. My life has been comfortable because of him and the career he has helped me to achieve. I live a life many Soviets will never have the opportunity to live. Like being here with you and enjoying a drink most Soviets could never afford."

"We know so little of the Soviet Union. What we do hear is mainly about the politics, poverty and how cold it is." She stifles a yawn. "Oh, I'm so sorry."

"I'm boring you?"

Larissa face reddens. "No, please don't think that. I'm feeling very comfortable here with you…"

He doesn't let her finish. Placing two fingers under her chin, he brings his lips to hers. She lets him kiss her.

What has taken you so long? I have been waiting all night.

He unzips her dress as he caresses her neck with his mouth. She throws off his jacket and is ripping at his shirt buttons. His chest is as buff as his arms. She runs her hands through his sparse chest hair and up around his shoulders. He holds her face towards his and kisses her tenderly.

She breaks away from him. Shame flows through her. She can't do this. Not on the first night. "Alexey, umm… sorry but I…" She clears her throat, "as much as I want you, I need to get to know you better."

So much for waiting all night. But it's just not me. I'm not comfortable with this.

His face shows disappointment. "Well, yes of course how rude of me. But I would like to see you again. That is, if you want to see me?"

"I would like that very much. I'm so embarrassed. I've led you on tonight, but this is not who I am."

"Please, it is fine. I will call you tomorrow afternoon. Is that ok?" he asks as he is placing his shirt back on.

"Yes, I'd like to see you again. Meeting you tonight was the second highlight of my night."

He bends down placing a passionate kiss on her lips before he leaves, "I'll call you tomorrow afternoon," he says as he enters the lift.

She closes her door, leaning her back against it. Placing two fingers to her lips she smiles and walks towards her bathroom. Looking in the mirror she knows she made the right decision, one-night stands are not for her.

Chapter Six

AMELIA

1980

Cuddled together, the bombs are almost insignificant while she is in his arms. With Vladimir she feels safe. No other man in her life treats her like he does. With kindness, respect and a real love, a love that permeates her whole body…

"Darling, wake up."

She hears another voice in the distance. Is that William's voice?

Suddenly a hand is on her arm shaking her awake.

"Amelia, you're dreaming, wake up. You were throwing your arms around yourself in your sleep, was it a nightmare?"

"Wha… umm. Oh…" she yawns, "Yes William, I guess it was. Sorry I woke you."

"No need to apologise. Are you ok? Do you want to talk about it?"

"It was just a dream," she assures him, "I won't bore you with details I can't really remember." Her aching muscles scream to be stretched. With her arms and legs splayed at full stretch, she says, "what I will do now that I'm awake is have a cup of tea, would you like one?" She does more cat-like stretches, waking up her limbs before placing her legs on the floor.

"Thanks anyway, it's too early. I'll stay in bed a little longer. Just as long as you're ok?"

The clock blinks five am as she places her robe on then bends down kissing him. "I'm fine, thanks darling." She isn't fine but she does not want to concern him. This is something she has to deal with on her own.

Before heading to the kitchen, she walks into their bathroom. Splashing her face, she stares into the mirror. Why now? Why is she remembering it all now? Her mind keeps going back to the worst time of her life. A time William was never a part of, a time she does not want him to know about. Turning away from the mirror, she walks towards the kitchen.

The kettle whistles as she places last night's dishes back where they belong. Outside the dawn light is beginning to oust the night. She yawns again making her tea then ambles out towards the deck. Making herself comfortable her thoughts return to the past…

They have been down in the basement all day. Staying in each other's arms even after the bombs stopped, as if they have no care in the world.

"You had better get back, your father will worry."

She gazes into his caring eyes. They are much brighter now, not hollowed shells as they were when she first lay eyes on him. "I know," she sighs, "All I want is to stay here on this blanket with you, but I have other responsibilities. How much damage do you think is up there?"

"Not too much in this area. The bombs sounded a long way off. I am uneasy about the future though, there will be a time when they will hit Naples. For now, we are safe." "With all this danger around us, don't you fear for your life during your missions?"

His top lip lifts in a slight smirk, "I try not to think about it. We all do what needs to be done. My comrades follow my orders and my orders come from the top brass. We will follow orders until such time as the partisans have enough power. We are rallying support. There are many more pacifists like us, we will prevail."

"What we need are leaders who are pacifists," she says as she raises her head from the comfort of his chest. Stretching her arms upwards, she hits the shelf. Dust unravels its way down on top of them. "Oh darn. Sorry, I do forget how little room we have down here."

"I'm not complaining Amelia. This basement keeps me safe and hidden. Without your help I would probably be dead by now."

She kisses his forehead ignoring his mention of death, there is too much of it around them, "I will bring you some food after dark."

"Only if it is safe. In fact, it might be best to wait until morning. Troops will be scouring around after the bombings."

She pulls him towards her. Kissing him passionately before leaving the basement. Her beautiful Soviet lover, a man who takes up twice the space she does, is not easy to keep hidden. She has only managed to do so because she is the only one with a key. There is no reason for anyone else to come into this basement.

Once outside, she scans the lane. Fear keeps everyone indoors. Vladimir had been right; the bombs were further away again. She also wonders how long before they hit this area of Naples. This war... there had been talk for years. No one believed it would happen. But it has.

At a brisk pace she returns to her apartment. All quiet. Teodoro, her father is not home yet. Her breath filters through her body again. She doesn't even realise how often she holds it in. Busying herself with preparing what little food they have left, she hopes this war will end soon. Food is already scarce, and the news reports don't give people hope. Taking out the wilted endive, one tomato and an onion she decides to make a stew with the chicken bones left from the chicken Teodoro had somehow acquired. She does not ask how. In fact, she rarely speaks to her father because when he is around, he is the one who does all the talking. Sober or drunk, he is the master.

Simona and Marco, her sister and brother-in-law will arrive soon. If Teodoro is not drunk when he arrives home, it might be a decent evening. Even Marco will not confront him when he is drunk. Instead, he and Simona leave to the safety of their own apartment. This is when Amelia has to deal with the abuse on her own...

. . .

"Looks like it might be another warm day. Are you feeling better?" asks William placing a kiss on her head.

She had not heard him walk onto the deck. "I'm fine, I told you that earlier," she answers patting the spot next to her on the swing lounge. They sit together peering out over the Pacific Ocean watching the honey colours of the sunrise. Amelia is grateful for the life she has now. William is her husband and they live in paradise.

Chapter Seven

Amelia sees her and blinks to be sure of what she is seeing. A reporter on the news. She looks like a younger version of Simona. It's painful remembering all the humiliation and hurt of her youth. Occasionally she has thought of her little sister who lives on the other side of the world, wondering what if? What if she had not left that day?

After years of ignoring her past, she is finding herself reminiscing about a time and place far away from her current life. The reporter has triggered these memories again, so her eyes stay transfixed to the screen. Dark brown eyes, large and bright. The same colour hair; burnt auburn. The same European features of high cheekbones and thick, rich hair framing her eyes. She is seeing Simona. The Simona she left all those years ago. Tears blur her vision. Her little sister has never been far from her mind. She has wondered whether to contact her, even just to hear her voice. Life, however, was always too busy. With two children and living in a different country, the time was never right. Now that Jacqueline and Todd are adults, she has time on her hands. More time to think about what could have been. Guilt too prevented her from calling. The guilt of being a selfish young woman who wanted a man and security more than the responsibility of looking after her own baby. The guilt of stepping on a boat for 'displaced persons' bound for Australia, a country she knew little about.

The fire of guilt rises through her body like dragon's breath. She stops herself right there. The past is the past! She left her doomed life and all the people who were a part of it, years ago. Leave it alone. Italy, along with the love of her life, is no longer relevant. He and everything else about that time is to remain just that. The past.

Amelia Brent lives in Australia and has no living relatives or friends anywhere else in the world. She repeats this over and over. This has been her story since she arrived here in 1947. She begins crying again. Her body shakes remembering the fear. Fear and distrust were a large part of her younger years.

She places both of her palms to her eyes. Stop, enough! The reporter is no one, just some random person. Anger fumes within her as she stamps over to the television switching it off. Why does she even bother watching the news? It is all doom and gloom. There was enough of that in her youth. She wipes her eyes and heads towards the kitchen.

William is sitting at the kitchen table peeling potatoes. "I'm making mash to go with the meat." He looks up towards her, "Are you ok Amelia?"

Her husband of thirty years doesn't miss much. It's one of the reasons she fell in love with him when they met. He always makes her feel protected and loved. "Yes, I'm fine. I was watching a sad movie. My eyes are still red?"

"Yep. But as long as you're ok. Jac and Todd will be here soon."

They continue preparing dinner together. She knows he isn't convinced, but he remains silent much to her relief. She's not in the mood to explain why she was crying. Not now. Their two children are coming over for dinner with their respective partners, a rare occurrence these days. Both Jacqueline and Todd have left home and living full lives working and travelling.

This is her real life. Her husband and her two children along with their partners. They show her love and respect, something she thought was foreign in her previous life. A life she has kept well hidden from them. Focusing on the present is what she needs to keep doing, this is how she keeps sane. Italy is all the way over the other side of the world, exactly where she wants it to stay. That part of her life is obsolete. Eradicated long ago. Her Australian family knows nothing of what happened to her during her childhood. Nor any of the awful events during the war. This is how it will stay. She will do everything in her power to keep their secret hidden. She made this pact with her little sister, a pact they both vowed never to break.

William has never asked her the reason why she left Italy. He is happy she has accepted the Australian way of life. As far as she is concerned, she is as Australian as her husband and her two Australian-born children. This country has kept her safe and secure. Even before she met William, a few days after arriving, she felt safe here. The signs of war were a long way away. The happiness she found, the family she raised along with the love William has given her is more than she could ever have hoped for back in Italy. This is her home; this is her life.

The reporter on TV is not Simona and has nothing to do with Amelia's life. Her children are coming, she will concentrate on enjoying their company.

Tossing and turning, she decides it's no use trying to sleep. She creeps out of the bedroom not wanting to disturb William. Tiptoeing down the stairs toward their kitchen she starts to remember. She doesn't want to, but since seeing that damned reporter, her mind has not let it go.

Making herself a chamomile tea, she walks out onto their deck, sits on the swing lounge and listens to the waves. The horrible memories flood in again...

Her world collapsed when her husband left for the war. He was her protector against the tyranny of her father, Teodoro. But she couldn't stop him leaving. He left with a sense of obligation like so many young men did. The war ripped many lives apart. Many hearts were broken. Day in, day out she was sick with worry about whether her husband would return and be her protector again.

War, the brutality of it all, makes you think, this is the end so live every moment. She was lonely, the war was dragging on and suddenly he was there. Vladimir. Her husband was away. Teodoro was in his usual drunken stupor. This Soviet defector was there on her stoop this freezing December night asking for food. He was so thin. She hid him in the basement. She helped him recover. He became her saviour. He was her sanctuary from the world at war and her abusive father.

Her husband did return. For this she was thankful. She was protected against the abuse once more. Outwardly he was in one piece. No missing limbs and no visible battle scars. But his scars were deep within him. She felt lonely after he left for war, but it was nothing compared to the loneliness she felt after he returned. His brooding would last for days, he shut her out completely. This neglect pushed her further into the arms of Vladimir. The basement became their private place. Here Amelia felt loved because Vladimir was kind and considerate of her needs. No other man had treated her this way. This type of behaviour was foreign to her, the men she knows don't treat their women this way.

The day the Americans came was the beginning. The beginning of hope. Hope for a better world. A world where love could grow. Where children could grow up without fear. She had already been away from Italy for four years by the time the Americans landed...

The tea has gone cold. She drinks it anyway, then heads back to bed. William is still sound asleep. His snores rumble but she slept through bombs in her old life, his snoring is not the reason she cannot sleep. Her memories are too vivid, too invasive of her current life. Her need to contact Simona is becoming more urgent. Maybe she will? Her little sister might be missing her too.

Amelia's life here in Australia, a life she could never have imagined back in war ravaged Europe, is now missing something. A call to her sister will ease her mind and help put a stop to these awful memories invading her life. This is her hope and with some luck, Simona will feel the same as her and be happy to reconcile.

Chapter Eight

They are naked on her plush peach carpet.

"You are beautiful," says Alexey with his face buried in her neck.

Larissa rubs her body against his as he, with his long muscular legs, wraps them around her own body.

Covering her with caresses, he runs his fingers down her décolletage and gently moves around her breasts. Her nipples react to his touch. She arches her back. His tongue is on her navel. She moans at his touch. He moves his fingers down and sensitively runs them through her soft curls. Rhythmically he caresses her within. She is writhing with pleasure as she runs her fingers through his thick blonde hair. Pulling him towards her she kisses him with a fury and a passion she has never felt before. Firm and aroused, he moves slowly, his motions bringing her to new heights. Larissa's moans come from deep within her. His deep groans join hers. They are entwined as one.

Holding each other both breathing heavily, they remain silent. Larissa breathes in his scent.

Alexey looks into her eyes, "you have blue eyes"

"They are amber actually. Some days they look more blue, other days green depending on my mood, or on the weather, or what I'm wearing…" She is babbling, and she knows this as she spirals her fingers around his few strands of blonde chest hair. She loves this euphoric feeling of a new romance.

"Well right now, they're blue, my mysterious one." Picking a strand of her brunette hair he places it seductively behind her ear. He nuzzles into it whispering something in Russian.

"Whatever you said it sounds enticing so be careful, you could start something again."

"Have I found a sensitive spot?" he teases whispering more words of… she's not sure what… but his murmurings are such a turn on.

"Ah hah, and there's more for you to find. Ah yes, right there. Keep going." Her guttural moans surprise her. What Alexey is doing feels divine. For a man a head taller than her and twice her weight, he is amazingly gentle.

Oh, please don't leave me Alexey.

He had called the day after the awards just as he promised. He was patient and the perfect gentleman. He is not like other men she has dated, for one he is pale and blonde. Very different to the dark, tradi-tionally handsome Italian men she has seen in the past. He is strong yet sensitive to her needs, his looks are not the only thing she is attracted to. This attraction is what has led them to this point. After seeing each other every day for a week, she wanted him. It was she who couldn't wait any longer.

"Hmm, something smells good," comments Alexey as he slinks out of the bathroom into her kitchen naked save for a towel covering his taught butt. "French toast with bacon. Hope you're hungry?"

"Hungry for you my Italian beauty." He hugs her slowly caressing her neck with his lips.

She turns towards him, "Behave, we need to eat some time." Placing both her palms on his chest, she pushes him away in mock horror.

"Ok, you win this time," he says raising his arms surrendering.

With their espresso and breakfast in hand, they walk over to sit on the small balcony. Overlooking the block's courtyard, light snow scatters onto the railing. Alexey is now squeezed into her oversized winter coat.

"Are you sure you're warm enough? My coat only just fits you."

"I'm fine. Don't forget I have endured much colder winters than this."

The balcony is protected by a small awning as they sit enjoying the late morning. She has learned many things about him in the past week. Alexey is twenty-three years old with no siblings. He lives close to his grandfather's home, having recently moved out into his own apartment. Generally, he is a loner and enjoys losing himself in his photographic work.

"You're only twenty-three years old yet you have travelled quite a lot? How is this possible given where you live?"

His face changes as a serious tone enters his voice. He tells her his grandfather is also an expert photographer. He taught Alexey many tricks of the trade well before his university studies. Vladimir is his mentor, his confidante and his parent all rolled into one.

She waits for a moment before she speaks again, seeing his anguish when speaking of his grandfather. "Tell me more about the Soviet Union?" she asks sipping her espresso.

"I live in Leningrad, which is the second largest city after Moscow. I've travelled since I was sixteen because I was given the chance to study in London. This was due to my grandfather and his contacts. I learned to speak English while studying. When I go to assignments, people do question how someone my age has a portfolio of work the size of mine."

"You have some valuable clientele under your belt. Your grandfather must be very proud of your achievements. When did you learn to speak Italian?"

"Vladimir is very proud, and I of his achievements. I enjoy studying languages, so each country I visit I learn at least their conversational language. Sitting in airports and aeroplanes gives me time to learn. I found Italian easier than some, your words are pronounced as they are written."

She makes a mental note to learn a new language soon. She is moved by his story and appreciates the fact that her parents, no matter how annoying they can be at times, are alive and well. They continue talking enjoying this Sunday together. As he speaks of his country, the hardships endured by many juxtaposed by its beauty and grandeur, she thinks about him leaving. He lives in a communist country; she cannot imagine what it is like. That feeling of being watched and controlled. He seems unaffected, seemingly comfortable visiting other countries and then returning to his homeland.

Chapter Nine

Opening the front door, she enters her apartment. As with many apartments in Rome, the façade is ancient and deteriorating, but once inside Larissa instantly relaxes. This is her little haven away from the spotlight. Relishing the peace and quiet after a busy day, she walks to the kitchen and pours herself a wine. Walking into the bedroom she eyes the message light. Oh damn, I forgot to call. Dialling her parents' home number, she already knows what she's about to hear.

"Hello Gee. Yes, I know. I'm sorry but this week was really hectic… I did mean to call you. I even mentioned it to James when I left work today." She conveniently doesn't mention Alexey, who is the reason for her forgetfulness. He has all but moved in. There had only been one night this week they were not together. Listening for a while to her mother's remonstrations her head is pounding but she doesn't dare hang up. Gee continues prattling about general family chitchat. Her father is fine and out with some friends in the piazza. Her brother, Philip is off on another one of his expeditions in central Africa. Gee worries about him constantly, he moved away three years ago. She tunes out for a while as she has heard it all before. Why doesn't Philip come home? What does he see in Cape Town?

Then, when Gee utters Simona's name, her ears prick up. "Laura has heard her screaming again. More than a few times?"

Gee tells her she is going to Naples to stay with Simon for a while, she has to find out what is going on. Even though her knee is improving, her arm is still in a cast. They cannot expect Laura to take the full load of looking after her.

Wondering whether this is a good idea in Simona's current mood, placing her index finger to her temple Larissa says, "How about I come over for dinner on Friday night? Maybe we can call Laura and she can tell us more about what she thinks might be going on." Her mother agrees about calling Laura. But either way she will go to Naples, who knows what this caller wants from Simona.

"You're right Gee and why is she being so cagey about it? Anyway, we'll talk on Friday. Thanks for calling, I love you. Give my love to papa." She replaces the phone onto the cradle. Alexey has been taking up a lot of her spare time since the awards night. Not that she is complaining, she is happy having him around. But her grandmother's problem needs to be solved. It will be the main topic of conversation at dinner Friday night.

Her lips curl into a half smile as she reflects on her parents. They are good people who do many good things within their community. This gives her mother lots of opportunities to hear gossip, which she loves relaying to Larissa. Gee will fill her in on the latest news of everyone she knows. As a journalist Larissa hears many stories and facts all day, every day. Idle gossip is not something she is interested in hearing. She is interested in real drama, not pettiness. What is happening with Simona is real.

With her head still pounding she pops another two painkillers with what's left of the wine. Then, back in the kitchen, she refills her glass from the bottle left on the bench.

Returning to her bedroom, she picks up the phone again. Propped up on her pillow, she dials his hotel. "Hello Alexey. Hmm yes I'm ok, how are you?"

"You don't sound ok, what's going on?"

"My head, I have a headache. Nothing too serious. I'll be fine with some rest."

"Well, maybe it's best I let you rest. I did want to speak to you about something relating to my grandfather, but it can wait."

"I've taken painkillers, they should kick in soon and I'm comfortable laying on my bed. What is it?"

"No, you rest. I'll come over when I finish processing this roll of film and we can talk then. It's probably better not to discuss what I have to tell you over the phone."

"Oh, ok. See you later," she says half wondering what he has to tell her. She replaces the phone, downing the rest of the wine as her eyes droop. Her head sinks into the plushness of her pillow. She pulls her bedspread over her head thinking of Alexey.

"Hi sleepy head."

His blue eyes come into focus as she wakes up. "Oh hi … mmm, what time is it?" She stretches holding her arms out for Alexey to fall into them.

He obliges and lightly kissing her lips he says, "It's 10 o'clock. Are you feeling better?"

"You're here so I'm definitely feeling better." She nuzzles herself into his abs.

He nibbles her neck as Larissa moans with pleasure. The tension that had taken hold of her body slips away. Alexey is exactly who she needs right now.

Two hours later she finds him in the kitchen making a midnight snack for them. "That was a hot way to wake-up." She cuddles up to him placing both arms around his waist. Her head resting on his back. "I'm more relaxed than I've been in a long time. You have a knack of loosening all my muscles with your magic touch."

"You're welcome," he says as he hands her a piece of toast. "And there is more of that whenever you need it."

"Thanks, I'm sure to need it often," she mumbles taking a bite.

He smiles, kissing her forehead.

They chat about his latest assignment and her worries about her grandmother. Then she asks how his grandfather is doing.

"He's ok, I guess. Like you are worried about your grandmother,

Vladimir is always on my mind. Now, speaking of my grandfather, I have to ask you something. It is very important for him to know about this as his health is failing fast."

Larissa listens as he recounts Vladimir's story of how artefacts became hidden in parts of Italy. Jewellery and other artefacts he rescued are buried in a basement in Naples. A basement that has something to do with Larissa's family. He explains these events happened early on in the war. Before anyone knew the war was going to drag on for years.

He hands her the key. She holds the key, turning it over. She's seen it before; Simona has one exactly the same. She contemplates what this story means for her family.

"Wait… you knew who I was at the awards? Why all this pretense? You seem to know more about my family history than I do!" She becomes wary as thoughts niggle… Why now? Why has Vladimir waited so long to retrieve these treasures if they are precious? Should she trust Alexey? "Your grandfather has had many years to do this himself. Why has he waited so long? Are you using me to find the artefacts and then leave?" She cannot conceal her anger, her voice catching in her throat.

Alexey takes a deep breath, "I know how this must sound. It took time for me to believe his story too. But he showed me photos of these and other artefacts that were rescued by he and his comrades. Also, photos of the museum when it reopened. You must believe me; I am not here to hurt you or your family. In fact, you are the last person I want to hurt. Please Larissa, help me to fulfil my grandfather's dream?"

She is staring at his face, a face showing genuine concern. Calming herself she answers him with caution, "This is an incredible story, but you must understand how I feel. Why didn't you just tell me who you were from the beginning? Are you really a photographer?

"Yes, I am, and I promise there will be no secrets from now on. My feelings for you are a pleasant surprise. Had I known this was going to happen, then I would have introduced myself on the night we met and discussed this with you." As it is turning out, there is more at stake here than returning artefacts. Alexey doesn't want to ruin what is beginning to happen between them.

Her heart skips a beat because her own feelings for him are becoming stronger every day they are together. She takes a moment before responding, she wants to stay in the moment of wanting to believe him. "There is another issue, your grandfather told you Amelia is my grandmother. My grandmother is Simona. Amelia was her sister and she passed away during WWII." She notices his face twitch as he is thinking.

"Forty years is a long time. You may be right Larissa. Age and his ailing health may be clouding his memory" He pauses for a moment. "Do you know of this basement? I'm not trying to pressure you, but my grandfather's health is of concern."

Again, his voice and his gentle touch of her arm, calm her fears. He is genuine, her instincts are telling her to trust him. She tells him the basement is in a lane way near her grandmother's apartment. It has been owned by their family for over two hundred years. She remembers helping out collecting firewood when she was a child. She and Philip played games like hide and seek. At times they pretended ghosts were down there, each trying to see who would be the most frightened. "When I speak to my mother I will ask if she knows anything about what might be hidden. Neither she nor Simona has mentioned there might be something valuable down there. And I'm not promising anything, please be prepared that nothing may come of this."

His face has softened further as he takes her hand, holding it in reassurance. "Yes, I appreciate this has come as a shock to you. Maybe at this stage, don't mention the artefacts. The less people know about it, the less chance anything can go wrong. I need to protect Vladimir's privacy for now. Also, we should consider your own family's privacy."

Her journalistic mind understands how important privacy is for people and their personal stories. However, if the treasures are valuable, the Soviet government will want them back. This is an amazing story if everything Alexey is saying stacks up. And, if they are in her family basement, her family's privacy will be at stake. She will need time to process this, but from what Alexey has told her of his grandfather's health, there is not much time.

She remains quiet while they tidy the kitchen. Negative thoughts start to niggle again. Is he really interested in her or is he using her to find whatever is hidden in the basement? Is this the only reason he is with her? Once he finds what he and his grandfather are looking for, will that be the last she sees of him? She is not sure how a long-distance relationship such as this will work. From what he said tonight, he is committed to her, something she had not expected him to admit.

She sniffs, wiping her eyes. The bottle of red she was drinking earlier in the evening is still on the bench. "Alexey, want some wine?"

"No thanks." She pours herself a glass. Its smoothness coats her throat. The empty bottle sits on the bench. Judging her. She ignores this thought just as she is now ignoring all her negative thoughts about Alexey's motivation. He is here with her now, so she decides this is not the time to be working through relationship issues that may or may not happen.

Chapter Ten

Arriving at her parents' villa Larissa decides to find out all she can about what is going on with her grandmother. Especially as she needs to ask questions about the basement for Alexey. As for mentioning she is seeing him. That is a definite no! She is not even sure how dating someone from a communist country is going to work. No, it's too early to mention him.

Parking her car out the front she walks down the cobbled path into the villa.

"Amore mia, you're here. Oh my, your eyes are gleaming," says Gee greeting her with kisses on both cheeks.

The smells of delicious home cooking mingle with the smell of her mother's perfume. Larissa immediately feels at home. Her mother is perceptive. Is she seeing through her? Being in the throes of a delectable new love affair, the glow Gee has noticed is contentment.

Larissa explains it away with, "I won an award Gee, what do you expect?"

Giovanna, or 'Gee' as everyone affectionately knows her, is an inquisitive woman. She will find any excuse to catch her two children out on something she should always find out from them before hearing it elsewhere. Gee always wants to be prepared for any impending gossip mongering. She wants to hear news first-hand from her children. If there is even a whiff of a problem within her family, she must know about it. Her reasoning for this is she will then do anything in her power to fix whatever *problem* they are enduring.

Larissa's father Joseph stands behind Gee with his arms outstretched, his face beaming with pride as she falls into his comfortable embrace.

"Mia tesora," he coos. Even though she is taller than him now his arms still envelope her with love, safety and reassurance. He is the first man who made her feel this way. The second is Alexey. Both men give her a sense of security. The reason she trusts Alexey is that he makes her feel secure in the same way her father does.

"How are you papa?" she says still in the midst of the hug. His receding hairline is greyer every time she sees him, but his round face always has a smile for her.

He looks up, "Always well when I see you."

"Joseph, I need you in the kitchen," calls Gee. They both walk into the rustic kitchen jovially discussing the events of the awards night.

"Philip!" Her shrill voice fills the kitchen. She is in shock not quite believing he is standing in front of her.

He embraces her, "Congratulations sis. You did well."

"Thanks, but… how are you here… when did you arrive?" It is such a surprise to see him. This is a rare occurrence, to have the four of them together.

"Gee called and told me your good news, so I thought I'd come over and surprise you. It's not often you receive a top award in your field."

Gee tells Larissa she thought she would call Philip to surprise her. Larissa smiles while hugging her little brother. She was glad Gee had called; she had forgotten to call him.

The champagne cork bursts as Joseph fills four flutes announcing, "To our star. Congratulations and may there be many more accolades to come."

Moving into the dining room, Gee had laid out her best white linen. The table is laden with preserved vegetables, fresh garden salads and her father's homemade wine. With Joseph's gardening green thumb, her parent's small yard produces fresh vegetables all year round. The preserves, hand processed by Gee, are from the vegetables of last year's winter crop.

Sitting down for dinner, Philip tells them of his love for a girl from Cape Town.

Gee spurts out her wine and Larissa glares at him. How many times has she asked him not to blurt out news to their parents without consulting her first? Especially when it's big news like a relationship.

"Rochelle's father is a well-respected doctor if it makes any difference to you Gee, but I know it worries you I may never come back home," says Philip.

Gee pulls her chair back and shuffles off to the kitchen without answering.

"You've done it again Philip." Larissa is furious, her cheeks and ears burning red.

"Calm down. I was just making conversation. You had big news, now I gave them my big news."

Joseph scrapes his chair out and goes to help Gee in the kitchen.

"You know Gee wants you home. If you have a girlfriend from South Africa, and it's serious, what do you think goes through her mind? She goes straight to thinking you may never come home."

"Well my news is out now. She can get used to it. Why she worries I'll never know. I will go wherever my work takes me. It won't matter where my partner comes from. Besides, Rochelle and I have only been seeing each other for three months. So far, things are going well, but who knows?"

Joseph walks back into the room and winks at both of them as he sits. Larissa knows he has calmed Gee. He has a knack of smoothing things over because he is an even-tempered man, one of the qualities she loves about her father.

Looking at the photograph Philip is proudly showing them, Larissa concedes she is beautiful. Rochelle's dark eyes fill a warm, round face and they are focused totally on Philip. She tells him she is happy for him. How Gee feels about his latest girlfriend is not her problem.

Joseph nods and tells him she is pretty. "So… when is the big day?" he asks.

"Me get married?" jokes Philip, "with the travelling I do in my job! Come on Papa, we've had this conversation many times."

Gee walks in and Larissa knows she has heard Philip's jovial comment. She forces a smile to appear on her face as she places more food onto the table, again not saying a word. Once she is seated, Philip ignores Gee's mood and continues packing praise onto Larissa, "I'm so proud of you sis but I must admit I'm also jealous. You know you've won an award before I have?"

"I always said I would. Remember I'm the golden child." Their little spat is over as they continue sparring with each other. Her parents are also full of praise for her achievements. Conveniently Philip's love life takes second place to Larissa's win so the evening flows with pleasant conversation.

She relaxes as Gee starts chatting again. The last thing she wants is for Philip to leave her mother in a bad mood. "I did predict this. Do you remember Larissa, we spoke about it? I had a vision you were going to win something."

Gee believes she has psychic powers and loves regaling stories of how she has predicted all sorts of family events, good and bad. "Umm, would you like to remind me of the vision?" asks Larissa with a wink to her brother. Neither he nor Larissa believe in such rubbish.

"I had a dream you were holding something up high and there was an audience. It was after the San Remo music festival we watched together. You commented on a dress one of the hosts was wearing and said for your next formal occasion you would wear a dress just like it." She continues saying it was that night the vision came to her.

"I sort of remember us discussing the music but there were many dresses, the hostess changed her outfit often."

"There was one dress in particular you pointed out. Anyway, it doesn't matter. The point is, I predicted you were going to win something, and you did."

Larissa looks at Gee wondering how a night of watching a television music festival meant she had predicted such a thing. However, she appeases her mother with a silent nod and raises her glass allowing Gee to believe she really did have some type of psychic power.

Her mother continues telling them stories of other recent events she has predicted, including the birth of a neighbour's grandchild. "I knew all through her daughter's pregnancy she was having a boy."

"You had a fifty-fifty chance," laughs Joseph.

As Gee prattles on, Larissa gives her father a cheeky smile, knowing he will pay for that comment later. When Gee finally stops talking, Larissa asks her about the basement. Her mother confirms the story of her great aunt Amelia dying during the war. However, there is still mystery surrounding it all, her body was never found. Nonna Simona doesn't like to talk about it. Of course, her mother asks why the sudden interest in the basement. Larissa doesn't want to give her any details yet, just as she had agreed with Alexey.

"Oh, nothing really. You discussing your psychic power reminded me of days at Nonna's house with both of you discussing these powers."

"Yes, and Simona's powers are stronger than mine."

Really? Then why doesn't she use her powers to find her sister's missing body? I can't believe in this crap but if it makes Gee happy, what harm can it do?

Larissa takes another sip of her wine and changes the subject to Simona's current health issues.

"So, you're telling us she is better now?" asks Philip. Gee explains to Philip how Simona broke her arm. She tripped on the top step of the basement, it is well-worn and slippery. Placing her right arm out to stop herself, she broke her arm and injured her knee. "She was carrying firewood at the time."

"Surely there is someone who can help her with these types of chores?"

"Your nonna is becoming more stubborn with age, Philip,"

explains Gee, "but I spoke to her yesterday, she is coping a little better each day. All I can say is thank God for Laura, her neighbour. Having her nearby has been a big help."

Philip stretches and picks up his plate. "Glad to hear it. I'll give her a call before I leave. Now, this has been great, but I have to go. I have appointments set up tomorrow before I fly out on Sunday morning."

Larissa has enjoyed catching up with Philip. Walking towards him she gives him a warm, loving hug. "Thanks for surprising me. And Gee, you did well in getting him here." She sees him out after he kisses both parents' goodbye. "Maybe we can catch up before I leave for the airport, Larissa? I'll call and let you know when." He waves as the car pulls up. She waits, waving until she cannot see the car any longer. With a deep sigh she heads back inside. It was great to see him. She misses him. More than she thought.

As she is heading back to the dining room, she hears Gee. She is in a heated discussion with Joseph. "What are you going to do about it? He is old enough to make his own decisions. Besides love is fickle, you say that all the time." Gee is about to answer but stops when she sees Larissa.

"Let it go Gee. You know how often Philip changes his mind about women."

"Larissa, this time it's different. A mother knows these things."

There is no use answering her. She lets Gee have the last word. Picking up some plates and glasses from the table, she helps clean up. They chat more about the awards night. Then they discuss Simona again.

"I'll call her and ask her about this basement thing. I'm not sure she knows anything. Anyway, I'll tread carefully. She is touchy at the moment as you know."

"Thanks Gee. I do have a deadline as always, anything you can find out will help. But more importantly we need to find out who is calling her. Let me know if you go to Nonna's place and I'll drive down with you. Maybe she will open up with both of us there? I'm really curious about who she is having screaming matches with."

Gee follows her to the car, "You know what Larissa, thinking about it, I might go to Naples on my own. I want to spend time with Simona one on one. She may think we are ganging up on her if we both go. I'll call you about the basement as soon as I find anything out."

Gee waves as she pulls the car away. "Whatever you think is best for Nonna. Goodnight, I love you," Larissa calls out from the driver's side window. She sees both her parents waving in her rear vision mirror and smiles. Joseph had joined her mother on the stoop of their front gate. They may fight at times, with Gee usually winning, but they have each other.

As she is driving home, she thinks about the basement. Gee gave her an insight of what it has been used for over the years. She has many memories of playing in the basement, but it's been years since she's been inside. Simona may not want to discuss the awful things that happened during the war, but she may know about Vladimir, the treasures and where they are hidden. She will let Gee handle things for now but her concerns about what is bothering Simona remain on her mind.

Philip is standing at the bar waiting for her. He indicates to the barista for another short black as she walks up to meet him. "Thanks," she says as she downs the coffee, "what time do you have to be at the airport?"

"I have an hour. Let's walk towards the station, I'm catching the two o'clock train straight to the airport."

She agrees then looks around for his luggage, he only has a small man-bag, "Where's your luggage?"

"Oh, I organised the hotel to send it ahead, I didn't want to drag it around. So, what do you think is going on with Nonna?"

She wraps her coat tightly around her, placing her hands in the pockets. The light snowfall has stopped since they started walking, their boots scrunching through it. Philip pulls at his beanie, covering his ears. "I'm not sure but someone seems to be harassing her. If we do try to ask who is calling her from overseas, she dismisses us as being busy bodies. Also, she is argumentative, more than usual. Gee is hurt, especially as she won't open up to her either."

He remains quiet as they turn into the next block. Whipped up by a gust of wind, snow flutters down from a rooftop onto them as they walk.

Steam ushers from his mouth as he finally speaks, "There is not much I can suggest, Nonna can be stubborn. Ha, actually they both are… maybe ask Gee to be more patient with her. She will open up eventually, won't she?"

"The accident hasn't helped. She feels helpless. But the bigger problem is the international phone calls. I'm sure they're not helping her moods. Philip, what if someone is blackmailing her?"

Arriving at the station, they hug each other with Philip saying she can call him whenever she needs to. "Larissa, stop making up stories in your own head. You are way ahead of yourself. Look, I'm not sure I will be much help, but if you need to talk, even just to rant, call me."

She nods kissing him goodbye. "Have a safe trip back to Cape Town." He may be right. The fact Alexey told her Soviet treasures are hidden in their family basement is clouding her judgement. Would the KGB really be blackmailing her grandmother? Her imagination is taking this too far. She needs more facts.

Chapter Eleven

SIMONA

1980

She sees her first just as she is stepping off the train.

Gee's face lights up with surprise, "I didn't expect you to meet me here."

They greet each other with kisses on both cheeks and walk out of Naples Central Station together.

"I felt like getting out. I told you I'm managing better. Look, the swelling has gone," says Simona pointing to her knee, "and the cast is off my arm. I am able to move it better every day."

"I noticed you weren't limping as much. Well, thanks this is a nice surprise." Gee places her arm through her mother's arm as they walk to the car park. Arriving at the car, Gee places her bag in the boot and offers to drive.

"Thanks, I'm fine to drive. I didn't realise how much I had missed it until I drove here today. It also feels good to walk without my knee hurting." This was a good idea on her part. Driving to meet Gee shows she can cope on her own. Now she and Larissa can stop worrying. Laura, her neighbour can stop coming every day too. She still pops in occasionally to check on her but doesn't stay long. When both her knee and arm were out of action, sure she needed the help. Not so much now. This weekend Gee will see how much better she is coping on her own. She had already decided to enjoy the time with Gee. Two days should be easy for her to keep calm and not let Gee get on her nerves. If she can convince Gee that she is fine, then this will keep her and Larissa off her back.

Unfortunately, because Larissa took Amelia's call, she had heard the international beeps. Now every time they speak, she asks whether there have been more calls. Honestly, she told her it was a wrong number! Laura has picked up the phone when Amelia has called, quite a few times. She has obviously told Gee and Larissa. Now they are all curious. Well, they can stay that way. Divulging who the caller is won't happen. It is none of their business.

Parking her car outside the basement, they head towards her apartment. It had been a quiet ride. Gee must have decided to keep this visit amicable as well. Before they reach the apartment, they see Laura.

"Hi," she greets both of them. "How was the train ride Gee?"

"Fine thanks. It wasn't too crowded. The Christmas rush hasn't started yet. Are you and Alessandro still joining us for lunch tomorrow?"

"Yes, we're looking forward to it. We'll see you then."

They continue walking up to the apartment after saying goodbye to Laura. Simona had suggested the lunch and Gee had agreed. Now she wasn't seeing Laura so often, Simona was happy to socialise with her neighbours again. The lunch will also be a buffer between her and Gee. Having other people to talk to will minimise them having a fight. Even though she loves her daughter, sometimes she can be overbearing. There have been times over the years when she and Larissa had wanted her to move to Rome. It had taken all her energy to convince them she is happy living in the home she shared with her husband and where Gee had grown up. All her memories are here.

She enjoys her independence, which is what finally convinced them to let her be.

This is why she has struggled since the accident, having to rely on others has not been easy. Now, Gee will see how well she has recovered. This weekend will be pleasurable, she will make sure of it.

Chapter Twelve

She holds the handset away from her. Staring at it, she wonders what she said wrong this time. Simona is making this a habit. She keeps slamming the phone in her ear. Eventually she places the receiver back on its cradle and walks onto the deck.

Amelia watches aimlessly as the waves crash over the rocks. It's a dull spring day and is threatening to rain. The weather suits her mood. Annoyed at her little sister, she breathes in the humid, salty air. Stubbornness was not a trait she remembered Simona possessing. Obviously, the years have changed her demeanour.

Staring towards the grey ocean, her mood thickens. How is she going to convince Simona to meet with her? Each time she brings up the subject, Simona refuses to discuss it.

Well, I can be just as stubborn. There will be more calls from me.

William is in the garage fiddling with his car. She walks towards him, and in a light-hearted tone she really isn't feeling, asks him whether he wants a cup of tea. He has no idea about Simona and the phone calls yet, so she feigns this cheerier tone.

His head is under the bonnet, "Give me a minute… just have to tighten this… ah there got it! Sorry, didn't hear you love, what did you say?"

She admires him as he wipes grease off his hands. He's working on an Aston Martin DB5, the model driven by Sean Connery as 007 in the movie Goldfinger. His two passions – classic cars and 007 movies – keep him busy in this garage. Memorabilia of the movies line the walls and when he is working on the car, the record player plays soundtracks over and over again. They have taken many road trips down the coast in this car. It's their thing to do on weekends.

"Would you like a cup of tea? I'm about to make one," she repeats her question.

"Thanks, but no. I'm heading down to George's service station, he ordered a part for the car and it's arrived. Do you need anything while I'm in town? I can pick up some things if you like."

"Actually yes, that would be good. There's a list in the kitchen. I'll just add a couple of more things to it, so I don't have to go down there tomorrow."

He follows her into the house wiping his hands with a greasy rag, "Leave the list on the bench, I'll take it on my way out. I'm going to clean this grease off first." He pads off towards the laundry looking the part of a professional mechanic in his grease-stained overalls.

She admires him. Although he has enjoyed cars since well before they met, he has only taken up fixing them in the last ten years. He studies manuals, goes to workshops and helps out at George's garage occasionally. At first, she felt nervous riding in a car he had fiddled with. But she had nothing to worry about, he is a natural mechanic and very good with his hands.

"Well that took some scrubbing," he says returning to the kitchen and picking up the list, "I won't be long," he says pecking her on the cheek.

"Thanks, you'll save me time tomorrow. Now I don't have to go back into town after lunch with the girls."

"My pleasure. You can spend more time with your girlfriends and enjoy a longer, boozy lunch." He chuckles as he leaves.

She harrumphs then smiles as he winks back towards her. After he's gone, she finishes her tea and sits on their deck again, swaying aimlessly on the swing lounge. Light rain is fluttering around on the humid sea breeze. A rainbow floats on the horizon. This deck faces east towards the beach and on a clear day they can make out the light house. Sitting here always improves her mood. It is serene, her own piece of paradise. How she wishes Simona could see this.

Reconnecting with her little sister has been worthwhile. Angry thoughts about their childhood and the decision they made don't abuse her senses as often as they did. There had been an absence of forty years between them, neither breaking the promise they made to each other during WWII. Phone calls between them are frequent now. Hearing Simona's voice has made her feel young again, it has given her a purpose. But Simona refuses to listen when she wants to discuss the past. She does not want to remember the war, especially as it caused them to be apart with no news for too many years.

As she walks back to the kitchen rain thrashes against the window. A far cry from the serene scene on her deck only ten minutes ago. Another summer storm has brewed towards the west. The black sky threatens hail. This is Australia, the land of bushfires, floods and fierce summer storms. Their home has survived well, occasionally they have had some flooding in the garage and the odd hail stone through a window. Bushfires too have come close; the acrid smell of smoke has infiltrated the house many times. Charcoal, ash and dust have floated down settling around their deck and on their cars. There was a particularly fierce bushfire only three years ago where they awoke to an ash covered lawn, a blackened deck and her white Mazda covered with a thick film of downy grey ash. This is nothing compared to others, many people suffer tragically when Mother Nature shows her full force.

Staring out the window she wonders why humans go to war? Why do we target each other when thunderstorms, cyclones, earthquakes and tsunamis can devastate us? There is no reason for humans to kill each other, nature can destroy us indiscriminately without warning. War is an unnecessary evil; one she hopes she will never have to suffer through again. Neither anyone she loves. In fact, no human should go through war or suffer atrocities at the hands of other humans.

Another disturbing memory creeps into her mind. She shakes it off as hail pounds her kitchen window.

Chapter Thirteen

Alexey is sitting in his tiny hotel room with the phone to his ear. Rain drizzles on the dirty window as he watches people down on the street hover under umbrellas, pulling their coats around them. With his hand on his forehead he massages his temple while he waits for his grandfather's number to connect. This room is closing in on him. He thinks of Larissa and her inviting apartment. The tension dissipates a little, she is a good antidote for his stress. Passion grips him as he thinks of her.

"Yes grandfather, I've met her," Alexey tells Vladimir. He must be careful not to reveal he is actually involved with Larissa. More involved than he had expected to be. He keeps his tone unemotional.

After a long bout of coughing Vladimir answers, his voice raw "Have you had a chance to go to the basement? Has Amelia been contacted?"

He explains the problem he is facing with Larissa's grandmother and how she doesn't wish to talk about what happened during the war years. "Amelia is Larissa's great aunt and she died towards the end of WWII. Her grandmother is Simona. Maybe your memory is not what it used to be?" he says as Vladimir gasps at hearing this news.

"I had the affair with Amelia. Simona is her younger sister. However, I only met Simona once. Amelia was protective of her and I met Simona in tragic circumstances, she may not want to remember me. Also, Amelia and I had agreed the less people we involved in what we were doing the better."

Alexey hears sorrow in Vladimir's voice as his coughing fills the line between them yet again. His grandfather must have harboured a thought he may have been able to see Amelia again. Sadness seeps through him, not only for his grandfather but also because of his own strong feelings towards Larissa.

Vladimir continues telling Alexey stories of people in Naples who helped him to escape dangerous situations. How Amelia had helped him through dark times, shielding him in the basement. He in turn protected her. The effects of war have tragic results. You are constantly in survival mode. People do things they would never consider doing in times of peace. Their love for each other was strong, but circumstances as they are during times of war, things were not meant to be. "My intention was to return to Naples. I was in Italy for a year before I arrived back home. By this time the war was raging. I witnessed so many casualties and the destruction…" Vladimir stops inhaling deeply. When he speaks again his voice is barely audible, "Your grandmother needed me." Alexey does not interrupt. "I kept up my contribution of saving our precious history by assisting the museum with their work. When the war ended, it was the museum's director who recommended me for the job at the NKVD."

Alexey doesn't correct him because it doesn't matter. Whether he calls it the NKVD or the KGB, Vladimir was a member of the secret police. His grandfather, although emotional, seems to be enjoying recounting his memories. Whether these are the skewed memories of an ageing man or whether they actually did happen, Alexey is not about to argue. He feels nothing but pride.

"It does not matter who owns the basement now, Amelia or Simona. Please find out if it is still in the journalist's family and make any excuse to see it. The treasures must be returned even if I am not around to see it happen."

Alexey assures his grandfather he will do his best to find out more from Larissa but then he is stunned by Vladimir's next statement.

"My grandson, I am not for this world much longer," he coughs, "you must fulfil my dream before my rival Colonel Bruskev hears of this. He is a dangerous man, especially as he is one of the agency's best infiltrators and spies. He had wanted my senior position for many years and never forgave me for accepting the post that he felt was rightfully his."

Alexey knows of Bruskev and the hatred he has for his grandfather. Bruskev never forgave Vladimir for being promoted over him. Alexey becomes worried as he had not realised Bruskev is still in the employ of the KGB. This bit of news makes him even more determined to find the basement soon. Apart from his grandfather's ailing health, he especially doesn't want to put Larissa's life in danger. Nor the rest of her family. "Grandfather, please look after yourself. I want to see you when I return."

"Yes, I promise to take care my grandson, but such things are out of my humble human hands. Bruskev knows nothing yet of why you are in Italy, so we are still one step ahead. Goodbye."

Alexey replaces the phone on the receiver. His hands are still holding it as he places his forehead down. He thinks about what his grandfather has revealed about Bruskev. He hopes his grandfather is right about Bruskev not knowing he is in Italy. He will have to do something about Bruskev, he doesn't want any more trouble for his grandfather. He'll deal with this issue at another time.

Sighing, he dials Larissa's work number, he has more important things to deal with right now. She answers and he asks her to listen carefully. He recounts his conversation with Vladimir about the basement.

"I was just on the phone with my mother. She confirmed Simona still owns the basement. She also confirmed my great aunt died but it was in suspicious circumstances. My grandmother doesn't like talking about what happened. This is making me even more suspicious."

"Do you think your grandmother will let us look around the basement?"

"Until I talk to her, I don't know. I'll see you later, let's discuss it then."

"Yes, we need to finalise things. See you tonight, I'll be over around eight." He hangs up the phone, grabs his jacket, and leaves the confines of this depressing room. He looks forward to seeing Larissa later. After the news about Bruskev, he is even more protective of her now.

Chapter Fourteen

"Well, Nonna you are certainly looking better than the last time I saw you," says Larissa greeting Simona with a kiss on each cheek as she walks into the apartment.

"Hello bella mia. I am feeling better thank you. It was such a relief to have the plaster off. I still have more physiotherapy to do but I'm better. And you, congratulations on winning the award. I haven't spoken to you since you received it."

Larissa answers as she places their lunch on the kitchen bench. "Oh yes thank you, what an evening! I'll tell you more in a minute. Now, I've brought us chicken soup and the crusty bread you like from your favourite salumeria. I'm starving, are you?" She moves about the kitchen grabbing plates and cutlery. "I have a couple of hours before getting back to the crew, which is plenty of time for us to catch up."

"Oh, I'm glad you don't have to rush. And yes, I am hungry now. This food looks and smells delicious."

Larissa watches on as her grandmother slurps the warming soup then dunking a piece of bread. Simona can be hard on herself. She says it was a silly accident due to her lack of concentration, stupidity on her part. However, it was probably due to the slippery sandstone. The ageing steps have worn over the years and can be hazardous.

Looking over at the knitting sitting on her tattered recliner, Larissa knows Simona will be happy to start knitting again. Somewhat of a recluse, Simona busies herself making baby booties and bonnets for premature babies.

"So how is the physiotherapy going?"

"Very good actually. I was surprised how the exercises helped my knee to heal. Once I was able to walk without pain, I stopped feeling so helpless."

Larissa and Gee know how much Laura helping out has saved them. The fact Simona may not have appreciated her is a bit of a nuisance, but they have argued enough. Larissa wants this time with her grandmother to be angst-free.

"That's good and once the physiotherapist has your arm moving better you can take up your knitting again. Won't that be nice?"

"I started some knitting this week. As long as I don't do hours on end, it's ok. Besides the other ladies in the group have kept up the supply to the hospital. I'm also driving again. Didn't Gee tell you I met her at the station?"

"Yes she did. It's great to see you back to your usual self again Nonna." Waiting for her to finish eating before she brings up the subject of the basement, Larissa slides her chair out placing dishes in the sink. She chooses her words carefully, "I notice you have more firewood, did Laura bring it up for you?"

"Umm, yes a couple of days ago. That is another job I'll be able to do by myself again. Only this time I will be more careful on those two steps."

Not wanting to think about her grandmother falling again, Larissa continues asking questions. "From memory it is quite a large space, what else do you keep down there now?"

"You remember it as a child my darling, it is not so large. I keep firewood, tins of tomatoes, some preserves and olive oil down there these days. I don't drink homemade wine anymore and most of what was left I gave away. The vats and some empty bottles are still there. Ah, the memories of good times down there. When we made wine, it was a social event. Our neighbours and friends all joined us."

"Sounds like fun. Philip and I talked about how we used to play down there."

"Gee told me he surprised you with a visit. How nice. He called me too. Lovely to hear his voice." Her face gleaming, she continues, "Ha, I do remember the two of you getting up to mischief down there. Oh, and the time you screamed because a rat ran past your feet. You vowed never to go down there again?"

"From memory I don't think I did after that. Besides I was only twelve and you all made fun of me for being scared. Especially Philip. Who ran out of there faster than I did by the way." Pausing, Larissa decides this is the time to ask, "speaking of the basement, do you know of anything else that is down there? Something that might be valuable?"

"What do you mean?" Simona is now guarded. "Why are you asking such a question? Whatever is down there has been in our family for years, whether any of it is valuable I have no idea."

Larissa sees she is visibly shaken and wonders why? This makes her think Simona is definitely hiding something from them. She decides to pursue her grandmother on this point because time is not on her side. Alexey needs her help now. Vladimir's health is deteriorating. "I didn't mean to upset you Nonna. People find all sorts of treasures in basements like yours, so you never know. I have a colleague who has an interest in valuables that went missing during WWII. One day we were talking, and the subject of our family basement came up. He is curious and asked if he could take a look."

"A colleague? He must be older than you if he has an interest in WWII history and he wants to go into our basement?"

"No, he's younger than I am. Anyway, what has age got to do with it? It's a hobby probably. Look, how about I make us coffee? Then I'll be going," she says sensing Simona has had enough of her questioning.

The strident ring of the phone startles her. Picking up the receiver from the wall, she hears the distinctive international beeps before hearing a long-distance crackle.

"Simona?" says the caller.

Stretching the handpiece towards her grandmother, Simona makes a gesture asking who it is?

Larissa shrugs, "It's an international call."

Simona shakes her head no.

"Sorry you have the wrong number," says Larissa to the unknown caller. After replacing the handpiece, she asks, "Who is calling you from overseas?" As far as she knows, her grandmother does not know anyone from overseas other than Philip. He only calls her on her birthday, which is not today.

"Like you said, it was a wrong number. It happens sometimes. Now I'm going to have coffee in the lounge. Please bring it over to me and then see yourself out. I need a nap."

The dismissive tone in Simona's voice takes her aback. She has witnessed her grandmother treating Gee in this way, but never towards her. First, she was annoyed when questioned about the basement and now being rude because of a strange phone call. Simona's short temper is unusual. Her thoughts earlier about Simona being back to her usual self was a little premature. Her curiosity is now piqued even more. She has two things to concentrate on. One is convincing Simona to allow Alexey access to the basement pronto. The other is finding out whether she is being harassed by an unknown caller. In Simona's current mood, neither is going to be easy.

Chapter Fifteen

"So, who was it that answered the phone?" Amelia asks. A letter she has written to Simona is sitting on the desk ready to be mailed. She placed a call to her sister before heading to the post office to mail the letter. The phone being slammed down in her ear the other day was still rattling her.

"It was Larissa. She was visiting and we had lunch together. I panicked when she told me it was an international call. That's how she ended up telling you it was a wrong number."

"Yes, obviously the beeps gave that away. It might have been better if you took the call. Now she is probably suspicious."

"I feel terrible. I panicked after that, I was awful to her. I've never been rude to Larissa, but my fear she and Gee will find out the truth… I can't… I won't…" Simona breaks down. Again. Her sorrow seeps through the line.

Exhaustion cloaks Amelia's body. Convincing Simona to allow her to meet both Gee and Larissa is going nowhere. Now, with Larissa poking around asking questions about the basement and taking the call, Simona is obviously spooked.

"Oh, Simona my darling little sister, please stop crying. Haven't we cried enough?" She pauses to allow her to regain composure.

Sniffles reach her ears, "So you want me to allow them to go down there and find them? Then Larissa will ask even more questions."

"Do we have a choice Simona? Vladimir wanted them returned after the War. I think we owe it to him."

"He was your lover, not mine. I don't owe him anything. I lost you because of him. Now, Larissa wants to bring another man into my basement. No, I won't do it."

What man is Simona talking about? "I thought it was only Larissa asking about the basement. Who is this man?"

"He is a work colleague apparently. I didn't have the chance to ask such questions. Your phone call interrupted us."

"Simona, find out more about this man. Why is he asking Larissa such things? Does he know something? Is he from the Soviet Union?"

She hears Simona give out a huge belly laugh. "Now you're letting your imagination run wild Amelia. Larissa said he has an interest in WWII history, that doesn't make him Russian."

"Well at least I've made you laugh. It's better than hearing you crying." Amelia wonders at the irony. Is it a coincidence? Has someone who knew Vladimir organised this man to talk to Larissa? Her mind fills with all sorts of scenarios – Does the agency Vladimir worked for know what he did? Is the Communist government involved? Are they in danger again? Does Larissa know this man's motives? "Simona please listen to me. We cannot change what happened in the past. What I am trying to do is make a better outcome for our future, yours and mine. I ache to see my daughter…"

"She knows me as her mother!" Simona is shouting once again.

Amelia composes herself before answering, "I appreciate what you did to bring her up, Simona. We can all know each other; we can be together without the angst of our childhood. I need to see you as much as wanting to meet Gee."

"Amelia, I have to go to my physiotherapy appointment," says Simona in a much calmer voice.

"Yes… umm ok Simona. I love you, please take care." Replacing the receiver, Amelia stares at it. Simona did lose her because of her love for Vladimir. The decision was made out of fear, now she fears for their lives again. How much does Larissa know of this work colleague?

Another memory floats through her mind…

She holds Simona tight. She is scared too. For now, they are safe in the basement. They ran from their father, Teodoro. He came home ranting and angry again. Hearing him before he saw them, they ran to safety. He won't find them. He doesn't even know they have keys to the basement, their mother showed them where they were hidden before she died. Outside it is a hot July morning. Sweat drips down her body as she calms Simona. They will stay as long as they need to. He will eventually fall asleep in a drunken stupor.

"He is always angry now Amelia. We have to tell someone what he is doing."

Simona's sad brown eyes look up at her. How she wishes she could take their pain away, "Who is going to believe us? There is talk of war, people have bigger problems to deal with. We have a place to live, food and a father who provides. This is what people see."

"But it's not true, look at what he does to you. To us."

"Our father has power Simona, for now we have to endure this. I am the older one, please listen to me and together we will survive this. I promise." She says this with more conviction than she is feeling. Her fear is palpable, but she must not show Simona. She is the strong one. Cuddling her sister, she falls into an arbitrary sleep.

It is mid-morning the next day when they leave. Entering the apartment, it is silent. Amelia breathes a sigh; her pounding heart slows. They both head towards the bedroom. Suddenly Amelia feels her hair almost ripped from her scalp. Pain sears through her as she is on the floor screaming, "Simona, run!"

She doesn't argue. Simona knows the routine. This has happened before…

Amelia picks up the letter. She rips it up, there is no use sending it now. She will find out who this man is first. He could be yet another obstacle to having Simona's approval for her to meet Gee.

Chapter Sixteen

A voice at her office door startles her.

"The show's on-air fifteen minutes early Larissa, there's a political speech at a quarter to seven," announces the studio floor manager, "get your butt into make-up asap."

Her mind had been on the script in front of her. She's not quite finished with the last story of the night but decides she can ad lib.

She realises an earlier start to the show means she will be home earlier. This lifts her spirits because she can call Alexey earlier too. He is on assignment in London. There isn't a minute he is away from her thoughts and although neither of them has mentioned anything yet, she knows their love for each other is growing. These elated feelings keep sweeping over her but he's leaving for the Soviet Union soon. What will happen if he is not able to return? He lives in a communist country. Who is to say if the government will allow him to keep working as he has been?

Alexey has promised her he will ask for assignments in Italy. She desperately wants him to come back to her. The love she feels for him is something she has never felt before. He has captivated her heart. With the warmth of this feeling, her face brightens.

I need to keep positive. He will return to me. I know already I can't live without him in my life.

Pushing her chair back from her desk, she heads towards the make-up department.

Returning to her office after the show to collect her bag, she notices the message light flashing on her phone. She clicks it hearing Alexey's voice. He is back in Rome. The assignment in London finished early. Her fingers dial his hotel number automatically. She knows the number by heart. "Alexey, hi. How are you?"

"I'm well. I missed you. How about we grab some lunch tomorrow? We need to sort things out with your grandmother. I'm leaving for home soon."

Her heart misses a beat.

I thought this was your home, you have told me how much you love being here. Doesn't that include being with me?

She keeps her voice cheery, "I missed you too. And lunch tomorrow? Absolutely. You're not coming over tonight?"

"Sorry no. I have to develop these films and deliver them in the morning. You do know I would much rather be with you?"

"So, come over," she jokes, "no… forget I said that. I know all about deadlines. They can be a curse. Ok, let's meet tomorrow at the Spanish Steps. Ciao darling." Replacing the receiver, she is disappointed. Their time together has been so short. If only he didn't have to leave. His looks are not the only thing that attracts her, although in her eyes he is the most handsome man ever! There is something different about Alexey. He is not demanding of her time. Other men she dated had been threatened by her career. Not Alexey, he seems to accept her and her career, which is another reason he is so attractive to her.

"I'm over here," she yells towards Alexey. "How about a pizza?" she asks as they kiss and hug each other, neither wanting to let go.

"Whatever you want. As long as you're with me, that's all that matters."

After finding a table at 'Il Re Degli Amici' on Via Della Croce, she tells him about her progress with her grandmother. "I went to see Simona while you were away. She was very cagey when I asked if something valuable could be in the basement. Maybe you have to come with me to convince her to open it for you?"

"We're going to have to do something quickly. Will you be able to organise another visit this weekend? We could take a drive down to Naples."

"I'll call her. Maybe we can tell her we are doing research for a show and you're my work colleague. I kind of already mentioned something. I don't think she will say no. At least, I hope she won't. She was in a very strange mood when I visited last. Then, when I answered an international phone call, she basically threw me out. Telling me to see myself out because she needed a nap."

"From what you have told me of her and how close you both are, I find that hard to believe. And do you think it's wise to lie to her?"

"It was weird. She basically shut me out and didn't want to discuss anything further. I was hurt. And I'm telling you, someone is harassing her. It was not a wrong number, the lady on the other end called her by name. As for lying to her, do you have a better idea? We're running out of time."

Their pizzas are placed in front of them. "Let's deal with one thing at a time Larissa. We'll do whatever it takes to look in the basement. I do have a key, we could take a look without telling her?" Alexey picks up a piece, folds it and eats it in two bites. "Oh, this is good."

Eating only two pieces of her pizza, she pushes it towards Alexey. "Have mine too, I'm not that hungry. And no, I want her permission. We can't go moving things down there without her knowing."

"True, it is better that she knows," he says, "And I will finish your pizza, if you insist." Alexey nods scoffing down her leftovers.

Simona's behaviour is playing on her mind. When she had mentioned the behaviour to Gee, she acknowledged it and said

Simona was frustrated. Her grandmother, although on the mend, was not dealing well with her injuries

"Let me know as soon as you can after you speak to Simona," says Alexey stuffing his mouth with pizza, "And please try not to worry too much."

She starts laughing. Stringy cheese dangles from his chin. Oily tomato sauce covers his mouth. Grabbing her napkin, she playfully wipes his mouth, then kisses him. "You really are enjoying this pizza."

"Sure am," he says licking his fingers, "the only way to eat a pizza is with your hands."

After having an espresso each, Alexey pays and they both walk outside. She will call Simona as soon as she is back in her office.

"I'll be at your place around seven," he says as he hugs her placing a passionate kiss on her lips, "Together we will sort things out with your grandmother."

She starts walking back to her office wishing she had as much faith as Alexey.

"Larissa, wait up." Heading to her office after another show wraps up, she turns to see Brigite.

"I keep meaning to ask you how things are going with Alexey? We haven't had a lot of time to talk. I guess you've been busy enjoying him."

"I sure have, but he's not here for long," Larissa tells Brigite as they enter her office. "Things are going well, he's very attentive and…"

"Attentive? I'd say sexy, yummy, delicious to look at and hot. I wouldn't use the word *attentive*."

Larissa smiles as she begins packing her briefcase. "Ok, you want to know the juicy stuff. Yes, he's all of that. The night of the awards we ended up back at my place and we haven't really been apart since. Only when he's away on assignment."

"Way to go Larissa. You snagged him the first night."

"Well not quite. We took it slow for a week. Then everything fell into place and I couldn't wait any longer. I've fallen hard. He seems to feel the same about me but…"

"He's leaving soon and you're not sure he'll be back?"

"Exactly. What if he's not allowed back into the country? I didn't expect this. He was meant to be a fling. A light romance for a few weeks."

"Wow, you have fallen for him, you haven't spoken about your other boyfriends with that look on your face. But you're making it a habit of dating unobtainable men."

"I am, aren't I?" she sighs. "He's been in London for three nights and he's coming over tonight. I know I won't be able to keep my hands off him. Oh, Brigite he's so adorable… and attentive."

"There's that word again," laughs Brigite. "Oh well, enjoy this… whatever it is, while it lasts.

As they walk out of her office, Larissa asks Brigite about her love life.

"Unlike yours, it's non-existent at the moment. Now go and enjoy yourself with your hunky, blonde beau," says Brigite winking at her, "And lap up all the attention he gives you."

Chapter Seventeen

After eating all that pizza, Alexey decides to do some shopping before going back to his hotel. He wants to find something special for his grandfather, and he should buy another gift for someone he hasn't thought about until this minute. He has been tackling with his guilt about mentioning this person to Larissa since meeting her, but he cannot tell her yet. Right now, he is enjoying being with her and wishing he didn't have to leave.

After a couple of hours of browsing and shopping, he passes a florist and decides to buy Larissa twelve rose buds in red cellophane. Walking out of the florist a blast of cold air hits his face. It's a shock at first but this Italian winter is nothing compared to the winters he has endured back home. Placing the roses carefully into the bag with his other purchases, he decides to walk back to his hotel.

As he passes Piazza Barberini, he sits near Bernini's Triton Fountain watching as people walk by. Many are rushing to get to the terminus station before their train leaves. Pigeons peck around him, an old man sitting near him is feeding them. He thinks of Vladimir. In another ten days he will see him again. He hopes he will be able to give him good news about the artefacts.

The old man who had been feeding the pigeons is shuffling

towards him. Bent over, his legs move slowly and with a lot of effort. When he does arrive where Alexey is seated, he asks for money. Rummaging in his coat pocket, he gives him all the change he finds.

"God bless you, young man." With this he shuffles off towards the station.

Watching the old man, he wonders where he would be today if his grandfather had not taken him in… homeless and penniless like that old man?

The chill wind is now swirling stronger, so Alexey makes a move towards the station as well. The train will get him back in a few minutes, which will give him time to organise his next assignment before heading to Larissa's apartment in Prati.

As he heads in the direction of the trains, he thinks about the fact he is in Rome. He has been lucky to see much of Europe. His position in life and his grandfather's position in the KGB, has allowed him to do this. He appreciates the sacrifices Vladimir made to take care of him after the death of his parents. How he misses them and wishes they could see him as a grown man. He knows he is lucky to be here in Rome, roaming free and falling in love. If only he could share this with them.

Holding the flowers, he buzzes her apartment. The front foyer gate clicks. Pushing the gate open, he lets himself into the apartment block. Larissa is at her door smiling broadly as he exits the lift. Her eyes widen when he hands her the roses.

"This time you know who they're from."

"Alexey, they're gorgeous, what's the occasion?" She places them in a vase carefully arranging them and tying the ribbon around the base. The roses take pride of place on the mantle as Alexey answers her.

"No occasion but I have a confession to make. I'm the secret admirer from the night of the awards."

"You? You sent those roses?" Her face changes to disbelief. "Wait… you knew who I was but how did you know where I lived?

And who let the delivery man into my apartment?" Her sharp voice is piercing, and she is shaking.

"Promise you'll calm down and I'll tell you the whole story," says Alexey placing his hands on her arms rubbing them trying to soothe her. He had not expected such a reaction.

Hesitating at first, Larissa does calm down, "Alright, I promise."

He proceeds to tell her his agency had provided file photos of the nominees for the awards. When he saw her photo, he decided a thing of beauty should be sent beautiful roses. With a little detective work he had found her address and with a few Italian lire her doorman was easily convinced to let the deliveryman into the block.

"You're a sneak, but a loveable one," she says, "and please promise me you won't scare me like that again."

"I'm sorry darling, I didn't know you had been stalked. We don't hear too much celebrity news where I live."

"No, I suppose you don't. But no more lies please!"

He holds his arms out wide, "Will a hug make you feel better?" She falls into his welcoming arms. All is forgiven and forgotten. Alexey breathes a sigh of relief.

They are sitting on Larissa's balcony, rugged up and warm sipping two glasses of port. Rome is definitely inviting; it wouldn't be hard to get used to living here. Alexey is listening to Larissa as she recounts her conversation with Simona.

"It took some convincing, but she finally agreed to both of us going on Saturday. So, the plan is to leave early Saturday morning, offer to help her clear some stuff out of the basement and, hopefully, we find the artefacts."

"You make it sound so simple. I'm sure they are well hidden, otherwise they would have been found before now."

"Or, Simona is hiding something and doesn't want us to find out? Don't you think it's curious that your grandfather chose this time to find them? I'm telling you they are hiding something from us. Anyway, she is the only person who goes down there."

"Larissa, your journalistic mind astounds me. Stop creating stories before you are sure what Simona knows."

"I've told you before, something is up. Laura told me she heard her screaming again. My grandmother doesn't scream. At least she hasn't until now. Don't question me about her."

"Ok, ok!" He picks up both glasses along with the port bottle and heads inside. Larissa follows behind him.

"Please don't be angry with me. You're lucky to have a grandmother who loves you. She is protective of her privacy and she doesn't have to tell you and Gee everything going on in her life."

"I don't like the feeling she is hiding something important from us. Why else is she being cagey all of a sudden?"

Leaving the bottle and glasses on the bench, he places his arms around her shoulders. Kissing her nose, he says, "Look, you know your grandmother best. I was out of turn telling you what to do." His eyes meet hers, the now familiar feelings rising up inside him. She leads him to the bedroom.

They undress, slowly caressing each other. Their heated discussion is now washed away by her kisses. His whole body is alert to her touch. They are together in a rhapsody of love and as they are holding each other close, Alexey whispers his love for her.

"I'll be honest, I've never felt this before. I feel like shouting at the top of my voice, 'I love you, Larissa Mina'."

She looks up admiring his face, kissing him lightly on the lips, "I felt that the moment I met you."

Alexey smiles weakly, "Um, there's something I should tell you."

"Really what? Not more lies I hope?" Her eyes plead but her face is soft with love.

Before he can speak the phone rings. She asks him to hold his thought. Alexey leaves the bedroom as she picks up the receiver.

He is in the kitchen when Larissa tells him the call was from James.

"I have to go to the studio; a big political story has broken. We're doing a special Saturday night edition of Roma Tonight. Sorry Alexey, I have to go."

"Oh, is it ok if I come too? I'd be interested in watching how one of your shows is produced."

"What a good idea, I'm sure it won't be a problem. James might even give you a job to do," she laughs. "Let's shower and get going because we're on air in three hours."

The studio is hectic. They are told by the floor manager this thirty-minute show is dedicated to the overthrow of the government. Italy is known for its political upheavals and this is another major event. James and the research team have already organised live crosses and interviews.

Larissa brushes up on as much information as she can whilst Alexey watches on. He overhears that the Christian Democrats are in government and seem to have survived. Many people didn't like the social reforms the current government is proposing but somehow the votes went the way the government wanted them. On this show they are going to report why this particular overthrow didn't work and Larissa will interview the President about his plans going forward.

The studio floor is cleared as directors and technicians move up into the control room. Make-up artists and production assistants move out of shot. Larissa is ready for the interview. Alexey watches in the shadows and takes it all in. His job as a photojournalist, which he enjoys, is solitary compared to what Larissa does. He marvels at the teamwork and how, although it is chaotic behind the scenes, the television audience has no idea because the stories that go to air are seamless.

The show ends, their job is done. Alexey is in awe of the work involved. He hears some of the staff suggest going out for drinks at the local bar.

"Great idea," agrees James, "let's go. Larissa and Alexey, are you joining us?"

"You bet we are," answers Larissa. Alexey, who is standing next to her gives James a thumbs up.

. . .

"What a buzz," comments Alexey once seated at the bar, "I thought my job was exciting, but a live show… you can't beat it."

"Yes, my heart's still racing," says Larissa, "There is no time to think, everyone has to pull their weight and make it work."

James offers a round of drinks with cheers from everyone. They discuss the current political problem and the possibility of yet another election. Alexey listens intently, never having voted in his life. What he would give to have a say in the running of his country. Watching all this unfold has stirred something inside him, something he thought he would never think of, let alone do. That is, up until he met Larissa. This thought has been getting stronger with each day he has spent with her.

"Alexey, shall we go. I'd love a weekend away?" asks Larissa.

"Huh, pardon, weekend where?"

"Earth to Alexey, are you with us?" jokes Larissa, "a friend of James' has a villa in Tuscany. He asked if we'd like to go next weekend."

"Sounds great." It will be their last weekend together before he heads home to Leningrad. He can see how excited she is about going, he would not dare to say no. Not knowing when he'll be back again, the more time they spend together the better. Being away from her is something he would rather not think about.

"Ok, I'll let my friend know. You two can leave on the Friday after work, I'll already be there because I'm going to make a long weekend of it."

"Oh… I see. So, this is a special friend?" she asks placing her head on his shoulder looking up towards him, "care to tell me more?"

"Maybe? How special this friend is remains to be seen? We'll just have to wait and see."

"Hmmm, I look forward to the weekend then."

Larissa lifts her head from James' shoulder and looks towards Alexey asking him what he was about to tell her before they had to leave for the studio.

"Oh nothing. After what's happened tonight, it's not important anymore." He hugs her close giving her a peck on her cheek.

Chapter Eighteen

They park the car on Via Posillipo. This street is within walking distance of Corso Garibaldi where Simona lives. Walking arm in arm towards her grandmother's street they see Laura heading their way. Larissa lets go of Alexey's arm. "Hello Laura."

"Hi Larissa, Simona told me you were visiting today." Laura looks Alexey up and down.

Feeling awkward for him, Larissa introduces him. "This is my work colleague Alexey."

"Pleased to meet you." He shakes Laura's hand.

"Is she in a good mood today?" Larissa asks Laura.

"I haven't seen her this morning. I went over yesterday to check on her. She actually thanked me for helping out."

"And she should, Laura. Gee and I certainly appreciate everything you have done. Hopefully now she is better her mood will lift."

"I'm sure it will. Now I must be off, I'm meeting my husband at the station. He is arriving home from a fishing trip up north." They watch on as she leaves then Larissa says, "Brrr, let's get moving Alexey." The few minutes standing on this street corner had chilled her. She wraps her coat tighter around herself as they walk towards her grandmother's apartment.

. . .

Heading into Simona's apartment she is happy to find the fire has been lit. Warming herself, she introduces Alexey after greeting Simona.

"Hello, nice meeting you. Was the trip from Rome ok?" she asks greeting them both with a huge smile.

Larissa breathes a sigh of relief. She *is* in a good mood. "It was fine thanks Nonna."

"It's nice to meet you too, Mrs Pittola. Thank you for allowing me to be here. I hope you are feeling better," says Alexey.

"I am better, thank you for asking. Now please, both of you sit. I have prepared some coffee."

"I'll organise the coffee Nonna. Here, you sit, I'll bring it over." She overhears Simona asking Alexey where he is from and what brings him to Italy.

"I'm a photojournalist from the Soviet Union. I take photos for a living. My job takes me to different places depending on the assignment."

"Yes, Larissa tells me you want to see my basement. Is there a particular reason you chose mine?"

Before he can answer, Larissa speaks for him, "Nonna, the TV station I work for has hired Alexey to take photos for a story we're working on. Remember, I told you about my colleague?" She places the tray on the side table. Alexey helps himself, but Simona seems transfixed, her blank eyes stare into nothing. Larissa notices her ashen face as she passes her cup, "Nonna, are you ok?"

"Yes dear, I'm listening to your friend, why do you ask?" Just like that Simona snapped back into the room. Larissa was sure her mind was elsewhere; she had not been listening to Alexey nor her. "Oh nothing, you seemed a little distracted."

"You know I'm not sure I want strangers to see what is in our family basement. Do I really want one of your film crew snooping around? People are nosy around here."

Alexey explains he is only taking some photos, "There is no need for a film crew, just me."

Larissa sits quietly watching Simona's face, she had ignored her. All this has already been discussed. Simona knew they were coming down to look inside the basement. Again, she seems far away. It's almost as if she didn't hear Alexey. Time is running out for Vladimir. Alexey needs to check the basement today. Why is her grandmother holding out? "Nonna, is it ok for Alexey to take a look? We can even help you sort some of the things you may want to get rid of. You told Gee and I you wanted to tidy up down there."

With a stern look Simona answers, "I don't see the need for you to go down there when I have assured you there is nothing to see. Just a lot of familiar stuff with lots of memories for me." She takes a sip of her coffee not looking at either of them.

"We just want to look Nonna. I'm disappointed you think we are going to do some damage." Larissa has had enough of her stubbornness and moves towards the mantle to pick up the key. "We only need half an hour at the most." Holding the key in her hand she continues, "Just a quick look, that's all we're asking." Still holding the key, she moves closer to Simona. She doesn't even notice Larissa standing next to her, that faraway look is in her eyes.

Alexey places his hand on Larissa's arm indicating she calm herself. She places the key on the table then she picks up the empty coffee cups placing them on the tray, "I'll clean these up and we'll be going. Sorry to have troubled you."

Simona turns to look at the key. She snaps out of whatever it is she is thinking about and gives an almost imperceptible nod.

"Is that a *yes* Nonna?"

She nods again and hands her back the key. "Half an hour. No more." Then she explains to them the basement is around the corner in the next laneway. "Turn right after Laura's house, then left into the lane. It is number 20."

Larissa is intrigued. Why the sudden change? She is finding it difficult to understand her grandmother at the moment. But she decides not to question her motives, there is no time. Larissa is committed to helping Alexey, and this is what she will focus on.

．．．

The rancid smell hits them as they open the heavy timber door. A wave of memories floods her brain as she steps down into the basement. She remembers how Philip teased her about feeling ill if she stayed down here too long. She finds the light switch. The bulb is dim. She shrieks as a rat scurries over her boots.

Alexey is behind her. "What's wrong?"

"Ugh, rats. It's so damp down here, there's probably masses of them. Philip and I played down here when we were kids. One ran over my feet back then too. This is the first time I've been down here since that day."

His face remains impassive, concentrating on their task. "As long as you're not hurt, let's get on with it. Now, Vladimir told me to look for a sandstone block on the floor. It has had the mortar removed around it. But finding it is going to be a problem, look at all this stuff. Where do we start?"

They keep looking around moving ancient wine racks and cheese brackets. There are also garden and farm tools, antique irons and vats covered in age-old dust as thick as moss. "Here, Alexey. This one, it looks different."

He moves the empty vat that is covering most of the stone. "Well spotted Larissa. I suppose the reason Simona thinks there is nothing down here is no one has moved anything in a long time. Look at my hands." His hands are black with sooty dust from the vat. He claps his hands together and she sneezes. "Bless you. Now, we are going to need some help to budge this block. We can't do anything about it today."

Larissa sighs. It looks like they are going to have to do more negotiating with Simona.

Chapter Nineteen

Making their way back up to Simona's apartment they see Laura again. This time she is with her husband, Alessandro. Larissa recalls he is a builder, so she seizes the moment. After introducing Alexey, she asks Alessandro if he has any tools suitable for lifting a sandstone block.

"I still have some tools, but they are at the farm. When do you need them and what exactly are you trying to do?"

"We need to lift a block that is on the floor of the basement. We're heading up to ask Simona's permission."

Alessandro gives her a quizzical look, but he does not ask the reason. "I have a lifting wedge. It's old but it should do the trick. Let me know when you need the tools and I'll drive up to the farm and collect them for you."

Larissa admires both he and Laura. They have been family friends since her mother was a child. Whatever has been asked of them they have been more than happy to oblige. Good friends like these are hard to find. "Thank you, Alessandro. Let me see if Simona is ok with this. I'll call you as soon as I know."

. . .

They find Simona in the kitchen. "How is this for timing? Exactly thirty minutes."

"Thank you for your obedience." She turns looking at both of them, "Would you both like something to eat?"

They answer in unison, "Thank you but no."

"Nonna, we did find something. There is a stone down there without mortar and I think there is a possibility something is hidden underneath it."

"I know the stone you are talking about. That has been like that since before your grandfather died. At least twenty years." Simona heads towards her chair. She sits breathing out a long sigh. "It is just normal movement of old soil. There is nothing hidden, I can assure you."

Larissa ignores her stubborn tone. "On our way back to see you we ran into Laura and Alessandro. He has tools and is willing to help us lift it. We will put everything back for you. Besides, do you need all the stuff you have down there? Maybe we can help you clear some of it?"

"Yes, I do. A lot of those items have sentimental value. The timber stacked down there I use for the fireplace, as you can see." She nods towards the warming glow.

"I understand you need timber but all those wine vats and cheese barrels - you don't make your own wine and cheese anymore so why keep them?"

Simona explains they are part of her memories, of times with her husband and all their family and friends making fresh cheeses and wine. "Sometimes I sit down there and remember. The memories come flooding back, they are so special. We had fun. So much laughter. They were good times," says Simona looking down towards her hands. As she raises her head, her eyes glisten with tears.

Larissa's face reddens, she feels awful for even mentioning it now. This is one of the few times Simona has said something good about her past. She rarely talks about her youth, merely stating how tough life was when she was growing up. How hard it was to survive each day. However, the problem remains. Time is running out and she wants the best outcome for Alexey. "What about if we place items outside? Once we're done, we'll put it all back for you?"

"This is a lot of trouble for something that may not be there. Alexey, why this basement? Who told you about it?"

Larissa is surprised at Simona questioning Alexey in this way. This makes her even more suspicious that Simona knows about the artefacts. "Nonna, why are you asking…"

Alexey stops her, "Larissa, it's ok. Your grandmother has a right to know." He bends forward, focusing directly on Simona, "I am from Leningrad. Many artefacts were removed from a museum during WWII. I am part of a group interested in retrieving these lost items. Yours is not the first basement I have searched." He looks towards Larissa indicating she remains quiet to let her grandmother process what he has told her.

After minutes of silence, Simona nods in agreement but with a stern stipulation everything has to go back, "If I find something missing, I'll be most upset. It is up to me to decide what to keep."

"Ok Nonna, thank you and please don't stress. I will call Alessandro and hopefully he can bring the tools down this afternoon. Alexey and I will find somewhere to stay tonight, and we'll get an early start in the morning. Are you ok with that Alexey?" Her words are racing out of her mouth. She wants a plan in place before Simona changes her mind once again.

"I have no problem with it at all. We will work as quickly as we can Mrs Pittola. The less disruption we cause you the better."

Larissa blows out a sigh of relief as Simona gives them final agreement.

The next morning a dust strewn Alexey is sitting with Alessandro on the stoop resting after hours of moving items out of the basement. Larissa has fresh panini and a beer for each of them. Taking their gloves off they accept the food.

"Thanks, I'm starving. I don't think I've worked this hard in years. How can one person have so much junk?" says Alexey taking a swig of the beer.

Larissa laughs and tells him her family is not known for throwing things out. "We do tend to hoard things. As you heard from my grandmother, she doesn't need all of this stuff, but she doesn't have the heart to throw it away. We are a sentimental bunch."

"We can start prying the stone out now. We've taken out as much stuff as we need to," Alessandro tells Larissa with a mouthful of bread, "By the way, is there a reason you are doing this? You can tell me to mind my own business, I'm just curious because it's a lot of work and nothing is being thrown out."

"It's research for a story on basements that Alexey and I are working on. That's why Alexey has been taking photos." She doesn't offer more information and he doesn't ask any other questions. As she heads back towards the apartment with the food tray, she turns towards them, "I'll be back as soon as I can to help you both."

Returning within ten minutes, she pops her head into the basement, "Simona is resting again. I can help you two for a few hours."

As she steps down, Alexey says, "Look what I found whilst you were upstairs." Larissa takes an old sepia photo from Alexey. "Is this your grandmother or maybe your Aunt Amelia?" he asks pointing to the woman in the photo. "I'm sure the young man is Vladimir. I've seen other photos of him in the same uniform."

She exclaims, "This is my Aunt! Look her name is written on the back."

They both examine the fragile photo. The faint ink marks do spell her name. There are other ink markings, but they are no longer legible. They both agree to show the photo to Simona later. Larissa doesn't remember there being any other photos of her great aunt around anywhere. Neither at Simona's nor her parent's home. She places it on the rickety shelf saying, "Remind me to take this with us when we finish in here."

After another hour of solid heaving, the stone is finally lifting. The stone itself is not wide, but it is the depth of it that surprises Alessandro. "This stone has been tampered with," he says, "it has been broken in half. Most of the blocks used for building in this area are deeper than this one."

Neither Larissa nor Alexey reply. Alexey is shining a torch into the hole. They are staring at a miniature glory box with rusted locks. Alexey lifts the box from its resting place. Insects scurry around frantically in and around the hole left by the box. Larissa cringes but by now is used to the smells and inhabitants of this basement.

"Larissa, you watch this while we place these items back in the basement," Alexey asks.

She is happy to oblige. Exhaustion has taken over, her legs feeling like lead weights. Not being used to physical labour, she has used muscles she didn't know she had.

"Ok, that's the last of it," says Alessandro clapping his hands. Dust furls from them making Larissa sneeze again. "Bless you."

"Ha, thanks. And thank you for your help today. This could not have been done without you and your trusty tools. Please let me offer you something for your time."

"Don't be silly. What are neighbours for? I've actually enjoyed using these old tools again. They sit at the farm doing nothing, especially this lifting wedge." With that he collects the tools and places them back on his truck. "I was happy to be of help. Good luck with the documentary, I look forward to watching it."

She is slightly embarrassed they have lied to him. However, he will probably forget all about this in a few days. She waves as he leaves and is happy he didn't hang around to see what was in the box.

"Oh, my aching bones. I'm glad to be out of there," says Alexey stretching, "but it was all worth it right? We have found the artefacts."

"Shouldn't we open it? What if it's not what you are looking for?"

"Vladimir gave me all the information about what it would look like. This is the box. He told me it was dark timber with this floral inlay. I saw a photo too. We better not open it here. Let's open it in front of Simona, without her agreeing to allow us down here this box would still be buried," he says.

The look on Alexey's face, one of pride and contentment, gives her tingles. He is fulfilling his grandfather's dream; someone Alexey loves with his whole being.

Larissa lets them both into the apartment.

Simona sees Alexey holding a box, giving him a quizzical look, "You found something? Am I going to be privileged to see what all the fuss was about?"

The look on her face does not mimic her cheery tone. In fact, she looks positively ill. "Nonna, you look like you've seen a ghost?"

"I have. The box… it belonged to my mother. I thought it was lost during the bombings."

Larissa places her arm around her grandmother's shoulders, "Oh, have we inadvertently found another heirloom?"

"It… seems… you have," splutters Simona beginning to cry. Larissa hugs her as Alexey places the box down in front of the fireplace and carefully opens the lid. Removing layers of aged newspaper, he finds items wrapped in fabric. There are three pieces. Each one is spectacular in its own right.

"They are quite exquisite, aren't they?" says Larissa as Simona gasps. "I agree but I'm in shock again. I recognise that fabric. It's from Amelia's wedding dress." Simona starts to sway. Larissa helps her to her chair, "I'll get you a glass of water." Her grandmother has suffered the loss of her mother and sister. Both in tragic circumstances. Then her husband died at a young age. This is so much loss to deal with. Larissa had not thought this through. Digging up the basement meant digging up Simona's past, a past she rarely speaks about.

Passing her the glass Larissa says, "I'm sorry this is affecting you this way. When you are ready, would you like to tell us about this box?"

Simona takes a sip then says, "Our mother kept it on her dresser.

The same dresser I now have in my own bedroom, the deep walnut one."

"Yes, I know it. Do you have any idea how this box ended up in the basement?"

"None at all."

Is her grandmother lying to her? Or is it true she has no idea? Amelia may not have told her about the artefacts to protect her. If they had been discovered during the war, then Simona would possibly not be here today. Larissa is thankful Amelia did the right thing in not telling her. But this does not explain why Simona was so insistent on them not going into the basement. Larissa is curious, what is she hiding? She will ask her another time and try to be more diplomatic, upsetting her grandmother isn't helping Alexey.

Whilst they are discussing the glory box Alexey is taking photos of the items. Then he carefully wraps them placing them back into the box saying, "Show your grandmother the photo, Larissa. I think we've found two precious items for her today."

"Oh yes, look what else we found besides the artefacts. It was in this envelope wrapped in more of the fabric." says Larissa handing Simona the photo of the couple, "Is this my Great Aunt Amelia?"

Simona regards the photo for some time without comment. Her eyes glisten once more, "Yes, it is," she whispers.

Larissa moves closer to her taking hold of her hand, "Nonna, I'm so sorry. This is a lot to take in."

"There are so many memories flooding my mind right now. However, this photo, I don't remember ever seeing it," she whispers again as tears flow silently down her face. She caresses her sister's face with her finger.

"I know it has been a long time, do you want to talk about her? I'd like to know what she was like." As she asks this, Alexey walks back into the lounge and sits beside Larissa. They both listen to Simona. She proceeds to tell them stories of her childhood and how Amelia became her protector after their mother passed away, "They were turbulent times. She had to grow up fast and take over our mother's duties. It was expected by our father." Simona goes on to explain the man standing with Amelia in the photo could be a man named Vladimir. Amelia helped him recover from wounds he received. "I can't be exactly sure because I only met him once. It is definitely not Amelia's husband; he was not as tall as this man standing next to her. Actually, he looks to be a similar age to you Alexey. There is a resemblance too."

Alexey asks to look at the photo again, "Hmm, I guess so," he says without committing either way, "if it's ok with you I will organise to have a copy made and have this one restored for you to keep if you like?"

"That would be lovely, thank you Alexey. I will place it in a frame and treasure it."

Alexey smiles, "Simona thank you for allowing us to do this. I have appreciated your hospitality this weekend. I'm honoured I was able to find this photo. It's a memory of your sister, one I know you will cherish." Then he turns to Larissa, "We need to go soon."

She nods towards him then turns to Simona. "Nonna, would you like me to call Laura? Do you need some company tonight? It's been a traumatic day for you."

"Thank you but no. I will be going to bed early. The two of you have a safe drive back to Rome. It was lovely to meet you Alexey."

"Lovely meeting you too, Mrs Pittola. Thank you again for allowing us to do this." Turning to Larissa he says, "I'll go and get the car. Please make sure we have everything to take back with us."

Larissa nods, "Yes ok." As he leaves, she turns to her grandmother and gives her a hug, "I know how stressful this weekend has been for you. Like Alexey, I appreciate you allowing us to trouble you like this."

Simona takes Larissa's hand placing it to her heart, "You are my only granddaughter. I know I am stubborn at times, but today you have allowed me to indulge my memories. There is one thing I ask you, whatever the photos are used for, please keep the basement's location obscure. Is that possible?"

"I'm sure that won't be a problem."

"Please do your best."

"I will Nonna. I promise we will look after your mother's glory box and have it returned to you."

As she finishes speaking, Alexey comes in and collects the box. "We certainly will look after it. You have no idea how much you have helped us today," he says bowing down to kiss Simona's cheek. Then, to Larissa he says, "Let's go. We have a long drive back."

Chapter Twenty

"These artefacts are extremely valuable," informs the Professor, "we estimate they are from late 19th to early 20th century… and they are definitely of Russian origin."

Larissa smiles at Alexey. The three of them are standing around a solid mahogany bench in the office of Professor Ortonio, who is enraptured by the tankard he is holding. She had taken his course on *Evolution and Sociolinguistics* as an extracurricular subject when she was a student at this university. The professor is more rotund, his head is now devoid of hair but he is still the amiable person she remembers. When she had called to make the appointment asking for his help, he obliged willingly.

The artefacts are carefully laid out on protective mats in front of them. The Professor picks up the tankard using gloved hands. He points to an inscription on the underside, explaining that its meaning is unknown. The tankard is designed with a flip handle lid made of pure silver. The lid on its own weighs several kilos. "This piece is early 20th Century, the *Bock* marking you can see means it was made by Karl Ioganovich Bock, who was appointed court jeweller to the Tsarist royals of the era. See this forest scene glazed into the glass and the etched silver, these are traditional features of his work. His silver workshop supplied the court from 1901. During the Russian revolution and the forced abdication of Nicholas II many precious items were destroyed, lost or stolen. This item is magnificent and is in almost perfect condition. Amazing... given how far it travelled." He places the tankard back on its mat, picking up the bracelet and handing it to Larissa. "The cuff bracelet is late 19th Century and it contains; gold, rubies, pearls and enamel. This was a high-fashion item at the time."

Larissa cradles the bracelet as Professor Ortonio continues. He explains the royals and wealthy women wore them on silk blouses with wide sleeves. The fashion at the time was to cuff the fabric over the bracelet achieving a ballooning of the sleeve. These blouses were made of silk manufactured expressly for the rich. "The necklace with the cross medallion is made of gold, rubies, emeralds, diamonds and pearls. This item is from Moscow and was made in the 1860s. You two finding these beautiful pieces is such a find, they are priceless," the Professor concludes. He is holding the heavily embellished necklace with both hands, treasuring it.

"Professor Ortonio, it was a pleasure to see you again. Thank you for taking the time to assess these items," says Larissa with a warm handshake.

Alexey replaces the artefacts back into the box. "It was nice to meet you Professor. On behalf of my grandfather I thank you. He spoke of these items with great pride. Preserving Soviet history was his passion during the war years."

The Professor smiles, "It is *my* honour to meet you Alexey. I understand your grandfather's motivations. There are not many who wish to save cultural treasures for future generations. To my mind your grandfather and his comrades were inspirational. I look forward to hearing about the safe return of these items back to where they belong."

Larissa is heading towards the door as Alexey says, "Wait a moment Larissa, I have a question before we leave." He turns back towards the professor, "My grandfather told me of friends who helped him to bring other art pieces to Italy. They were scattered throughout Europe. Was this a regular occurrence with the partisan armies?"

"Yes, the partisan armies helped many people to escape the tyrannies of war but also helped to preserve valuable pieces of art and history. Your grandfather was one of many such heroes. As we speak there are people looking for such artefacts. We hope they are successful as you have been."

Larissa watches on. Alexey is beaming with pride for his grandfather's heroic efforts. He continues telling them how Vladimir had been against the war but was forced to enlist. Many of his fellow comrades felt the same, which is why they joined the partisan army. They all wanted a quick end to the war.

"Even though Vladimir was a high-ranking member of the NKVD, now known as the KGB, he abhorred violence against innocent people. He told me many stories of the innocent he saw tortured, bullied and killed. He thought, as many did at the time, the war had drawn out far too long and he wanted to do good, not harm."

The professor nods and clearing his throat says, "Unfortunately, many people throughout Europe know someone who suffered atrocities during the war, my own family was not immune."

"Again, I especially would like to thank you for your time Professor. I appreciate you assisting us with this."

"It is my pleasure Alexey. My thanks to both of you for allowing me to care for these treasures, and if you do need anything further you know how to contact me."

Alexey opens the heavy door for Larissa as they exit the Grand Hall, "Here give me the box. Now we can concentrate on having these precious artefacts returned." Larissa braces against the wind as they walk to the car. Alexey's eyes are full of sorrow. He wants Vladimir to be with him for the handover to Russia, but from what he has told her, his health may not allow this. "This is a story needing to be told. With your permission I'll speak to James about dedicating a show, maybe a special one-hour show. The public should know of people like your grandfather and the good they did during this horrible time in history."

Alexey is hesitant, "My grandfather is a private man. I'm not sure he will want a public ceremony at all. Nor doing it through your show. Please give me some time to think about how to return the artefacts."

This is a sudden change of heart she had not expected. When they had discussed this after finding the artefacts, he was open to her ideas. She has already started organising a scheduled special. She decides to let this slide for now, she will pick a better moment. The story will be told, one way or another she will make it happen.

Chapter Twenty-One

Viktoriya is at Pulkovo Airport to greet him but she is the last person he wants to see. He kisses his fiancé on the cheek. As they walk out of the airport, she threads her arm through his. She chats about insignificant things. Alexey remains silent. "Grandfather is waiting for you at home," she says, "I've prepared a meal you won't forget. I was able to buy meat early this morning."

Not even the mention of food snaps him out of his silence. He is aching from travelling eight hours. Missing his connecting flight out of Vnukovo Airport, delayed him. Viktoriya drives them home in silence. He knows she is annoyed with him but in his surly mood he wants to avoid a fight. He has more important things to deal with.

"Welcome home my grandson."

"Thank you, are you well Grandfather?" asks Alexey even though he knows this is a futile question.

"For one who has lived as I, one cannot expect to be better."

This is true, Vladimir has lived every minute of his life to the limit. Alexey knows his grandfather is lucky to still be alive, he has made many enemies over the years. His medals and achievements had only compounded the other comrades' hatred and disdain during and after the war. Still, he seems a happy man having lived the way he wished.

Viktoriya serves lunch and they sit quietly eating the rationed but delicious stroganoff. She is a country girl who moved in with Alexey a few months after arriving in Leningrad. They had met through friends. He was attracted to her shy demeanour. Had he not met Larissa, things may have worked out for them. At twenty-five years old, she looks younger than her age, with a petite figure and long blonde locks reaching her buttocks. She is not unattractive, but Larissa is on his mind now, so how can he stay with Viktoriya?

She is attempting to make conversation and is especially interested in hearing about Rome. But he ignores her. She is becoming annoyed by his short, abrupt answers. She makes one last attempt at conversation. Again, he ignores her. "My apologies to both of you but I must get some sleep. Grandfather we will speak later." His grandfather nods his acceptance and Viktoriya just glares. He chooses to keep ignoring her. He knows what she is thinking by being in a relationship with him. Having a fiancé who is a photo-journalist means a possible key to the West. This is Viktoriya's dream. She has mentioned many times her wish to live in Italy, or possibly France. He knows he is the vehicle to make her dream come true.

Reaching the bedroom, he hears her announcing to Vladimir she is returning to work. She works at a local bakery, and even that does not ensure they have enough fresh bread for the three of them.

Lying down on their bed he moans, stretches and makes himself comfortable. Sleep comes easily, leaving Larissa has exhausted him emotionally and physically. More than he thought possible. He is truly under her spell.

He wakes to see the sun setting, having slept soundly for hours. Sitting up he pulls on a t-shirt and leaves the bedroom. He finds his grandfather watching the small television sitting up on the kitchen shelf.

"I trust you feel better. Viktoriya left for work soon after you went to sleep."

"I do, thank you." He grabs a bottle of vodka and two shot glasses from the cabinet in the kitchen. Placing them in front of his grandfather he says, "to our health."

"To our health."

Their glasses clink then they down them in one gulp. Alexey feels the burn down his throat. There is nothing like Russian vodka to pep you up. He then proceeds to tell Vladimir what he was able to find out. Confirming how Simona was reluctant to talk about the war and her stubbornness about the basement. "She eventually allowed us to enter. We were lucky and found them in one weekend. One of Simona's neighbours helped us."

Vladimir nods his head, "It was an awful time for the whole of Europe, too many people died and those who didn't die, saw too many atrocities. Such things are hard to be unseen." He pauses then continues, "You say you needed help from a neighbour? Was this wise?"

"He is a friend of Larissa's family. His wife was good friends with Amelia, and they keep an eye on Simona. These people are not dangerous, they will cause no problems. Now, I will need to return to Rome again. My next trip will have to be longer than six weeks. The handover of the artefacts will take time." Even as Alexey says this, he worries about leaving his grandfather again.

"It is important for you to go. I do not want anyone else to handle those treasures. They are with Larissa I assume? Does anyone else other than Simona and her neighbours know about them?"

Alexey shakes his head no. "The least amount of people involved with the treasures the better. You told me this already. Had the stone not been a problem to move, I would have uncovered them myself."

Vladimir coughs. His nicotine breath wafts towards Alexey, "It must be you to return them to Russia in my name. Then, if you wish you might want to convince our government to find the other treasures hidden in other parts of Europe by my comrades."

Alexey tells his grandfather not to worry, he will organise another assignment with his agency. Vladimir continues coughing.

Alexey goes to the sink and fills a glass with water, handing it to him.

"Arrghh! Water, it is disgusting. Pour me another vodka."

He fills his grandfather's shot glass again and smirks at how resilient he is, no matter how sick, he keeps going day after day. But his concerns of Vladimir's health now take second place. Larissa is his number one priority. He thinks about seeing her again. She is the one he desperately wants to be with.

His thoughts turn to Viktoriya. They have been engaged for six months. The engagement was her idea and he was happy to go along. Then. Not now. His life has changed. He knows what real love feels like having met Larissa. Hearing his grandfather's story about the love he felt for Amelia and how he was prepared to give everything up for her, Alexey feels this same love for Larissa. His heart is racing just thinking about her. He will find a way to be with her permanently. He had not been strong enough to tell Larissa he was engaged. Having drummed up the courage only once, the phone had interrupted them. Now, engaged or not engaged, he doesn't care. Viktoriya is not his future. Larissa is, she is the love of his life.

He does have one concern. How is their relationship going to work? Will she ever move to the Soviet Union?

This is unlikely, I have to be realistic, if I was in her shoes would I move?

No, he would not expect her to give up her freedom. The more he thinks about this situation, the more thoughts of defecting become apparent to him — but what of grandfather and his dream of having the artefacts returned?

Putting all these thoughts aside, he picks up the phone and calls his agency.

Chapter Twenty-Two

"Colonel Bruskev please"

"Is the Colonel expecting you?"

"Tell him Alexey Dubrovnik wishes to speak with him."

Alexey sits at an awkward angle on the lopsided antiquated chair in the sparsely furnished reception area and waits. None of the official offices are ever inviting and this office is no exception. The wall clock ticks relentlessly as he waits.

He is wondering whether Bruskev will even see him when, an hour after sitting down, the receptionist finally walks him into his office.

"Mr Dubrovnik, to what do I owe the pleasure? Sit, make yourself comfortable."

Alexey glares at him with the contempt fit for a man of his calibre, "I hear you went to visit my grandfather." He sits in the cracked leather chair, sinking further into it than he expected. Doesn't the KGB know how to buy decent chairs?

"Is it a crime to visit an old friend?"

"For what reason did you ask of me. Since when have my movements concerned the KGB? I am a photographer and you know the agency I work with. They are reputable."

"Alexey… if I may call you by your first name?"

He makes no response. How he is addressed is of no importance.

Bruskev continues also unmoved, "We were conversing about your family in general, it was an innocent inquiry."

There is nothing innocent about neither Bruskev nor the KGB. Alexey keeps up his guard. Even though he is sitting a good metre away from him, he sees Bruskev's top lip is shiny with sweat. Is he threatened even though there is a large wooden desk between them? The thought that Bruskev might fear him is amusing. "My grandfather is very ill, he does not need any undue stress. If you wished to speak to me you should have contacted me directly. Or through Dusitrovii Agency, my agents."

"Please, I had no desire to harm your grandfather. Nor you for that matter. It was because of his ill health that I paid a visit."

"KGB business does not concern Vladimir Dubrovnik any longer. You have no right to disturb my grandfather in this way." Alexey pushes himself out of the uncomfortable chair and turns towards the office door. He stops as Bruskev speaks again.

"It is no secret Vladimir and I have had our differences over the years but that is in the past, all forgotten…"

Alexey decides not to listen and doesn't bother looking back, he knows whatever Bruskev says is just a smoke screen. A man such as Bruskev is not to be trusted. Ever.

Entering his apartment, he is greeted by a joyful Viktoriya. She is excited and wants to give him some good news. He asks her to wait until he's spoken to his grandfather, handing her a small gift he had purchased. She thanks him telling him how appreciative she is for such a present. He just nods giving her a half smile, now wishing he had not bothered. Did he buy it out of guilt? Probably.

Vladimir, who is waiting for him in the small lounge, greets his grandson. They begin discussing the events of his trip. "We hope the show airs next month. Larissa is working on the handover with her team. The two Presidents have to coordinate their schedules before there is a firm on-air date. I will keep you informed. Now, what did Bruskev say to you?"

Vladimir had not wanted such a fuss over the artefacts being returned but had agreed after he heard his grandson's enthusiasm for the journalist and her idea. Had he not been proud to save some of Russia's historical gems? It took some convincing, but he eventually came around.

"He wants some of the credit for the artefacts, I guess. Especially now in view of the way they are being returned. He was always one for the limelight. Why else would he visit me after so many years?"

Alexey smiles. Yes, Bruskev is a man who seems to be wherever he needs to be to move his career forward. He had a knack of sticking his nose where it shouldn't be. This handover being one of them.

Both agreeing Bruskev had nothing to do with the partisan army's efforts and so deserves none of the credit, they stop discussing him and concentrate on matters that are more important.

"Grandfather, we found this photo in the basement. I'd like you to confirm it is you standing next to Amelia. Simona has already confirmed the lady in the photo is her sister."

Vladimir takes the photo. Staring at it, tears slip down his face.

Alexey is stunned by his show of emotion and places his hand on his grandfather's shoulder.

Vladimir clears his throat, returns to his stoic self and confirms it is indeed he who is standing next to Amelia. "My only regret is never seeing her again. In those troubled times it was not easy keeping promises," he says as he begins recounting stories of how he managed his return to Leningrad. How he returned without injury is mainly due to the partisan army taking care of their own.

Alexey is horrified as his grandfather recounts how he helped to bury many unrecognisable, bombed bodies. How maimed, bloodied people were assisted in makeshift medical areas. Buildings were rendered uninhabitable, but these same buildings became temporary shelters for those left without homes. Innocent children, alone and without parents, were homeless and terrified. In the year after Vladimir left Naples, the atrocities he witnessed are forever in his memory. "No one trusted anyone, and it was difficult to help some people, but we did what we could. Your heart becomes hard and you do what needs to be done. Seeing children suffering was the worst." Vladimir sighs and remains quiet for some time.

Alexey cannot fathom the terror people endure during times of war. The generations born after this destructive and cruel world war are the benefactors, generations such as his own. Listening to these stories he realises no one actually won. However, he marvels at how resilient human beings can be. People like his grandfather did survive to tell their stories. Stories that should never be forgotten.

Still holding the photo, Vladimir asks to be helped to the spare bed. Alexey begins to say something, but Vladimir's hand is up stopping him before he can start speaking.

After making sure Vladimir is comfortable Alexey finds Viktoriya preparing dinner for them in the kitchen. He helps with chopping some vegetables and comments on his grandfather's worsening condition. "I don't think he will be with us much longer," sniffs Alexey overcome with emotion.

Viktoriya tries to reassure him saying, "Your grandfather is ill and there is nothing we can do to help except be with him, give support and help him to be comfortable. We can take care of his needs but that is all." She puts down the pot she is holding and then gently places both her hands on his shoulders and looks him in the eye, "Maybe what I have to tell you will cheer you," she says placing a light kiss on his lips, "I'm pregnant."

Alexey is stunned! Did he actually hear her say she is pregnant? Frozen to the spot he is numb with uncertainty.

"I'm three months. No one knows yet. You're the first person I've told because I wanted to be sure."

His mind is a blur. A baby… three months. It happened before Vladimir's story, before the Italian trip, before Larissa.

"Alexey aren't you going to say anything? I know it's a surprise…"

"Viktoriya I… it's just a shock. Of course, I'm thrilled. But umm, very unexpected. We haven't even discussed having children," he blurts out. Nor have they discussed a date to be married for that matter. He walks towards the lounge area needing space, trying to piece together his thoughts.

"These things happen. I'm thrilled too. Can we organise a wedding date now? What do you think, before or after the birth?" asks Viktoriya following him.

This cannot be happening now. He has Larissa, the artefacts, his grandfather's dream to fulfil… how do you fit a child into a life like this? He suggests to her he needs to get used to the fact she is pregnant before they start considering marriage plans.

She nods but disappointment floods her face.

On top of Vladimir's ill health, Bruskev and Larissa, this is not what he needs right now. He notices disappointment spreading over Viktoriya's face as her happiness turns to dismay. She turns away from him without a word and storms towards their bedroom.

Alexey sits at the kitchen table with a bottle of vodka and doesn't move until Viktoriya comes in to prepare the table. Without looking at him she asks him to wake Vladimir. Obeying her, he is still stunned by her news. She is also fuming over his non-reaction.

Whilst skolling vodka glass after glass, he has been trying to work out what his next step will be.

Entering the room where he had left his grandfather sleeping, he finds him with the photo pressed to his heart. "Grandfather, would you like something to eat?"

Vladimir whispers, "No. Alexey find Amelia; tell her I love her."

Alexey leans over and touches Vladimir's arm. He again tells his grandfather Amelia is dead but Vladimir splutters with his last breath, "I love you Alexey, look after your…"

"No. No grandfather, not now. Not yet." He is whispering, his body wracked with sobs, "No."

With his head down, his shoulders shudder as he cries silent tears. His voice has abandoned him, and he is paralysed, not wanting to leave Vladimir's side.

Eventually spent and exhausted, he walks out of the room leaving Vladimir as he found him, clutching the photo of he and

Amelia to his heart. He returns to the kitchen pale-faced, "Grandfather is dead."

Vladimir Dubrovnik's funeral is a public event. Friends and foes attend the military-style ceremony as the few members of the Dubrovnik clan follow the procession. His brother, Nicolai, comes to pay his respects. Alexey ignores his uncle. Too little too late. Where was he when his brother needed him.

Walking behind the hearse, they enter the cemetery where his parents were laid to rest. His boots crunch the snow, compacting it to muddy slush. Viktoriya has her arm through his. They have spoken little since her news, which is fine by him. His grief for his grandfather is enough to deal with. Larissa, too. He aches for her. The pain of leaving her is as deep as his grief of Vladimir's death. Devastated by his feelings of loss and Viktoriya's untimely news, Alexey goes through the motions. The funeral is a blur of mixed emotions for him.

He is speaking to Larissa with this hand over the mouthpiece, he doesn't want Viktoriya to overhear. Hearing her voice takes him out of his grief. He listens and is glad to hear how she is progressing with the handover. She is waiting for him to return so they can discuss the presentation of the artefacts to the dignitaries. He knows he needs to be back in Italy. Tears well in his eyes as he explains to Larissa his grandfather has passed away. They were too late; Vladimir will not see his dream. They cry and each remains silent, both giving each other time to take in the news.

He tells her about the funeral, "I think he would have been pleased. The agency did everything they could to honour his legacy, right down to his retired comrades being in full uniform. It was very moving."

"I'm so sorry Alexey," sobs Larissa, "you wanted him to see them being returned, but time was against us. It's lovely you were with him. He would have taken comfort with you being…"

Suddenly, there is no tone, the phone line goes dead. Alexey curses and slams down the handset, staring at it. He shakes his head deciding not to call her back. They will be together again soon, he must return for the handover. Now, it is even more important for him to do this right. His grandfather's dream will happen.

Chapter Twenty-Three

Simona is sitting in a restaurant near Lungomare looking over to Vesuvius. Christmas lights are being connected to the outside of the restaurant. She picked Pizzeria Visconti for this meeting because it's usually a quiet restaurant away from the main tourist traps. Why she has even agreed to meet is still troubling her? The past is the past, which is where they agreed to leave it. Why is Amelia coming here after all these years? Apprehensive about what this means to her family, it's too late now. She sits waiting as a small part of her is fired up and excited to see her sister again. Nervous about their meeting, she had changed her outfits four times. How do you dress for such a meeting? Is there a dress code for reuniting with a long-lost sister? Her wardrobe is full of primarily black and dark colours. Since her husband's death she could never bring herself to wear something bright again. Even though he died years ago.

Watching the entrance, an elegant woman is being directed towards her table. It is her older sister, Amelia. Dressed in a bright red coat; her hair is shorter and lighter in colour, but there is no mistaking who she is. Amelia looks younger than Simona, who now feels drab and old in her grey woollen dress. She strides behind the waitress, her face lighting up the instant she spots Simona. Amelia walks towards her and as she stands in front of her, Simona's resolve melts. She falls into her sister's arms and the years slide away. Both sob openly. Both oblivious to people staring.

Simona eventually motions for them to sit down. The waitress immediately asks if they would like to order after placing two menus on the table. "Please give us a minute?" The waitress nods with an apathetic look but Simona decides to ignore it. "Thank you, I appreciate it." Then she looks at Amelia and asks, "How was the flight? How exciting being on an aeroplane."

"Tedious. Australia is a long way from Europe. You have no idea," she looks at Simona with tears still glistening in her eyes, "But now I'm here it's worth the trip. I'm so happy to see you."

"I am too but I have been anxious about this. So why now?" Sitting this close to Amelia, fine lines around her eyes come into focus. She too has suffered.

"You have never been far from my thoughts. Lately though, I have needed to see you since I saw a reporter on one of our news services. She was a younger version of you. I couldn't let it go. Honestly, it was driving me crazy."

"Amelia, you are dead to my family. That was our story, don't you remember? You asked me to stick to this story and, with much difficulty, I have. It was you who wanted to leave. You left me with all the mess whilst you went on your adventure to find Vladimir. Well, I cleaned up the mess and now you want to come back into my family?" Simona remembers the phone call eight years after Amelia left. She had called wanting to reconnect, letting her know she had survived and was living in Australia. As much as Simona was relieved to hear from her sister, eight years is a lifetime to a child. Gee knew Simona as her mother, and this is how it was to remain. She explained to Amelia that her husband accepted Giovanna as his. To change this would not help anyone. And what about Amelia's new husband? How would he feel? They had argued but eventually she saw reason. In the end, it was Amelia who suggested they keep the secret between themselves.

"I wasn't going to come here at all Simona. Up until seeing the news reporter, our phone calls to each other had been enough. Hearing your voice was enough. But not anymore. I need to know who she is; I need to see my daughter again."

Simona remains silent. She fidgets, her eyes down towards the cutlery. She adjusts it for no reason.

Clearing her throat, Amelia's voice is hoarse, "We made a tough decision. Both of us had been through a lot of trauma with our father…"

Simona places her hand on Amelia's arm, "Don't! We agreed to never speak of him again."

Amelia stops and nods her head sombrely. Again, an awkward silence rests between them. The waitress is hovering once more asking for their orders. They order but Simona is no longer hungry.

Amelia takes Simona's hand in hers and looks straight into her eyes, "I need to see them, just once."

And there's that look Amelia perfected. Simona remembers that look from years gone by. It always unsettled her. This was the look Amelia always used when she wanted her own way, "Are you crazy Amelia? If you are to meet Gee and Larissa how do I explain you are not dead? They will know I have lied all these years and they will want to know why? I'm not prepared to dig up the past Amelia, you were the one who left. This is what you wanted. You should never have come back." She clenches her fists, her jaw firm. Simona fumes now wishing she had not agreed to this meeting. As much as it is wonderful seeing her sister again she does not want her to meet Gee and Larissa. They are her daughter and granddaughter, and this is all they will ever know. Imagine the trauma they will go through if they learn the truth. Something she and Amelia buried long ago. No, she will stand firm. Their secret will remain just that, a secret.

The waitress dumps their food on the table and Amelia makes a comment about the lack of service, but Simona is not open to small, insignificant chitchat. "Amelia, you are not to stay, do you hear me?"

"Listen to me, she is my daughter. I had her, not you," says Amelia with tortured anger. Hurt floods Simona's face. Tears flow again. Amelia's voice softens, "You cannot know how it feels to have given her up. Remember all those times I saved you. That basement was both our sanctuary and our gaol. What happened has affected us both."

Simona doesn't answer right away. She is thinking how crazy her sister is to even contemplate this, after everything she has done to make a life without her. Doesn't she realise how hard it was for her to pretend she was dead, to forget she even existed? "Amelia, you have a family in Australia. What about them? They don't know anything about this. Do you really want to hurt all the people you love for something we cannot change? And what about me? The family I have here now?" Simona is screaming this time. She doesn't care about the people staring at them yet again.

Amelia drops her eyes and remains quiet sloshing pasta around her plate. Simona has also left her pizza. Amelia must know she is right, there is no sane reason to reveal their secret. She waits. Amelia's face is a torment of emotions. There is so much to consider. How will Gee and Larissa respond? They only know one story; the one Simona was forced to live with, to pretend her sister mysteriously disappeared. This was all Amelia's doing. No, she would not allow her to meet them.

"Maybe this has been a foolish idea? I had this romantic notion all would be forgiven and we could be a family again. But it was too long ago. Simona, I guess you are right. It was wrong of me to come but I'm in Rome for another four nights, will you come and stay with me? We can spend some time together. For old times' sake."

Amelia's hand is on her arm again. Her sad eyes imploring her to answer. Years of bottled-up emotions wrack her body. Tension tightens the back of her neck like a vice. She tries to massage it free, but instead tears begin to flow. Does she forgive Amelia? Having her here is surreal, almost like all those horrible years didn't happen. She is back to being Amelia's little sister, the one who always needed protecting. Wet, salty tears roll down her cheeks as she agrees, "Now that my knee and arm have healed, I will be able to catch the train back to Rome with you. But there are conditions; we do not mention this to anyone, no more talk about our father, then you go home to your family and leave me here with mine."

Amelia nods without a word. Simona is not really sure whether Amelia will stick to this plan but for now she will enjoy being with her big sister again.

Chapter Twenty-Four

He is dishevelled and unshaven sitting about his apartment missing his grandfather. Since his parents' death when he was twelve years old, Vladimir had taken care of him. It was just the two of them looking after each other. He had failed him. He should have brought the artefacts home and given them to Vladimir to do the handover.

He takes another swig. Vodka bottles are strewn around. He is despondent. When will he see Larissa again? Will he ever see her again? When he left they were still discussing the handover of the artefacts. She needed an answer. Did he want a public handover? Since Vladimir's death this seed of doubt had implanted itself into his psyche. Was he being selfish wanting to take the glory after his grandfather had told him to protect his privacy? Vladimir wanted the artefacts returned to their rightful home, but he was happy to remain in the background. Should Alexey follow in his grandfather's humbleness? Stay in the shadows? But how? Who is left to do the handover if he doesn't? And there is no way he will allow Bruskev this glory! Even if that is a long shot, he won't leave any loopholes. Bruskev would take advantage, of this he is absolutely sure.

Amelia had been his grandfather's true love. This fact Alexey had found out too late. He doubted his grandfather's love for this woman, thinking he was being a senile old man holding onto faded memories. Now he is in love with someone he may never see again. This severe longing in his heart is probably what Vladimir had felt when he left Amelia. A life without Larissa is an unbearable thought. It's another loss. A loss he cannot bear.

He watches through bleary, drunken eyes as Viktoriya flits around. She probably takes his behaviour as part of the mourning process. She had spoken to her parents and was beginning to make wedding plans. Alexey didn't have the energy nor a good reason to stall her. She looks different, pregnancy agrees with her. Her slight figure, one of the reasons he had been attracted to her, was beginning to give way to the growing infant. Her face glows. Admittedly, he had thought of having children and becoming a father. These thoughts crystallised soon after meeting Larissa. He wanted to have children with her not Viktoriya.

Sitting on the floor with his elbows on his knees and hands in his hair, he sighs. All he can think about is this emptiness that has taken over him after losing his grandfather and Larissa, both at the same time.

"Alexey are you ready?" she is yelling at him, "I've called you three times. Answer me."

He looks up. She had asked him to drive her to the obstetrician's rooms for one of her first check-ups. Deep in his thoughts he had not heard her. Reluctantly he puts Larissa out of his mind and follows Viktoriya to the car. He will do his duty for his unborn child.

"Alexey, how much have you had to drink? Stop swerving, you are scaring me. Stop the car! Let me drive."

"I'm fine," he slurs with a swish of his hand. As he heads into Leningrad's main street rain pelts the windscreen. His mind is again on Larissa. Could he live in Rome? How inviting it had all been. These thoughts of defection are becoming stronger, something he thought he would never feel as a proud Soviet.

A car horn blasts from the car behind. The traffic lights had changed to green and he had not noticed. He decides he had better concentrate on the slippery roads, the wipers swishing frantically in front of him.

Viktoriya, calmer now, starts chatting about wedding plans. He has no interest in listening to this. How could he consider marrying Viktoriya when he loves Larissa? Is he really duty bound to stay? He knows the answer to this question. His responsibility now lies with the unborn child. Leaving his unborn child forever is not an option. He can see no alternative to this sad situation he finds himself in, Viktoriya will be his wife.

Arriving at the doctor's office, Alexey chooses to stay in the car even though Viktoriya wants him to be with her. She scowls at him as she leaves the car muttering, "what use are you?" under her breath.

The rain eases as she slams the car door. He watches her as she stomps through puddles towards the grey office block. He knows she is cursing him; she has a habit of whispering retorts under her breath. Let her be angry, he does not care.

Wiping the driver's side window with his arm, he looks out. The easing rain sprinkles into puddles on the road. For him, Leningrad is beautiful even when it rains. The wide streets; the turrets, the baroque Winter Palace, the Neva river… and when it snows, to Alexey's photographic eye, it is at its most beautiful. Compared to many Soviets his life here has been comfortable. He had no reason to leave. But now his feelings for Larissa are pulling him away. He closes his eyes and dreams of seeing her again.

The car door opening startles him. Viktoriya sits down. She is in a better mood and starts talking right away, telling him all is well with the pregnancy. The doctor said her youth and being healthy are a plus. The baby's heartbeat is strong. Alexey is grateful for this small mercy; a healthy child is what they both want, and he makes this clear to Viktoriya.

She smiles holding his hand tenderly. Her face flushed with

happiness. Guilt rears into Alexey's mind but he pushes it away as he allows her to keep holding his hand.

Driving back to the apartment, they make a stop at the market to buy a few essentials. Viktoriya is asking him what he feels like eating but he isn't in the mood to answer, his head heavy, the vodka taking its toll.

"We've been lucky today, some of the vegetables are fresh," chirps Viktoriya, "and this queue isn't too long."

He smiles absently, hoping the queue moves along. He just wants to be back home, so he can keep drowning his sorrows. With only a month since his grandfather passed away, the grief is still raw. He misses him as much as he misses Larissa.

He decides to take some assignments that keep him in the Baltic region. Accepting the jobs, he is glad to have something to keep his mind off Viktoriya, their wedding and the baby growing inside her. Even with all this happening, Larissa is always with him. His passion to be with her has not waned.

Returning from an assignment of the Crimean Mountains and the Black Sea, he is placing his jacket in the drying room when he hears Viktoriya's screams. He throws his luggage in the hall and runs towards the screams. "Viktoriya, what is it?"

He finds her on the bathroom floor. A blood-soaked towel under her. Her body is wracked with sobs. "I'm calling a doctor," he says panicking while he runs to the phone and calls emergency. Then he races back into the bathroom to find Viktoriya trying to get up. "No, don't try to move. A doctor will be here soon." He tries reassuring her holding her head in his arms. She is weak, closing her eyes her breathing slows, "Viktoriya, stay awake, please. They'll be here soon. Help is on its way." Feeling useless, he counts the seconds in his head. Please hurry.

The door buzzer sounding jerks him into action, "Don't move," he says to her. Viktoriya gives him a weak nod.

He rushes to open the door. Two paramedics walk in and he leads them to the bathroom explaining how he found Viktoriya like this when he returned home. Both paramedics look at each other as they take in the scene. Straight away Alexey knows the situation is grim, worse than he had thought.

The first paramedic, who seems to be in charge, asks him how long she's been on the floor as the other paramedic heads back down to the ambulance. He returns with a stretcher.

Alexey is overwhelmed answering, "I'm not sure. I found her like this when I returned home. Is she going to be ok?" he asks choking back tears, "Why did it happen?"

The paramedic replies in a monotone voice, "Until we do further tests, we won't know. Sometimes there is no answer, these things just happen. We'll take her to the hospital where they will run some tests. She will get rest and will be ok, don't worry."

"Ok. Yes, umm… thank you."

As he waits in the hallway of the ward to see Viktoriya he feels strangely apprehensive about seeing her. What will he say? He is feeling emotions foreign to him; how do you grieve a child you haven't met yet? Deep in thought he doesn't hear the nurse as she asks him to follow her.

Entering the room where Viktoriya is resting, she whispers an apology.

"Shhh, don't talk, just rest." She closes her eyes while he holds her hand. His feelings range from anger to disbelief. The loss is overwhelming. His body is trembling and nausea grips him. First his parents, then his grandfather and now the death of his child. The hospital room closes in on him. He rubs his face with his hand, sniffing and wiping away tears. His emotions unsteadying him. Anguish and anger drive a thought through his mind. No matter how hard he tries to quell it, it is too strong. He looks away from Viktoriya, letting go of her hand. She doesn't stir. Letting out a sigh trying to silence the thought, it is no use. The sigh is full of misery. He decides he will leave. What is keeping him in this country now? His grandfather is gone, he has no other family, and he no longer loves Viktoriya. The hospital stench of bleach, antiseptic and medicinal chemicals wash over him. Dizziness overwhelms him. He breathes deeply, stopping himself from fainting.

Opening his eyes, he turns looking at Viktoriya. She still has not stirred. She looks peaceful in her drug-induced state. How is he going to handle her once she wakes? What is he supposed to say when all he is thinking about is leaving her? She has endured a traumatic experience. They both have. But he is not in love with her. This is his truth.

Chapter Twenty-Five

Alexey's assignment is cancelled due to a snowstorm. He is on his way home early. He hadn't phoned Viktoriya to let her know, deciding to surprise her. His behaviour towards her after the miscarriage had been cruel. He decided to make it up to her, the trauma she suffered is ongoing. She has been physically and mentally drained since he found her.

Turning the key in the front door he hears Viktoriya laughing. What a pleasant sound, she has not laughed since it happened. In fact, she had hardly spoken to him. They had basically ignored each other. He should have made more of an effort to support her. Besides, he wanted to find the right time to tell her his plans. Her laughter is coming from the bedroom.

"Viktoriya, surprise!" he calls as he opens the bedroom door.

She sits up stunned. Picking up the sheet to cover her bare breasts, she looks from Alexey to Mikhail then starts talking falling over her words, "What are you doing home? Err, I mean, hello…" Her head spins between both men, mouth agape.

Alexey is stunned into inaction. He stares at them. To think he was going to be kind to her. To be more respectful of her pain. And this is how she treats him?

Still holding the door handle, he yells, "Get out of my house!"

Now, he is truly free.

Chapter Twenty-Six

Amelia sits alone on the deck, coffee in hand. Staring at the waves, the humid easterly breeze gives some relief from the heat. This morning William had questioned her about the phone bill. Why the sudden spike? She told him about her calls to Simona. He asked why the secrecy? What did she think he would do, not allow her to call her own sister?

"I thought you were having an affair. Especially when you went on that sudden trip with your girlfriends. Do you realise what a relief it is to hear you are calling your sister?" he had said.

She did lie to him about her trip. William thought she was going to Thailand with her girlfriends. At the time he was organising a car trip down to Melbourne with his own mates, so had not taken much notice of her trip. In hindsight, she should have confided in him. None of this was his fault.

Her latest conversation with Simona this morning was a short one. There was no arguing. They spoke of trivial matters even though Amelia wanted to say so much more. The urge to be with Simona again as well as meet Gee and Larissa, was occupying all of her thoughts.

Something her mother said flickers in her mind, "No child should see what you have seen." The words echo as loud as the day they were uttered as she recalls that day…

Cowering in her corner hiding spot she can hear him in the kitchen. Throwing and bashing things. Her mother, where is she? Is she alive? Worry whirls around her mind. The hate she feels for her father makes her surge with ideas on how to rid him from her life. But what about her mother? How can she leave her to deal with him?

Anger and worry combine to freeze her to the spot. In this corner she is invisible. This is the person she becomes when he does what he does. This is how he affects her. She hides away in this cupboard, from herself as much as from him. No one knows he is abusing her as well as her mother. Who's going to believe her? Her father is the town's mayor, he has status and trust. Who's going to believe a fourteen-year-old over an adult? Children don't have a voice, especially not girls.

She begins to worry about her sister. She's at school and will be home soon. She will walk into this. She can't let that happen. Simona must not know he has abused her as well as their mother. She has to do something right now. Before she arrives home.

Pressing her head to the cupboard slats, she listens. There is silence. Slowly she unfolds herself out of the cupboard and creeps towards her parents' bedroom. She still hears nothing but takes care opening the door. He might be in there.

Creeping into the room she sees it is empty. She breathes, relief empowering her to keep searching. Where is her mother? Then she hears a whimper from the bathroom. She finds her sitting on the hard, tiled floor holding her head. Creeping towards her she whispers, "Mamma."

Her mother looks up towards her. Tears stream down her face, which is black and blue, the bruises clearly visible. Amelia holds her by the shoulders in silence. What does she say? How does she comfort an adult? And how does she protect them from his tyranny?

She has to be the strong one. She will be the one to confront him, their mother has been abused for too long. Three months later they buried their mother. This is when Teodoro turned his anger and twisted idea of love towards his two daughters…

Sipping the last of her coffee, she watches as their neighbourhood kookaburra flies from the gumtree to rest on her balcony railing, cackling his morning song. His size belies the tone and strength of his song. It was her mother's size that was against her. Although tall, she was slim and frail with chronic arthritis. Teodoro took advantage of this frailty knowing she would not fight back. The kookaburra cocks his head watching her, "I'll give you my awful memories, please fly away with them. Take them far away from me." As if he understood, he flies off. She watches him until he is out of sight, her mind still whirling with memories. No, I guess you didn't understand.

Her thoughts turn to Vladimir. To the morning he left her forever…

Fate brought them together when she was nineteen. She was already married to a man many years her senior. He was away fighting the stupid war. Vladimir's war wounds were superficial, but he was malnourished and weak. She cared for him; his blue eyes became brighter as his strength returned. They were both lonely. He protected her whenever bombs threatened. They remained cuddled in the basement. Many of those nights she thought were her last. She wasn't frightened whilst in his arms. If they died, they died together.

In the mornings she always went back to the apartment, back to be a dutiful daughter. But she kept sheltering him. No one knew Vladimir was in the basement - until that day. The day the bombs hit, then the morning her father…

She stops. Taking a deep breath, tears sting her eyes as she keeps on remembering that fateful day…

The devastation was everywhere. For some reason their street was saved from the worst of it. Once quaint cobbled lanes were now rubble. Building after building reduced to blackened dust. Fires burned. Stunned people struggled out of shelters, crying and clutching each other. Or what little belongings they had managed to save. The stronger helped the weak; the injured were stretchered to makeshift medical areas, the dead were piled onto military trucks.

They came out of the basement to help. Dressed in one of her husband's uniforms; too short in the arms and legs, Vladimir helped with no one questioning him. Together they assisted as many people as they could. She lost many neighbours and acquaintances that day.

The next morning was when it happened. Her father, Teodoro was dead.

Vladimir left that morning. He ran and kept running but not before he told her he would return for her after the war. They would be together again. He promised.

She was left looking at her father's dead body as he ran…

She stops, clutching her hands together. Tears flow. She is sick of crying, but they keep flowing strong and clear, just like her memories. The void that she felt when Vladimir departed has mellowed but the memories remain, they never actually leave.

Chapter Twenty-Seven

James and Larissa are in the boardroom with their team discussing the night's top stories when they bring up the subject of the Soviet artefacts. Larissa explains how the handover of the artefacts will happen, how the show will proceed and the whole rundown of this special event.

"Wow, what a story," comments one of the reporters, "I definitely look forward to working with you on this."

"Thanks, I'm going to need assistance from all departments. James and I will keep you all updated."

With the morning meeting almost over, some of the crew leave for their assignments. She asks the remaining team members who wish to work on the artefact story to stay for more details. Not surprisingly, no one leaves.

Alexey had called her from Leningrad saying he had decided on a public handover. Vladimir is now dead, what does it matter if Bruskev and the KGB don't agree with his motives? The fact remains, artefacts were saved for future generations to enjoy. He is proud of his grandfather's choices. She told him she and her team would give his grandfather's story the kudos it deserves. This is the beginning of the end of Vladimir's story, his heroics and his gift to humanity.

Once everyone is settled in again and ready to listen, she continues the meeting. Alexey will present the items to the Italian President, Mr Mantana, who will in turn return them to the Soviet President, Mr Breshnev. She explains there is already a team working on making sure the Presidents will be available. Asking everyone to be alert and make sure everything goes like clockwork on this story she says, "We only have a short window of time. Both Presidents and their entourages will be on a tight schedule. Everyone at the station will be briefed on protocol when both presidents are in the studio. There will be security surrounding all of us, and only staff with work permits for this story will be allowed on set."

"Any questions?"

She fields a few questions and eases everyone's mind about security. "Ok thanks for your interest in this story. I won't have final details until the research team come back to me and then we'll organise a time line. Brigite will keep everyone informed and give you final run sheets for the show."

Everyone in her team is buzzing with anticipation and Larissa feels elated. What a historic event to be showcasing on Roma Tonight. She will keep her personal involvement out of the story, this is Alexey's time to shine.

Arriving home to an empty apartment yet again, the buzz of the day exits from her body. She misses Alexey, they haven't been together for three months. This long-distance relationship is harder than she thought it would be. And it *is* a relationship, one that she desperately wants to work. But how it will work, she has no idea. She has no intention of moving to the Soviet Union.

Grabbing a glass, she pours herself a shot of scotch while mulling over her thoughts. James and Clara had broached this subject with her. They were concerned, knowing she has fallen for Alexey. She told them she had not given it any thought yet; the relationship was still in its early stages. This is a lie. It is constantly on her mind. Her love for Alexey is growing each time they are together, but does their relationship have a long-term future? At this point at least, it doesn't seem feasible.

Love is a fickle thing. She had learned this from her last two relationships. With Alexey it is a different feeling. She feels comfortable around him. This has been the case from the moment she met him. He makes her feels special. And it's not only a physical thing; they connect on other levels as well. They can talk for hours or be silent for hours. There is no pressure to be someone other than themselves. This is the difference with this relationship, there is no pretence with Alexey. If only he lived in Rome.

It is 2.30am in Leningrad, should she call him and discuss her concerns? Taking another swig of the scotch, she decides to sleep on it. This is a discussion better left to a time when they are together again. How she has missed him. His company, his smile and their conversations. Breathing deeply, she decides to be patient. He will be here in a few days. This thought cheers her.

Walking towards her bedroom she suddenly feels exhausted, the alcohol helping her to relax. Peeling off her clothes, she slides into bed naked. She falls asleep dreaming of Alexey.

Chapter Twenty-Eight

Larissa is talking about her family and some issues she is experiencing at work. Alexey isn't really listening to her. Since his return to Rome he had not had the courage to tell Larissa what occurred back in Leningrad. She is oblivious to the fact he was engaged and was to be a father. And, he hasn't revealed the most important thing, the fact he is never returning to his country.

"… I was nervous for you, but my adrenalin took over. Meeting Mr Breshnev is one of the highlights of my career. Look at this certificate of honour and medal you received on behalf of Vladimir. Your grandfather will be honoured posthumously. Oh, Alexey this is all so exciting, don't you think?"

The handover of the artefacts was successful. Mr Breshnev accepted them on behalf of the Soviet people. They now reside back in the Hermitage Museum where they belong. His grandfather's dream is finally accomplished. What Alexey will do from now on is concentrate on Larissa and his growing love for her. "Umm, yes I know of these honorary certificates. They are not given out lightly," says Alexey sniffling, "it is indeed a great honour." An overwhelming ache takes over his body. Logically he knows he is in Larissa's apartment but in his heart, he feels he is back in the Soviet Union with his grandfather. So many conflicting emotions are attacking him. He is torn between his heritage and his passion for his Italian lover. Even though being with Larissa is what he wants, the Soviet part of his life, especially growing up with his grandfather Vladimir, will always be a part of him. He has to try and lock these thoughts away in a compartment and leave them in his past or … or what?

She has stopped talking now. Her hand brushes his face, "Sorry, I wasn't thinking. I'm blabbering about things…"

Wrapping his arms around her he realises she is his lover and also his best friend. Kissing her passionately his feelings for this woman overwhelm him. He blurts out whilst tears fill his eyes, "I love you very much Larissa Mina, please marry me."

"What? Alexey I…"

He waits for a better response to his question. She tells him she needs time. He remains quiet. Is his love for her greater than hers for him? They had not yet discussed their love for each other in terms of a long-term commitment. He fears he has rushed into this decision without thinking.

She places both of her hands on his face, "We are both emotionally exhausted, there is no need to rush into this. It is a huge decision for you Alexey, do you really want to defect? Your grandfather is to receive an award, who will it be awarded to if you do not return?"

"I will still return to receive the award, but there is nothing else to keep me there. I want to be with you. I will deal with all the authorities and paperwork. I have worked in Europe for years now. The Soviet Government has never stopped me from travelling."

"Travelling for work is very different to living here. Alexey you come from a communist country and you have a high profile because of your work. Your grandfather's many achievements too; they will take all of this into account. I don't think they will make it easy for you. You need to think about this further and make sure the authorities of both countries don't cause problems."

He nods his head in agreement, their foreheads now touching. She is a high-profile celebrity, so the tabloids will have a field day with a story about her marrying a defector. She is assuring him of her love and tells him keeping things as they are for now is right for their relationship. "My feelings for you are strong, Alexey. I love you too but the fear of losing you has been on my mind. I've tried to think how to make us work, how our relationship can grow. I am not saying no to your proposal, maybe we need to think this through first."

"Larissa, I don't want to leave you. Unless you come and live in Leningrad with me, how else can we be together?"

"We both know I won't be doing that. Marriage is a big step. And so is defecting. Give yourself more time, that's all I'm asking."

They keep discussing and reassuring each other of their feelings. Larissa tells him trust is what makes their long-distance relationship work. She assures him she trusts him as she heads towards the bedroom.

He hangs his head in shame. He has abused this trust by not being totally honest. But he decides Viktoriya is a conversation for another time.

Chapter Twenty-Nine

Colonel Bruskev listens intently to his informant as he reveals facts of Alexey Dubrovnik's overseas trips. He learns that under the guise of work Alexey had organised the retrieval of artefacts and how there is talk of the late Vladimir Dubrovnik being bestowed with a posthumous award from the Soviet Government.

This is preposterous. Slamming his fist on his desk with such force it causes the paper holder to fall. It thuds to the floor. The informant watches on as sheets of paper scatter.

"He stole artefacts and now our Government is saying thanks with an award?" fumes Bruskev.

"This is not confirmed. I assume it is hearsay, probably a rumour started by his grandson."

"I will ensure it is not a possibility. There are people in our Government who preach openness with the West. This will not happen, not while I have the power to stop such idiotic ideology.

The informant completes his report leaving the folder on the Colonel's desk. He salutes as he exits the office.

The KGB building at Lubyanka Square houses his office. He looks out of his window. He sees other neo-baroque buildings such as this one. People who work in these buildings huddle against the cold as they go about their daily business. Most of them, just like him, work here every day. They are proud Soviets. He is the one who has served his country for years in the right way, in the true and just way. But where is his recognition?

During the war years, Dubrovnik's top job as 'Chief of Leningrad Directorate' of the NKVD was given to him under false pretences. Vladimir was not a war hero he was a common thief. How was he allowed to take precious items out of Russia? The gall of the man.

"That job should have been mine," he screams smashing his fist on his desk once more.

Picking up the folder left by the envoy, he sits. Reading what he has already been told fuels his anger. It is obvious to Bruskev that Dubrovnik had never told his superiors about this scheme. He concocted it all for his own personal gain and now, with the help of his grandson, he looks like a hero. He climbed the NKVD ladder as a liar, tricking his way to the top.

Picking up the phone he calls the Foreign Intelligence Office. Once he has the information he needs, he starts compiling a list of things he has to do to get the wheels in motion. He will shame the Dubrovnik name. Vladimir will not be known as a hero; he will make sure of it.

Chapter Thirty

Viktoriya picks up a note laying on the dining table.

"I write this only because of the love I once felt for you. That love has now died, along with our baby. I'm sure you have your reasons for your actions with Mikhail, which shall remain your business. Prepared as I was to become a father and to be a faithful husband, it is beyond my comprehension that you should wish to have another man in our bed. Especially so soon after my grandfather's and our own child's deaths. You had a miscarriage and we cried together at how much suffering it caused us. This is how you show your suffering… by bedding another man? Take your things and be out of my apartment within the next two days. When I return from my current assignment, I want you gone. Viktoriya, I leave you forever. Do not ever try to contact me again. Alexey Dubrovnik"

She scrunches the note, throwing it to the floor. There goes her only chance of living in the West. Her dream to leave this oppression of her measly life is now gone. Alexey gave her an insight into something better with his gifts, things not available here. She had overheard conversations between he and Vladimir of the riches in the West. How could she have been so stupid? Why hadn't she checked to see whether he was on his way home? She could have waited a few more days to see Mikhail. Alexey did come home from assignments earlier than planned occasionally, so why had she not thought ahead this time?

She clasps both her hands into fists as anger surges through her. Mikhail does not have any contacts in the West. She will have to find another way to achieve this dream. For now, she just waits for Mikhail to arrive. He is helping her move out.

"Here Mikhail take this box. That's all of it. My whole life is in those three boxes in your car." She watches as Mikhail does as he is told. Taking one last look around Alexey's home, she sheds a tear. A tear for her lost hopes. Closing the door behind her she decides there will be no more tears. Her dream of living in the West will come to fruition, at this point she is not sure how. But she will find a way, there must be another way to achieve this dream.

Chapter Thirty-One

Colonel Bruskev phones the bakery asking Viktoriya to meet with him after she finishes work. He would like to meet at her apartment.

She knew of Bruskev as she had overhead Alexey and Vladimir speak of him many times. She had met him once when he visited Vladimir only weeks before he died. She was surprised he had remembered her.

Her palms begin to sweat. A KGB official wants to talk. Is it about Alexey? She cannot think of any other reason. Or she hopes there isn't. A customer is asking for bread. She puts aside her anxiety focusing on her work. She will find out soon enough what it is he wants.

A sliver of thought pops into her mind. Maybe she can turn this meeting to her advantage?

"Please come in," invites Viktoriya.

"Thank you for seeing me at such short notice. This won't take long."

They sit in the tiny lounge area, Bruskev declining offers of a drink. Viktoriya listens closely to the Colonel as he offers her an opportunity she cannot refuse.

He finishes with, "…will you help me with my investigations?"

She muses over what he has told her, "What's in it for me?"

"You name it and I will make it happen. I have many resources at my disposal."

"A new identity, new job and a home in the West once you receive the recognition you deserve. I would prefer Italy but anywhere in Western Europe is fine. As long as it's away from here."

"I may be able to arrange it."

"Guarantee my terms or there's no deal."

He places his fingers on his chin, thinking. Rubbing it slowly he agrees to her terms, "My pretty young thing, there is one condition. You are not to fail in helping me damage the Dubrovnik name."

"Give me the tools I need to succeed, and it will be done." She also informs him of her martial arts experience and how she has used it to her advantage in the past.

"This skill will come in handy but may not be necessary for you to use. As long as you ensure this assignment is successful. Revenge against the late Vladimir Dubrovnik must be mine."

"My dear Mr Bruskev, revenge will taste as sweet for me as well."

They shake hands sealing their deal. Viktoriya seals it even further – right on his lips. He seems to have enjoyed it but makes a move to leave.

Viktoriya takes his hand and leads him towards the lounge, "Let's seal this deal properly." She removes her uniform revealing sensual red lace underwear. Sashaying towards him, she unzips his trousers and grabs him firmly. She massages while rubbing her breasts in his face.

He removes her bra and with both hands brings her breasts together as he smothers his face into them. Viktoriya smirks as he is quickly spent. He is an old man; it is to be expected.

Bruskev wakes hours later. She is standing in her robe watching him.

He clears his throat. "I seemed to have fallen asleep," he says. Naked, he waddles towards her placing his arms around her. She allows him to place a kiss on her neck. This is one person she needs on side at all times until this deal goes through.

She keeps looking at the wall, "I must get ready now. Thank you for coming and seeing me."

"Oh yes. Yes of course, I will be going." With that he waddles back to the lounge collecting his clothes.

A few minutes later she is closing the front door after him. With a broad smile on her face she muses over her luck. I am going to be living in the West and I didn't need to marry Alexey Dubrovnik to get me there after all. Bruskev is her ticket out. There is no need to involve Mikhail, who would have been a noose around her neck. He would have slowed her down. Not that she had any qualms of disposing of him had he become too much of a hindrance. In the end, her ticket to the West came from an unexpected source. And sooner than she could ever have planned.

Chapter Thirty-Two

It is five in the morning when Larissa wakes to the shrill of the phone.

"Hello," she drawls still in a sleepy stupor. Her voice is gruff from the smoke of the nightclub they had been to the night before. She hears her mother's voice screeching through the phone… "No Gee, no!" Larissa doesn't want to believe what her mother has called about. Her father… "No Gee, please tell me it's not true."

Alexey, lying next to her says, "Larissa, what's wrong?"

She doesn't answer. She can't answer him, the shock of hearing her father has passed away is overwhelming.

"I tried calling you all night, your machine wasn't even on," she hears her mother.

"It hasn't been working," replies Larissa in a disembodied voice, "how Ma, how did it happen?" She places her hand over the mouthpiece and whispers to Alexey something awful has happened. Holding his hand, she asks him to stay close.

Gee is explaining through sobbing attacks how Joseph had gone to the piazza to spend some time with friends. He had walked down there as he always did. This was his weekly routine. But last night was different. On his way home, he slipped and fell.

Hitting his head on a rock near the side of the road. He died instantly.

Larissa tightens her grip on Alexey's hand. He places his other hand around her shoulder. She continues listening and is comforted he is here with her. Hearing bad news is never easy.

Gee became worried when Joseph had not returned home. Calling one of his friends, he came over to help her find him. It didn't take long. She and Joseph's friend found him dead on the roadside.

"I'm on my way. I'll be there as soon as I can."

Alexey is still with her. She sits with his consoling arms around her. In shock, she tries to imagine life without her father, and as she does her tears drench Alexey's chest. Lifting her head, sniffling she says, "Alexey please stay home until I call you."

"Are you crazy? I'm not letting you drive in this state. I'll drop you over. Is there anyone you need me to call? James and Clara for instance?"

"Umm, yes ok," she answers trying to gather her emotions.

"I'm here Larissa. Whatever you need, just ask."

A sea of tears well behind her eyes, "Oh Alexey… this is horrible. Yes, please drive me over. I need to be with Gee."

Arriving at her parent's villa, Alexey holds her tight, "Would you like me to walk in with you?"

"If you don't mind no, I'd like to be with Gee on my own. We need to speak to Philip and… oh I'm sorry. I really don't know what we need, or what Gee wants me to do."

"It's ok Larissa, I understand. James and Clara are waiting for me. Call me if you need anything, anything at all," he says gently kissing her forehead.

She is at the front door. A surreal feeling comes over her as her hand hovers before she knocks. Only Gee is left in her family home, her father won't be greeting her. Ever again.

Her face is wet with tears when her mother opens the door. They fall into each other's arms. "Gee, he was too young. How dare he leave us," cries Larissa.

Gee nods imperceptibly without answering. Larissa is drained, not yet able to comprehend what has happened.

Gee eventually clears her throat and whilst wiping her eyes she whispers, "Your fa …., your father is at the funeral home." Cracking sobs come from deep within her.

When Gee composes herself, Larissa asks, "Have you let Philip know?"

"I tried but no answer. The funeral home… they umm, they're looking after details for now. They will come over tomorrow and discuss our wishes" she replies having regained more of her composure.

This is so sudden. Almost as if she is suspended in a capsule of grey fog. An uneasy feeling of dread takes over Larissa. They have to call Philip now; he has to know.

"You two look after yourselves. I'll be out on the first flight I can book. I love you both, don't worry, together we'll help each other cope."

"I'm staying with Gee as long as she wants me here. See you soon Philip." She looks over at Gee whose eyes are focused on nothing.

Larissa feels the same emptiness. "I suggest we get some rest because as news spreads throughout today, friends and family will call and pass by to give their condolences."

"Leave me here. This was his favourite chair. I want to rest here."

"Sure, whatever you want Gee." Larissa moves to head to her old bedroom but decides instead to lay on the lounge. She wants to be close to her mother now.

She tries to remember how old she was when she stopped calling her mamma. Her friends have always addressed Giovanna as Gee. Philip and Larissa grew up knowing their mother by this short version of her name. Everyone closest to her knew she preferred this rather than Giovanna. Joseph would occasionally call her by her full name during arguments, more out of frustration than anything else. They always knew their parents were having a serious argument if this happened. From memory it was Philip who started it. It was before he left for Cape Town, it was a few months before. When she didn't correct him, Larissa started. Ever since, everyone who loves Gee calls her by the nickname. Who is going to call her Giovanna now Papa? Somehow, she feels Gee will miss everything about Joseph, even their arguments.

Overwhelming sadness seeps in as she drifts into a fitful slumber.

The three of them hug. Philip holds onto them in silence. He arrived early the following morning, causing another round of tears. Like Larissa, he found it hard to believe.

Now, as they sit quietly in the lounge, Larissa feels blessed they can be together like this. Gee still sits in Joseph's favourite chair. She is calm yet tears still flow as she remembers why they are together, "He's not coming back is he?"

After Philip, the first close relatives to arrive are Joseph's sister, Sofia and her husband, Alfredo. They live in Como and took the first train heading south to Naples. Sofia and Joseph were not particularly close but to have him die suddenly like this has visibly upset her. She and Gee hug each other with Sofia offering words of comfort. Also, practical advice on how they should all care for themselves during this time. She promises to help them all through these first difficult days. She and Joseph lost their parents when they were very young.

Simona arrives soon after. Gee runs to her mother. Larissa watches as Simona consoles her daughter. She and Philip help them both to sit. The four of them remain silent as Sofia and Alfredo bring them tea.

Joseph's funeral is a quiet ceremony on a bleak December day. Light snow is falling, the cold wind whipping it up into drifts. Larissa feels the tickle of flakes on her cheeks. Normally this would make her smile. Not today.

· · ·

She is holding onto Gee as they throw dirt along with white roses onto his coffin. Philip is on the other side with Simona. The three of them each trying to keep it together to support Gee.

Many of their family members live the world over so there are more floral tributes than actual people in attendance. The few mourners who are there huddle together bracing against the wind.

The priest leads them away from the grave. He announces to the remaining mourners a wake will be held at Gee's home. They all walk back towards the waiting black cars, their footprints leaving a fresh path in the snow.

Once back in the house Larissa is talking to James and Clara. She tells them stories about Joseph, which are more for Clara's benefit, James had met her father many times.

Together, they then listen as others speak of him. He was a good husband and provider as well as a loyal friend. Larissa, Philip and Gee nod through more tears acknowledging all their caring words. Simona sobs as well. Larissa knows they were close; Joseph had a soft spot for his mother-in-law. They shared gardening tips. She cannot remember them ever having a cross word between them. If there was an argument, Joseph took Simona's side before Gee's. This infuriated her mother.

Aimlessly walking towards the kitchen, Larissa is stopped by James.

Giving her a hug, he offers, "Larissa, take all the time you need. Don't come back to work until you are ready. With Christmas next week, you know that we're only setting up stories for next year. If we need to know anything, we will call."

Grief has swallowed her words. She nods towards James. Work is the last thing on her mind, but she appreciates his gesture. Getting through the next few days is going to be tough. She wants to be with Gee as much as possible.

Alexey was already in the kitchen preparing them all tea. James sends Larissa back to the others. He stays back helping Alexey with the tea.

Again, they continue sitting quietly listening to Joseph's friends. Philip thanks everyone for being there with them knowing Joseph would be humbled to hear these stories.

Larissa knows her father enjoyed being with his friends. She knows he lived his life for Gee and his family, they were his pride and joy. His friends' stories portray this of him.

James and Clara are the first to leave but not before offering more help. Larissa thanks them saying they will manage. Between Aunt Sofia, Alexey, Philip and herself they will help assuage Gee's grief.

Gee hugs them both, "Thank you so much for coming, and James, I appreciate you allowing Larissa some extra time with me."

He smiles, "Not a problem, the show can wait. Especially at this time of the year. Christmas is a time when family is important. You need your children now. Take care of each other."

Alexey and Rebecca decide to leave as well. He tells Larissa they should have some time to themselves, it's been an emotional two days with very little rest. "I'll go back to your apartment and grab us some clothes and other essentials. Besides, I need to make some calls to the agency. You spend some quiet time with Gee and Philip tonight, I'll come back tomorrow."

She nods in agreement suddenly feeling exhausted. Her shoulders ache from the weight of her grief. A weight she has never experienced.

Gee suddenly pipes up, "James, Clara, please come over on Christmas Day, join us for lunch?"

James looks over to Larissa who nods yes. It will be a tough day for them. With Alexey, James and Clara around for company, they might get through this first Christmas without Joseph.

She watches as they walk up towards the front gate. The four of them had grown a special bond over these last months. Alexey and Clara bonded over their love of classical music. Larissa doesn't want to imagine her life without Alexey in it. A pang hits her heart, especially now she has to learn to live without her father.

The next few days are filled with tributes and more flowers from family and friends the world over. Larissa had not realised her quiet, unassuming father knew so many people.

After helping Gee with final details and the necessary paperwork, Gee tells her it's time she returns home too.

"Are you sure you're ready?"

"Of course, my love. You have been of great help to me. Life goes on. Unfortunately we must learn to live without him. Joseph would not want us to suffer more than we have. I appreciate you have stayed longer than Philip and Rebecca. It's time for me to move on."

"Ok, but I'm ready to come back if you need me too."

"That's fine, thanks. I will be ok; you have done so much in these past days."

Returning to work has helped to allay some of the grief. As she walks towards her office, her colleagues give their condolences. She fights back tears. Walking into her office, the phone message button blinks and written messages adorn her desk. They are from fellow journalists, with others are from fans.

Breathing deeply, she allows soft tears to flow down her cheeks. "I love you Papa, please give me strength to move on without you." Pouring herself a glass of scotch, she raises it above her head, "Here's to you Papa."

Chapter Thirty-Three

Amelia walks out to her post box to collect the mail. Flicking through the usual advertising brochures and junk mail, there are some bills and then… her heart stops. A letter is addressed to her. It's from Italy. But Simona said she would never write? Their phone calls to each other were enough for Simona to deal with, she was adamant about this. And she is still adamant Amelia is not to meet either Larissa or Gee, even though Amelia desperately wants to.

Wait? Simona doesn't know my address.

She panics. Her breathing becomes erratic as she runs to her kitchen. Holding onto the bench, she stares at the letter. Really stares at it. Does she open it or not? Is this the past finally catching up with her? Until she opens it, she won't know.

Deep breaths calm her nerves while she keeps holding onto the bench. Slowly, she moves towards the kitchen table, falling into a chair with a thump. Things are a blur as her tears spill onto the letter. She turns it over and over as if something might change, as if the postmark won't be from Italy.

Amelia just open it and get this over and done with. Maybe once you open it there will be a clue as to who found you?

Opening it at a snail's pace her nerves hit fever pitch. Then the envelope is open. Unfolding the letter, it is an impersonal typed note on plain white paper. Holding it trying to stop her hands from shaking, her name comes into focus.

"My dearest Aunt Amelia, if you are reading this letter and you know who I am, then I have found the right person. Your sister, my grandmother, has spoken of your phone calls. Gee (my mother) and I are both concerned about Simona's erratic behaviour towards us as well as others she has known for many years. Everyone who loves her is concerned. We feel if you two are to meet in person again to discuss your differences, this will benefit everyone...

There is more but she cannot read on. Gee must be Giovanna. Her daughter, the baby she left years ago. The time when too many horrific things happened to her at the hands of men who purportedly loved her. Giovanna is a consequence of her love for Vladimir, the love of her life.

Taking more deep breaths, she folds the letter and places it back in the envelope. Heading to the bedroom she drops the letter into her bedside drawer. She'll deal with it later. Then, back in the kitchen, she grabs her car keys, heads to the garage and drives.

As she walks towards the top, she hears the waves swell and burst into the Blow Hole. A wave spurts into the air spraying the surrounding boulders. Some foolish tourists are too close to the opening... those boulders are slippery. They're ignoring the warning signs. She is about to warn them but doesn't need to, their tour guide is shouting at them, waving them back away from the spray.

She sits looking out to sea and gathers her thoughts. Staring out over the gleaming boulders, the horizon is blurred by the salt spray and her tears. Her vision is blurred but her memories flood in with clarity...

He was on her stoop, thin and exhausted from the heat. Black circles line his sunken eyes. His cheeks concave in a pallid face. They belie his age. He asks her for help. If she doesn't help him, he will be dead within days. It is early 1940.

"You are so kind. Where are you able to find food?" asks Vladimir.

"There is a women's network. We know where to find food. We help each other to cook and bake things that will last. There is enough to feed us for now, but only because we ration as much as possible." She omits telling him about her father, the Mayor. He has a way of procuring things, especially alcohol, in ways she would rather not know about. The less she knows the better when it comes to Teodoro, 'il Sindaco'.

"Please feed yourselves first, I do not want to burden you."

Then he explains to her how and why he is in Naples. She listens to his tale and promises not to reveal him to anyone. In fact, she offers to help him with his mission.

She also tells him he can stay in her basement; she is the only one using it. No one will find him there.

As summer ends, they are both thin but at least they are alive. She visits him in the basement every day. He is polite and respectful to her. This is something she is not used to from men. They slip into an affair of passion and need.

When her husband is relieved of his war duties early in 1941 due to severe depression, he is moody and sleeps his life away. Lonely even though he is back she turns to Vladimir, who is there for her. She confides in him about how her father treats both she and Simona. Hearing this, Vladimir's face flares red with anger. He wants to confront Teodoro, but she forbids it. The danger of him being caught and killed is too much for her to bear.

Hidden in the basement and with Amelia's help, Vladimir manages to hide some beautiful treasures. He is covering them when Amelia walks down into the basement with a blanched face.

"He's dead. My husband has been found hanged at his parent's farmhouse. I am a widow." She falls into his arms crying. As the grief surges through her body she wonders why? She thought her feelings for her husband were gone. Vladimir and his missions had been her life these past months. "Now I am vulnerable again. He was my protection against the abuse. Who is going to stop my father now?"

Vladimir vows to protect her, "Me, I will protect you."

"You are very honourable, my love. I know you are stronger than my father, but I do not want you to reveal yourself. You're a deserter and you will be killed. Teodoro is a dangerous man. A dangerous man with power."

But he did protect her. She remembers the anguish she felt when her father hit her in front of Vladimir. It felt like flaming arrows piercing her face. Things then became ugly…

She sits staring out to sea as the Blow Hole surges once more. Even though Vladimir was only in her life for a short time his impact changed her life forever. Silent tears tickle her cheeks. She remembers his embrace and what might have been. Damn it! I wish my memories would stop. Wiping her eyes and breathing deeply she makes a pact with herself. She will leave her memories where they belong. In the past.

Arriving home, she heads straight to her bedroom. Taking the letter out of the drawer she places it in a shoebox, then hides it in the corner of her wardrobe. This is not the time to be dealing with Larissa's request.

She hears the garage door open. He is home. Walking into the bathroom she showers her memories away. One day she will have to deal with the letter but not today.

Chapter Thirty-Four

"Simona I'm calling you from a public phone, I don't want William to hear this conversation." Amelia scratches at the graffiti on the glass of the phone booth, watching cars whizz by as she waits for her sister to answer.

William was annoyed with her. He was fed up by her surly manner. Now he wants to know about her past. She had almost told him everything the last time they had argued but she decided to speak with Simona first.

"After our last conversation I was wondering whether you would call again," answers Simona.

"We both said things we regret. Let's leave them be for now." Simona harrumphs in her ear. Amelia chooses to ignore her; she refuses to argue today. It doesn't matter who is right or wrong. They have more important things to discuss. "Something you said when I was in Italy with you has haunted me. When I mentioned our father, you quickly stopped me. We didn't discuss him again. I think we have to Simona. Especially as you told me about Larissa's new relationship." Amelia is pleading down the phone line. She wants her sister to understand how important it is for them to find out the truth about Gee's father. "I have doubts that Vladimir is Giovanna's father. We made a decision back then and now it is coming back to haunt us. Do you understand Simona?" Amelia hears crackling down the line and adds more coins. She has brought enough money with her to have a long conversation. This one is too important not to have.

She waits, holding her breath until Simona answers in a whisper.

"It is an embarrassment to both of us, please leave it all in the past Amelia, I beg you. You were not here to pick up the pieces. I saw Gee grow up. My husband took her as his own. Gee and Larissa don't know you."

Amelia remains calm even though fury is burning her insides, "This is not about you and me, it is about how our past affects their future. Simona, we have to find out before it is too late for Larissa and Alexey."

Amelia understands what their father did to them, and to their mother, is something they want to forget. She had shielded Simona from the worst of his tyranny. He was the mayor of Naples, a powerful man hiding behind his status. But now she refuses to let him get away with what he did.

Italy after WWII was in ruins. Many women were left without their men. Without Teodoro's wage how were bills to be paid? This is why she left to find Vladimir. They had to survive. Their homes were damaged. How were they going to pay for the repairs? Let alone buy food. This was how she was rescuing them. She would find Vladimir and they would both return to Naples to be with their daughter. He had promised her they would be together.

"Larissa and Alexey are happy together. They, nor Gee, need to know about our horrible past. Please I beg you, leave it be. Our father is dead. What good will come out of digging up the past? If you want us to keep in touch, we can discuss things between ourselves. What do you think about that? We need to think about the consequences," continues Simona.

The fury bursts out of her. She shouts down the line, "You can't know how it feels to have a child Simona. I was the one who gave birth to Giovanna. How do you think I feel? I lost everything; my home, my child, my lover… and you." Her words trickle down to a whisper as her fury subsides and she wishes she could take her words back, "Simona, are you still there?

She hears a slight whimper… "I had miscarriages. I do know the feeling of being pregnant." Simona coughs and in a stronger more determined voice says, "You left me all alone. I was a child myself and you left me with a baby to look after." Then she clears her throat again and yells, "You gave me no choice. What was I to do? Come chasing after you with a baby?"

Amelia listens as Simona spurts out yet another tirade aimed at her. How she sacrificed her own needs so the baby would survive. How she missed her, wondering whether she was alive. Telling everyone she disappeared presumed dead. Then the relief to find out she was alive. And then the disappointment of finding out she lived in a country so far away. What their father did to Amelia, herself and their mother haunts her life too, but he is dead. He cannot hurt them any longer. "And now Larissa is in Australia. Against my wishes. She wants to meet you. This is your fault."

"My fault?" screams Amelia, "our father's abuse is my fault? Look what it has caused. The two of us living apart, me inventing a new persona in a new country on the other side of the world and you living alone as a recluse. He was a man of power. Our lives should have been comfortable and secure." She adds more coins in the slot but hears nothing, "Simona?"

"What good will come of dragging our families through our sordid past?"

Her sister's pained voice makes Amelia remember how the abuse started. It was soon after the death of their mother. He told her it was normal. This is how daddies look after their daughters. He told her not to talk to or tell anyone. This was love and this was how daddies showed it. At sixteen years old she escaped into the arms of the first man who showed her kindness, even though he was twice her age. When she left Naples, she placed her trust in one of her father's colleagues. He assured her of his help to make sure she made it to the Soviet Union safely. Stefano had been supportive after the death of their father. She missed Vladimir desperately. Blinded by this she accepted Stefano's help to accompany her to Rome. He had contacts who would organise her papers, or so he told her. Trust me he said. She had not told Simona the truth about how she ended up in Australia.

"It will help us heal. It will help Gee…"

She is interrupted by another outburst from Simona, "How will it help Gee? The only father she knows is my late husband. Please Amelia, stop this."

"It's too late Simona, Larissa is on her way to meet me. She is arriving this afternoon. I think it is time we heal, both of us. The hurt has ruined our lives, we have lost too much time. All those years of not talking to each other. There was too much anger tearing us apart. I have missed you ever since I left."

"You've made up your mind already? What is the point of this conversation? Thanks for not thinking about my feelings."

"If you didn't agree then why did you tell them I am still alive? You were the one who blurted out our secret." Hearing Simona sobbing, she wonders when this nightmare will end.

"It was Christmas, Joseph had just passed away. We were reminiscing. Larissa can be very persuasive. She is good at asking the right questions. Besides, I was vulnerable and emotional. Joseph was a good man."

"So deep down you agree with me? Our conversations must have been in the back of your mind."

"Whether I do or not, it is too late now. You are meeting Larissa today."

Simona sounds so distraught. She is right though, there is no turning back now, "Obviously Larissa is worried about your well-being, why else would she go to the trouble of finding me? I have to give her the time she deserves."

"Well it's time you should go to meet with her. Whatever I say will not change a thing. Goodbye Amelia."

She hangs up the phone. Standing there she has never felt so alone. She weeps. The little sister she protected has managed to survive without her. But she needs Simona now more than ever.

Chapter Thirty-Five

The waves foam over the rocks. Young children paddle and frolic near the shore under their mothers' watchful eyes. The sun filters through the giant fig tree they are seated under. At any other time, she would be enjoying this idyllic spot.

They both agreed to this meeting. They have been sitting on this bench under the shade of this giant fig since their awkward meeting at the phone booth. It was Amelia who suggested walking to this spot.

Outwardly her Great Aunt looks calm. Larissa is wary because Simona's outbursts and behaviour towards her and Gee are still raw. She wants to avoid antagonising her grandmother's sister and wonders how things have become so messy.

"I didn't plan any of this. We were so young. We made the decision together, despite what Simona has told you."

Her grandmother is playing the victim card. This is why Larissa is here. She wants to know both sides of the story. Staring out towards the electric blue Pacific Ocean she listens to Amelia's side…

"His love was just for me and mine for him. He was married, I was married. Our love was forbidden but it was right for us. When we were together, nothing else mattered. Then, suddenly I was a widow. I was never in love with my husband, he was my escape. I used him to break free from my father. Running off to marry young wasn't an answer to my troubles, all I did was I trade one torment for another. With Vladimir I had real love and as a widow, I was free to be with him. This was all I wanted. War is a living hell and it makes you do things you never thought you would. Things you would not contemplate in times of peace. We both hated the war, but it brought us together. Our love for each other gave us hope. We despised the fact innocent people were killed daily. Also, the fact history was being erased throughout Europe. This is why artefacts were being saved by Vladimir and his comrades. We all faced an uncertain future. There was devastation everywhere. Bombings wreaked havoc. Men and women of the armed forces returned crippled or mentally unstable. Or worse, they did not return at all. There are no winners. Everyone suffers, win or lose.

My world collapsed when Vladimir left. He had to leave. He killed Teodoro, our father. Teodoro was assaulting his own daughter. Vladimir was my lover and proved his love by defending me. Him protecting me was how I lost him." She fiddles with her bag. Tears flow freely, her face flushed.

Larissa turns towards her, placing her hand on Amelia's knee, trying to give some sort of comfort. What kind of man assaults his own daughter? No wonder her grandmother has never spoken of her parents. The heirloom coffee cup – the one only her great-grand-mother used – this is why it is special. This is Simona's memory of her murdered mother.

Amelia continues, "Vladimir left on a grim day. It was March 22, a day I will never forget. Your mother was born on a freezing morning the December of the same year. The war was dragging on into the second year." Amelia stops and sighs heavily, placing her hand on top of Larissa's. "What sort of world was she going to grow up in? Where is the hope when war rages around you? We needed food and shelter. Two very basic things. Food was scarce and our shelter was always threatened. We women kept ourselves busy with household chores. This was futile. There was no one to share our homes.

Life was miserable no matter where you looked. People left for countries that were safer and promised work. The three of us were alone. I had to keep us safe and I knew I couldn't do it on my own. I had to go and find Vladimir. Simona agreed to look after Gee until we returned. This was the choice we made." Amelia takes her hand away and stares out to the ocean.

The tears have stopped but her face still carries the pain. What do you say to someone who has suffered at the hands of her own father?

They sit on the bench, both staring out to the ocean. There is only the sound of the waves, the mothers and children have left. The waves foam over the rocks, the rock pool fills. It is high tide.

The glass glistens as the bar lights hit it. "Another one, thanks." The bartender obliges.

Sitting at The Marble Bar, she has one more night at The Hilton before flying back home in the morning. Meeting her aunt has made the situation more complicated. Where to from here if Simona does not agree to meet with her sister? She has a whole other family in this country. Yet, she sits by herself in that apartment doing nothing about the person who wants to be a part of her life again. Larissa doesn't understand why Simona keeps holding a grudge.

Indicating to the bartender she wants another drink, she hears someone behind her.

"You really know how to knock those back. It's sad to drink on your own, how about I join you?"

Oh no, this is the last thing I need. The bar was empty when she walked in, this is the reason she is sitting here instead of drinking alone in her room. A dark space, this bar is perfect for drinking alone.

Without waiting for an answer, he sits on the stool next to her. Looking around, there are a few other people sitting at tables. She had been so deep in thought; she didn't notice others had entered the bar.

"A scotch on the rocks, thanks. Another for you?" She declines, keeping her eyes on her cognac. "I'm Max," he says shoving his hand in front of her.

"Listen, I won't be great company. I'm not in the mood to talk." She hopes he takes the hint as she is trying not to be rude.

"Now come on, someone as pretty as you can't drink on her own. It's not right."

She looks over to the bartender, who nods and heads in their direction.

"Mate, the lady wants to be on her own. What don't you understand?"

Max backs off the bar stool, hands in the air, "Ok, just trying to be friendly but if the lady wants to be difficult, fine." As he walks away from her backwards, he spits out, "Drink by yourself. You sad, lonely bitch."

Her eyes remain on her glass. She feels the eyes of the others in the bar boring into her back. Looking over at the bartender, she mouths, "Thank you."

He taps two of his fingers to his forehead in a salute, "You're welcome. I sensed you wanted to be alone."

Downing the remains of her drink, she waits a few minutes before leaving for her room. Making doubly sure the annoying Max has gone, she doesn't want a confrontation.

Swaying towards the lifts, she places her hand on the wall to steady herself. Would Max have wanted company if he had just met someone who was meant to be dead?

Chapter Thirty-Six

He finds her in the bathroom. Her reflection smiles back at him as she says, "Good morning. Thanks for waiting up for me last night."

"I fell asleep early so I could be awake when you arrived home. Australia is a long way; you weren't exactly around the corner. And you're up early, aren't you exhausted after such a long flight?"

She turns towards him, placing her arms around his neck. Kissing him with passionate fervour, he melts into her caress.

Then she says, "Jet lag is setting in, I can't sleep. And yes, I was on the other side of the world so my sleeping pattern is totally stuffed." She places a gentler kiss on his lips, "I missed you."

"Me too," he says cuddling further into her, "So, was it worth the trip? Want to talk about meeting your Great Aunt?"

"Umm, I need to speak with Gee and Simona first. There are a few things I want to confirm. Simona's version of events doesn't tie in with some of what Amelia told me."

He nods placing a kiss on her forehead, "That's fine. I'm here when you're ready." Then he tells her he has some photo assignments coming up, one of which will take him to London. "I'm going to be away for three weeks. We've been apart enough. How about coming over for a weekend? We can have short break, just the two of us?"

"Let me look at the dates, I can't promise yet but with everything going on, a weekend away with you would be bliss."

He smiles then steps into the shower asking her as she walks out, "What would you like to do today?"

"As little as possible. Is it ok with you if we hang around here, maybe watch an old movie?"

"Whatever you feel like is fine by me." A day together with no interruptions sounds like a great way to be together. He can think of no other person he would want to be alone with. A wide smile glides over his face. Things have worked out beautifully for them; their relationship is strong and enduring. This is something no one expected, least of all him.

Finishing his shower, he looks in the mirror rubbing his chin. I won't bother shaving if we're staying in.

Grabbing a towel and tying it around his hips, he walks into the kitchen. Larissa is still in the bedroom, probably crashed out on the bed again. It is not just the jet lag making her tired, meeting her grandmother's sister and everything that goes with that, has taken a toll on her.

A toll on her mother and grandmother as well. He had kept a close eye on them whilst Larissa was in Australia. Gee was already vulnerable after Joseph's death. In his view, Simona blurting out that Amelia was alive and living in Australia only a few days after his death, was tactless. She had kept quiet about the secret for forty years, why now?

Preparing the cafeteria, he places it on the cooktop then goes to check on Larissa. He was right, she is sprawled sideways on their bed, naked and sound asleep. His body tingles with admiration for her, he does not regret his decision to defect. The Soviet Union was his home, but now it's his past. A past he will never forget. However, returning home will never be an option. Vladimir and his parents are in his heart forever.

Viktoriya fleetingly crosses his mind. He is sure she has survived without him, not that he cares. She is not someone he needs to remember.

Chapter Thirty-Seven

Sitting with Alexey at Pruniers restaurant she is relishing them being together. "This is beautiful, just the two of us for the whole weekend."

"I'm glad you made the time to be here in London with me. Now, there are rules – no discussing work or family, and no phone calls to Italy. I have plans to spend every minute with you and do with you whatever I wish."

"Oh, sounds intriguing. Hmm, I look forward to letting you have your way with me," she coos running her finger under his chin.

This restaurant is known for celebrity spotting. As they are discussing this, Raquel Weattson, an English actress famous for her four marriages as well as her acting ability, walks in with her entourage. They overhear the security guard at the door yelling at her fans to leave.

"You are disrupting our patrons who are trying to enjoy their meal. Stop blocking this doorway." He is also asking the paparazzi to move on.

As they hold hands across the table, Larissa says, "I have fans come up to me occasionally, but it's nothing like what is happening out there. That poor woman cannot go anywhere without being followed by hordes of people. It was hard enough when I was being stalked. Believe me Alexey, fame is not everything."

"Well, famous people have kept me in work for some time now, although I don't go seeking out celebrities like the paparazzi. Anyway, I am your number one fan and I keep telling you I will always protect you," he says kissing her hand.

The waiter brings their entree and as they enjoy the blini with caviar there is a raucous at the Weattson table. One of the men is screaming at the waiter, "You! Come here." He is pointing to the waiter who had served them. "This fish is raw. Take it back, I asked for it well done. In a restaurant of this standard I expect a lot more."

"I'm so sorry sir. I will alert the chef, my apologies."

Larissa and Alexey watch as the waiter, shaking with nerves, carries the offending plate back to the kitchen. He has a horrified look on his face as he walks past their table.

"Poor guy," says Larissa, "he looks young and inexperienced. Did you see how embarrassed he was? Is there any need to be so rude?"

"Another perk of fame I guess," answers Alexey, "you can treat others like crap. How about we leave? I know we've only had entree, but we don't need to put up with this. Besides, it's time for me to show you how much I've missed you."

"Lead the way. I'm more than ready," she answers slipping her arm through his.

Stepping outside, Alexey is accosted by a screaming woman. She slaps him across the face. Placing his hand up to his reddened cheek, he is stunned. A lone paparazzo is snapping photos as Larissa is trying to put her hand over his camera.

Alexey is attempting to calm the woman, but she starts yelling again, "Why did you leave me and our child!"

Larissa reels. This woman's accent is thicker than Alexey's. She is from the Soviet Union.

He is telling Larissa not to listen to this mad woman. The woman keeps attacking him with words as well as her fists. From what Larissa can decipher this woman is Alexey's wife. She wants him to come back to pay his dues for the sake of their baby.

Alexey flinches in pain as the woman keeps hitting him. At the same time, he tells Larissa not to listen, "She's lying Larissa, don't believe what she is saying."

But she is frozen to the spot watching this scene.

You haven't said you don't know this woman. Why aren't you telling me who this woman is?

This is her boyfriend who she is now finding out is supposedly married with a child. He has been lying to her all this time. Through tears she stares at this bizarre scene unfolding in front of her. Meanwhile the paparazzo keeps taking photos. Alexey and the woman are screaming at each other as Larissa asks the security guard, who is looking on enjoying this commotion, to call her a cab.

In a trance-like state, she heads to the main road. Alexey yells out for her to wait. She turns. He is holding both of the woman's hands in one hand, keeping them away from his face. And he is trying to grab the paparazzo's camera with his other hand. This is the last thing she sees as she turns and keeps walking towards the waiting cab. She hears him yelling, "I can explain, this is all a big lie, this crazy woman..."

"Did you know the woman who attacked you?" she asks with a calmness she is not feeling.

They are both back at the hotel. She is packing to go home. Swigging at the last of the scotch courtesy of the mini-bar, she hurls the miniature bottle towards the bin close to where he is standing. The force twirls the bin around, both bin and bottle ending up on the carpet.

"Easy Larissa!"

"I was aiming for you. Now, answer my question." She shoves more items into her suitcase, pummelling them in. How could he? Yet another boyfriend who has lied to her.

"Her name is Viktoriya and she is my ex-fiancé. Did you hear me? My ex! She was pregnant but lost the baby before I came back to Italy to be with you."

How can she believe him? Why would this woman risk coming to England from a communist country to be with a man who has defected? Why has she come over to be with someone who doesn't want to return?

"Alexey, I have booked a flight back to Rome, I am leaving at six in the morning." She throws a pillow and blanket at him. "You are not sleeping in bed with me. I need to process this. Why didn't you tell me you have a child?"

"Larissa you have to believe me… I don't have a child. Viktoriya lost the baby and then slept with another man in our bed. I didn't leave my child; I left a whore who lied to me."

Looking at his distraught face she wants to forgive him. But two of her ex-boyfriends have lied to her. She cannot do this again. No, she won't forgive him, not yet. "I'm leaving in the morning. I need to process what has happened tonight. Please leave me alone." She watches on as he hangs his head and shuffles over to the sofa. Her heart is splitting in two.

James is in her office. He is incensed the tabloids are running the photos with the headline 'Defector leading a double-life with respected Italian news host'. "This is not the type of publicity we need Larissa."

She tells James she couldn't give two hoots about what type of publicity this has caused right now – she just wants to find out the truth. Does Alexey have a wife and child living in the Soviet Union? "How do you think I'm feeling right now? You're meant to be my friend, but all you can think about is how this looks for the show."

James speaks again, this time toning down his attitude towards her explaining the 7Oro board members are not happy with this situation. This type of publicity can ruin things. The board doesn't need much of a reason to replace Roma Tonight with some stupid game show. A TV show that will probably make more money for the shareholders.

"I understand what you're saying James. I don't particularly like my personal life being dragged through the tabloids either. Alexey said the woman is lying. Let me find out what is actually going on. Right now, I am angry, confused and sick of being lied to again."

Chapter Thirty-Eight

"Defector to be Deported"

"Reporter's Boyfriend is a Spy?"

Viktoriya is reading the tabloid headlines to Bruskev. He had called her after hearing of her success in London.

"You have done well my young friend. I will now liaise with the Italian authorities to have Dubrovnik extradited. He must answer for the crimes of his grandfather."

She listens to him droning on, but as long as she remains in the West, she really does not care what happens to Alexey. She has helped to ruin him. This is all she wanted to do. What Bruskev does with him now is of no consequence to her. With a passport and a permit to work in Italy, she will make a new life for herself. Tomorrow she will look for a job and put the Soviet Union, Alexey and her old life behind her.

The tiny flat Bruskev organised for her has been fine. It is near Termini but without a job, she will not be able to afford the rent. He has given her a month, then she must move. There are a few bakeries nearby, she will begin with those.

A knock at the door interrupts her planning. Placing the latch on she asks who it is before opening it.

"Signorina Viktoriya, we are from the Italian Interiors Ministry. May we speak with you please?"

She opens the door a sliver. The first things she sees is a holster, then looking up she sees only one man with a thick moustache looking at her. He said "we"?

Opening the door slightly wider, she gasps. There are three of them, and one of them is Alexey.

Slamming the door in their faces, she turns running to the bedroom. This is futile but because panic has set in, she can't think of another option. She cowers next to the bed shaking. Then the front door is smashed open.

"Put your hands in the air," shouts the man with the moustache.

Slowly her hands go up as he and the other man in uniform come towards her. One is pointing a gun at her. Alexey is handcuffed to the other. Alexey speaks to her in a defeated voice telling her not to do anything stupid, it is no use. They are both to be deported to answer charges of spying.

Bruskev has double-crossed her. Energy surges through her veins as her anger takes charge. No one treats me like this and gets away with it.

Chapter Thirty-Nine

Gee's knuckles, white and raw, clutch the kitchen sink, "You are joking right? You're leaving me alone to deal with everything? Simona is a handful. You know how difficult she is right now. And, I'm still grieving the loss of your father."

Once again Gee makes it about herself. Larissa is grieving the loss of two people she loved. And Gee is worried about how she is going to cope? "You are over reacting. England is not the other side of the world, it's only three hours by plane. Besides, I need to move for me, this is not about you or Papa. I miss him too." She stops, her words catching in her throat. Raw rage seeps through her as she thinks that her mother could not be more selfish.

Gee's shoulders droop, silent tears ping onto the sink, "Don't do this to me Larissa." This time her voice is hushed, barely audible.

Seeing her mother like this, Larissa's rage mellows to irritation before she continues. "This is about me coping without Alexey. We will never be together again. You and Papa had a long time together. Alexey and I were still getting to know each other." Without waiting for her mother to answer, she heads to the lounge. Picking up her bag, she heads for the front door. She had been about to leave earlier when she casually mentioned she was thinking of taking a job in

England. This is the result. Her mother has a habit of catastrophising and piling on the guilt. But this is her life she is talking about, a life without Alexey now. She has to deal with this in her own way.

Gee had followed her. She exhales throwing her head back, "Why do you need to be so far away? Can't you find a job closer? Like that one in Milan you mentioned." Her pleading face is drawn, wet with tears.

"Gee," sighs Larissa, "the job in Milan is a three-month assignment. Please stop trying to guilt me into staying. Anyway, it's no use discussing it further, I have placed a deposit on an apartment."

"Well, there is no more to say is there? You are moving to England," says Gee. Placing both hands on Larissa's shoulders she sighs heavily, "you do what you have to do." Then she beckons her out the door.

Larissa stares at her mother's hand indicating she leave. Stunned, she walks out. The door slams behind her. Standing for a moment, she contemplates going back inside. Deciding against it she heads towards her car and drives away. Gee can mull it over for now.

"No, she didn't take it well and I haven't spoken to her since," she tells Clara as she doodles on the notepad in front of her. A glass of scotch and ice sits on her desk. With half an hour to spare before she has to go into make-up, she had placed a call to Clara.

"Did you expect her to understand Larissa? You, Gee and Simona have always been close. Now without your father, we all know how much Gee is struggling. Have you spoken to Philip?"

She thinks about her brother, the one who left to follow his dream of an international career. Gee wasn't happy when he announced his intentions. Occasionally she whines to Larissa about him never returning.

She chugs back what is left of the scotch. "Yes, and he is supportive of me. He says the change of scenery will do me good. Gee will come around. Philip told me she doesn't bother him about coming home as much as she used to."

"At least you have his support. James supports your decision too. You know that, right? Although he will miss working with you."

Looking down on the pad, she has scribbled Alexey's name. Why? Why is she even thinking of him? He is in a communist country. In one of the prisons no less. They will never be together again. Yes, it is definitely time to move, she needs a fresh start.

"I will miss James too, both of you actually. And I'll miss Gee. Simona too, although I won't miss her current mood. This will be good for me; a new job will give me something different to focus on."

Brigite pops her head into the office, "Make-up will be ready for you in five minutes Larissa." Without waiting for a reply, she is off rounding up everyone else needed for tonight's show.

"I have to go, duty calls. Thanks for listening Clara. I'll see you on the weekend." She places the receiver back on its cradle and with a sigh of relief, she knows she has made the right decision.

Chapter Forty

The river is a leaden grey. Rain is forecast again. As she sits in the kitchenette of her apartment in Hebden Bridge, she looks out of the one and only window. The tiny kitchen overlooks the Calder River, it's the best feature of this drab space she now rents.

She ruminates over everything that has happened over the past year. After Alexey was deported, she needed a break from everything and everyone. The issues with her mother, grandmother and great-aunt escalated to epic proportions. Without Alexey by her side, she did not want to deal with the issues befalling her family. She now wishes Simona and Amelia had kept their secret to themselves. To top it all off, Gee still holds a grudge for her moving away. Exasperating comes to mind. Her mother is one exasperating woman.

So, here she is in the United Kingdom working on a nightly news service for a local network. It's not as high profile as her last job but after everything that happened with Alexey and his ex-girlfriend, this is enough for her right now. She wanted to lay low, this was the reason she moved to this sleepy town.

When everything went haywire in their relationship, Alexey did profess his innocence but, in the end, them breaking up was out of their control. Alexey was deported to answer charges brought to him

by Bruskev, who claimed he was an accomplice in the stolen artefacts. He also claimed Vladimir used his power in the NKVD to
further his career, by means of a crime, a war crime. Bruskev wanted
Vladimir stripped of his award and his status within the current
KGB. Viktoriya was his pawn in this game of revenge. Ironically
both Alexey and Viktoriya are also being charged for spying. Before
Alexey was deported he told Larissa that Viktoriya was furious with
Bruskev. He had promised her a home in the West in exchange for
punishing Alexey. In reality all Bruskev had wanted was an excuse
to have Alexey deported.

She was emotionally drained and couldn't forgive Alexey for not
telling her about Viktoriya and their baby. Did she want to wait
around in case he might return when the likelihood of him returning
was so slim? Her family was in tatters and so was her love life.

The tabloids kept the story going for months, which placed even
more pressure on her. Alexey left to answer the charges and
promised he would return. After all his efforts to help his grandfather return the artefacts, he is now in trouble. The Soviet Government has the artefacts safe where they belong, and Vladimir has been
stripped of his achievements. Alexey had told her the story of
Bruskev's hatred for Vladimir. Why had they not seen this as a threat
to Alexey?

Now, all she wants is to be with him. How she wishes to have
him in her arms again. Her body aches for his touch. Yes, she was
angry with him, but she did not want him where he is now. In
danger. If only he had told her about Viktoriya, maybe things would
be different?

These thoughts go around and around in her head. She makes up
many scenarios of how this outcome could have been averted.
Moving away has been a change of scenery, but her love for Alexey
is not waning.

James and Clara visit regularly along with little Matthew, their
two-year-old terror whom she adores unconditionally. James is still
the producer on the show and fills her in with all the gossip about
her old crew. They are arriving soon.

She walks into her powder room. She cannot call it a bathroom, it is miniscule. Taking out her compact, she pats her face. Looking at her reflection, she smiles. Having dinner with her goods friends will lift her spirits.

"Brigite is happy to be co-producer. Didn't I tell you she was after my job?" jokes James.

They are at The Olive Branch restaurant enjoying a Mediterranean feast and little Matthew's mouth is awash with hummus. Their waitress is gushing over him as she pretends to eat his food.

"Yes, she was always an ambitious young thing, but I'm happy for her. She put in the effort whenever it was required so she deserves to be where she is now."

They continue talking about her ex-colleagues and how the show is doing in general. The new anchor of the show is also female. The formula is obviously working because the show is still on-air. James tells her there were some small issues after she left but now things have settled. The show is doing well enough to keep the Board members happy.

Then he turns the subject to how she is doing and whether she still thinks about Alexey. Her heart races as it always does when his name is mentioned. "Of course, I think of him. Often in fact, but I need to move on. He is in a Soviet prison and I'm here with you three." She averts her head towards Matthew, taking hold of his chubby hand. He giggles.

After the Viktoriya incident in London she saw Alexey twice. He was in a holding cell. Both he and Viktoriya were waiting to be deported. The meetings were tense. Her anger prevented her from accepting Alexey's side of the story. Since then both James and she have received sketchy information about Alexey's wellbeing. A part of her hopes he isn't being tortured or in exile somewhere, but she really has no way of knowing.

"Just say the word Larissa and we can help you with your lawyer. It's been a year and we can tell how much you miss him. Has there been any further news?" asks Clara.

"He says he has a top team working on the case. Governments,

Soviet or otherwise, don't take lightly to spying. What I fail to understand is, Alexey did a good thing by returning the artefacts back to them. How is this spying?"

"Bruskev has concocted a story. He wanted revenge no matter who it involved. Look what he did to that woman he recruited."

"Yes, you're right James. I think he used Viktoriya as a pawn too. Not that I care what happens to her. Clara, I'll be speaking with my lawyers next week. Thanks for offering, I'll certainly need all the help I can get. All I want now is to have Alexey back with me. Alive and safe." She drops her eyes; the hurt is still so raw. She had thought moving away would ease the pain. Away from familiar surroundings and all the places they had been together. She had hoped this would help erase him from her memory. Almost the opposite has happened, she pines for him more. Loneliness arrived when she moved. She is away from everyone she has ever loved.

She had thrown herself into her new job and had made some friends since moving to the UK. Moving to a small, rural town after living in a large cosmopolitan city like Rome had not been such a good idea. At the time she was hurt by Alexey's lies and wanted a complete change. When Brigite mentioned she had an aunt living in a town in England where creative people thrived, she had decided then and there to check it out. Looking back on it all now, everything happened quickly. She and Brigite flew over. They met with her aunt who helped her to find the apartment she is now renting. With Brigite aunt's contacts she found the job, and voila, she was living in England before she knew it. However, there is one positive to come out of all this, her English has improved out of sight.

James and Clara both smile when she tells them this. "Well you did mention a few times you wanted to learn a new language."

"I know Clara, but I already knew English reasonably well. It doesn't count as a new language." She continues telling them she doesn't dislike living in this part of the world, she just misses her friends and loved ones back home.

James and Clara had finally convinced Gee to forgive her. Things remained strained between them until the first time Gee came to visit. She thawed out after a few days of staying at Larissa's place, especially as she saw how she was moving on with her life. She also told Larissa how calm she looked. "I can see you're doing well. I guess I was being selfish, but your timing was not great," her mother had told her.

It probably was not the best time to leave Gee alone, but it was the best thing for Larissa.

Now that she is on speaking terms with her mother again, she is not as homesick. When she speaks to Gee, who has visited her a few times since, she hesitates about going home no matter how lonely she feels. There is still no resolution between Simona and Amelia. In fact, the rift between them keeps burgeoning with the chasm between Simona and Gee deepening as well. They argue every time Gee tries to convince Simona to speak with Amelia.

"By the way, I wanted to thank you both for helping with Gee. How did you convince her?"

"We told her how much you were missing everyone and especially her. She was adamant at first, but we whittled her down," explains Clara.

"Clara is being modest Larissa. She can be very convincing when she has to be, believe me I know."

"Oh, really now James?" Clara elbows him, "this is not a time for jokes. Larissa needed us and we helped."

"What? I was paying you a compliment."

"Now you two, don't have a domestic dispute in front of me," she chuckles, "whatever was said, it worked and that's all that matters." She explains every time she calls Gee now they have laughter filled conversations. The tension only appears if they discuss the rift, which Larissa keeps to a minimum. Ironically, the distance between them has helped them become closer.

"You have Gee onside again, which is great. Are you going to concentrate on yourself now? Have you made any friends?" asks James.

She has spent most of her free time setting up meetings with the lawyer. Some of her work colleagues have asked her out, which she has said yes to a few times. "The people I work with are fun. The rest of my time is taken up with researching information I can supply to the lawyer."

"It won't be easy convincing authorities Alexey was not spying for the Italian government. We may have to convince them it was totally on his grandfather. Will Alexey want to compromise his grandfather's legacy?" asks James.

"From what he told me, Bruskev was going to make sure Vladimir's name will be trash. This was the main reason Alexey was going to accept the accolades on behalf of his grandfather. To help cement his good reputation. Unfortunately, Bruskev got to Alexey first." The thought of Alexey rotting in a Soviet prison sends shivers down her spine.

"We'll help with any research," says Clara. James nods in agreement.

"I'm lucky to have you as friends. Thank you." She stands up giving them both a hug. Then, she scoops Matthew into her arms and they walk out of the restaurant. One day maybe she will be back with Alexey. And maybe one day, Simona will forgive Amelia. Secrets and lies have invaded her life, but she still hopes to fix things. She wants her grandmother and great aunt to heal their rift, she wants to meet her Australian cousins and she wants Alexey back in her arms. Miracles do happen, don't they?

Chapter Forty-One

Looking directly at the presiding judge who is dressed in full military garb, Alexey is listening. Bruskev is on the stand testifying against the late Vladimir Dubrovnik. There are two assessors, also in uniform, taking notes for the judge. Bruskev is posturing how stealing artefacts allowed Dubrovnik to scale the ladder of the agency then known as the NKVD, under false pretences. He states Vladimir is not a war hero, and he also implicates all four of his comrades who helped him in this thievery. However, Dubrovnik especially, as the leader of the scheme, should be stripped of all honours bestowed on him. He conspired with the West; he was a spy. He also implicates Alexey as a spy. Before his passing, Vladimir had sent his grandson to Italy. This proves he is a spy just as his grandfather was. Bruskev points towards Alexey as he spurts out this lie. Next, he hears Bruskev tell the judge of Viktoriya's spying. He explains she had no knowledge of the artefacts nor of Alexey's involvement during his spying assignments set by his late grandfather. However, she had been tempted by the spoils of the West, joining Alexey and his journalist girlfriend to conspire against the Soviets.

Alexey fumes. Bruskev is telling lie after lie. He wonders whether

Viktoriya knows how much trouble he is causing for both of them. He continues watching the judge as more evidence is provided by other retired NKVD agents. The judge flicks through photos placed in front of him. "We will take a ten-minute recess."

"All rise," announces the Bailiff.

Alexey takes the stand. He enthuses confidence because he knows he has done nothing wrong. He speaks of his late grandfather with all the pride he can muster. This was a man who had brought him up to believe in justice, to believe every person has a right to a fair and decent life. He disputes Bruskev's lies and even defends Viktoriya. He tells the judge how Bruskev conned her into this assignment promising her things he knew he could not deliver. His position in the KGB cannot give someone the right to live in the West. He assures the court, had she known this, she would not have agreed. Why would she place her life in danger?

He continues disputing he is not a spy. "I am a photo-journalist. Your honour, you have been given examples of my work. My only reason for being in Italy was to return historical items saved by my late grandfather. The journalist, Larissa Mina, whom Bruskev has mentioned, assisted me in recovering these artefacts. There was no spying involved. I was doing my duty in returning these items. These will now be viewed by many Soviets; part of our history has been returned thanks to Vladimir Dubrovnik's foresight. I am proud of what my grandfather saved for his country and I'm also proud I was able to fulfil his dream. Bruskev should be ashamed, he is lying about my motives. I have done this for the good of our history. There has been no spying involved on my part."

After he is back at his seat, the judge announces, "Court will resume tomorrow," with a loud tap of his gavel.

Tomorrow will be Viktoriya's turn to state her case. Alexey hopes she hears of his defence of her actions. He also hopes the judge takes his word against Bruskev's. He knows Viktoriya was stupid to believe his empty promises, but she didn't know him like Alexey did. Bruskev cares for no one, which is why he hopes he said enough to help his ex-fiancé. It is Alexey's fault she is in this position.

Chapter Forty-Two

"Oleg has everything ready," whispers the guard.

They are at the door of his prison cell. Alexey nods without answering. The less is said the better. He has worked hard at being a model prisoner and keeping his nose clean, he does not want to jeopardise anything at this late stage. The plan has to work, otherwise he is a dead man.

Oleg is the son of one of Vladimir's good friends. He heard about Alexey's plight. The Dubrovnik name is all over the news in Leningrad. Having heard stories of Vladimir from his father, and how much Vladimir helped his mother when she was widowed with four boys to bring up, he wanted to repay some of the kindness. He and his prison guard friend, along with Oleg's mates, formulated a plan to help Alexey escape. Alexey has been careful right down to the fact he does not want to know the guard's name. He knows him as Oleg's friend. Just in case anything does go wrong, he does not want the guard implicated in any way.

Even though he is not a spy, the evidence against him is irrefutable. Bruskev and his KGB cronies have concocted a strong case against him. This escape plan is the only way he will ever see Larissa again. It has to work.

The guard slips a pill into his hand as he walks into his cell, "Take this tonight, it will take affect by the morning. Oleg will be here then to take you to the medical centre. Good luck."

Alexey is groggy. He has thrown up several times during the night. The pill has worked, now all he wants is for the nausea to stop. Lying in his vomit-soaked prison bed, he barely hears his cell door open. It is Oleg. Dressed in the medical uniform of the prison ambulance service, he takes Alexey by the arm whilst holding his mask in place with his other, protecting himself from the stench. As they exit the prison cell, Alexey, propped up by Oleg, hears a voice from further down the cell block.

Footsteps hit the pavement with excess force, becoming louder as the officer nears them. "Stop, where are you taking the prisoner," asks the officer.

Alexey hears more footsteps. Other officers are running towards the scene.

"To the medical unit, can't you see he is ill. Now have someone clean up the mess in this cell. We do not want others becoming ill as well."

The first officer sends the other two to organise a cleaning crew. He then places his finger under Alexey's chin, "How sick is he?"

"Remove your finger, don't touch him. Are you crazy? He is contagious," Oleg screams as Alexey drops his chin with exaggerated force.

"Look, we have to get him to hospital before this bug travels throughout the prison."

As the officer is listening the cleaning crew arrives. Alexey, right on cue, throws up in front of them.

"Go. Go now," says the officer waving his hand furiously at them, "and you four make sure you disinfect this whole area." He keeps barking orders as Alexey is whisked away.

Light-headed, Alexey falters. Oleg urges him to breathe, they are almost out.

Then they hear another command. "You there stop. What authority do you have to take this prisoner out of his cell?"

This time Oleg yells back at the officers, "Come near us at your peril. This man has a contagious disease."

"He's right, don't go near them."

Alexey hears the voice of the first officer who had tried to stop them. "His cell is being disinfected now. Don't worry, he'll be back in there once he's cured."

"Yes sir, as you command."

"Get back to your duties. You, medical officer, proceed to take the prisoner and make sure he is not brought back until he is clear of this infection. I do not want my prison infested."

Alexey hears Oleg take a breath. He too had held his own breath.

There are more officers at the front gate, both look at Alexey and hold their noses. "Go," says one of them, "we've been told not to keep you here any longer. But we'll be here waiting for you once you are better."

Alexey nods, again having held his breath.

The ambulance is waiting. Once Alexey is bundled into the back of it, he is given an anti-nausea drug. Laying on the stretcher, as the effects of the drug clear his head, he is handed his papers to enter back into Italy. Checking them, everything seems in order. Alexey thanks his accomplice.

"Please Alexey there is no need for thanks. What your late grandfather did for my family after my father's death will never be forgotten. I will always be at your service, wherever you are in the world."

Alexey is humbled but doesn't respond. His grandfather had avenged all of his accomplices' deaths because he felt responsible for what had happened to them. He had made sure the families were well looked after but especially the family of Vladimir's best friend, whose son is now driving him to freedom. This is all his grandfather's past and even though it is a part of his own history, it is time to move on with his own life. It is time he makes his own memories.

Oleg is transporting him as far as the Ukraine border. From there

Alexey is to meet Oleg's cousin who will help him cross into Hungary and Austria. Once in Austria, he will be on his own to make his way down to Italy.

He rests his head on the pillow hoping Oleg made the right decision about not letting him fly back to Italy. Oleg had worried someone might recognise him and alert Bruskev or the prison. The trundling of the ambulance along the back roads of Moscow is lulling him to sleep. As he drifts off, all he wants is to be back with Larissa. This time for good.

<h1 style="text-align:center">Chapter Forty-Three</h1>

She is lying next to Jack, err no John. She thinks his name is…? Oh, no she can't remember his name. She was that drunk last night. This is a new low for her. She had attended another work function and as seems usual these days, she drank more than she can handle. This has been a trend since moving to England. She drinks to forget her family crisis. She drinks to forget Alexey. There is a distinct line in her life – with Alexey and after Alexey.

This 'after Alexey' part of her life is made easier with alcohol and the occasional one-night stand. Jack/John, or whatever his name is, is one of these one-night stands. He is next to her sleeping and blissfully oblivious she is even there. He probably doesn't remember her name either.

Details of last night are slowly coming back to her as she walks around his bedroom looking for her belongings. She sneaks out of the room as she tries to dress herself, she's really not in the mood for small talk if he wakes up. She leaves as quickly and quietly as she can.

He was at the pub she and her work colleagues were at after the awards ceremony. He came up to buy them drinks, recognising her and two other reporters. She accepted his offer. She should have known better. She was already well on her way to being drunk even before hitting the pub. Her will power to say no to alcohol is lacking more and more. Being around people who enjoy drinking is addictive. She wants to forget, and this is how she forgets.

Outside his apartment block trying to remember if she had driven last night he yells from his balcony, "Thanks Larissa, too shy to say goodbye?"

"Err sorry, didn't want to wake you. Thanks, but I have to go. Umm… see you around."

He gestures with a shrug of his shoulders, "Yeah sure," he says giving her the finger.

She is fine with him not wanting to see her again but a small part of her is a little hurt. This single life isn't all it's cracked up to be, she misses being a couple. No one comes even close to the feelings she still has for Alexey.

A discussion with the lawyers about securing his release had been positive. This gave her some hope.

Placing the key in the driver's side door, her stomach heaves. Running to the street verge, the grass changes from green to brown sludge as she slumps her head towards it. What were her colleagues even thinking getting in the car with her last night? Obviously, they had been as drunk as her and had not cared.

She drives the short distance to her apartment and parks on the road not bothering to go into her parking area. She will need to freshen up before heading for the studio. The first thing she grabs before heading into the shower, is a glass of water and drops a soluble aspirin into it.

"Hello Larissa, congratulations on another award," says the production coordinator as she is walking into her office. Giving her a smile, she is thankful she doesn't mention anything about the drinking afterwards. Her head throbs as she reaches for a fizzy vitamin B tablet in her drawer. She throws it into a glass of water. Hangovers are not fun, but she had seen others in the studio who looked just as bad as she felt, so at least she is not alone.

The award is sitting on her desk and she picks it up wondering where she will put this one, there are already three others on her office wall. Professionally her life is great, she is at the top of her game and is still one of Europe's best investigative journalists. This gives her immense pride; her job is her life and she is grateful that at least one part of her life is on track. Personally, though she should probably do something about the drinking before it starts to control her. She has already had one hiccup in her career with leaving a prime time show for this local job. She is conscious her need for alcohol will ruin things for her. She needs to take control.

Chapter Forty-Four

Her producer, Tim, is shaking his head. Cowering opposite him, his booming voice reverberates in this tiny office. Her ears ache.

"This might be acceptable behaviour for anchor's in big cities like Rome but not here Larissa. This station does not need this type of publicity."

Awkward silence fills the space where his voice leaves a void. "Well?"

"Is saying I'm sorry enough? How did I know a paparazzo was following me?" Six months into her new job and another tabloid disaster threatens her. 'Scandals Corner' reported seeing a 'local female anchor hurling on verge... and it's not the first time'. This gossip column in the local paper does not name names nor show a photo, but she is the only female anchor in this town.

Tim launches at her again, "You're meant to be a professional. We could not believe our luck when you accepted our offer as anchor for our show, 'Bridge Scene'. Someone with your star power, someone known through most of Europe. You were meant to raise the profile of our show. But not like this!" He hurls these words towards her. His spittle assails her face.

"Tim, you are right, it was very unprofessional of me. Will it help if I tell you it will never happen again? I can promise you this because I'm getting help." This is not a lie. She has signed up with an AA group and is attending weekly. "I started with a group. I attend meetings on Thursday nights."

"What? Are you telling me you're an alcoholic?"

"Yes, and once I admitted this to myself, I was able to begin with the group." Her nerves are on edge, has she revealed too much?

He shifts in his chair. Rocking back into his black executive chair, his fingers tap the desk. She stares at his fingers hoping she has not lost her job. As he remains quiet the tension heightens. She now focuses on the wall clock, anything not to look at his face. The incessant ticking and his fingers tapping makes her uneasy. Sweat forms on her palms.

Eventually he speaks. She exhales expecting the worst. "What you did is not acceptable, but because you've confided in me, you seem willing to make amends. I am sorry you are going through a tough time, but this is a tough business as you know. Just remember, this is your only warning, if it happens again, I will fire you."

"Thanks Tim. Again, I apologise again. Believe me, you have my word, it will be professionalism all the way from now on."

"Hmmm, don't disappoint me again Larissa. I'll organise our publicity department to counter this, we'll place a good news story about you in the paper. The girls will contact you for some quotes."

She nods. Then, looking him directly in the eyes, she shakes his hand saying, "No problem, and I appreciate you supporting me like this."

He looks down and already moves onto his next issue, the back of his hand waving her out of his office.

Rising from the chair, she tugs at the fabric of her pants suit because sweat is causing it to adhere to her legs. With relief flooding her body, she walks back to her office.

"So, spit it out. What did the boss have to say?" asks her colleague Joanne. Standing at her desk, Larissa holds the corner to steady herself.

"Whoa, are you ok? Your face is as white as paper." Joanne walks towards her placing her hand on her shoulder, "Sit down and put your head between your legs. Let me get you some water."

Returning with a glass of water, Larissa accepts it from her. Sipping some, she looks up, "Thanks Jo. Tim was brutal, but I still have a job."

"You're lucky. He is known for throwing people out for less."

"I know, he has a reputation, and the way he was yelling, I thought I was going to be one of his scalps."

"Look, it's almost lunch time. How about we go out to get some fresh air?"

"Sure," she beams up at Joanne, "let's go and sit by the river." Her job is safe, and she will ensure it stays that way.

She turns the token over and over. It is a six-months token awarded to her by her AA group. She has not touched alcohol since starting with them, and she has kept her promise to Tim. The first few days without alcohol were unbearable. How she managed to go on-air is testament to how much she was able to cover up what she was going through.

Joanne was the only one who noticed her trauma and kept a close eye on her. Joanne noticed the palpitations, made sure she took her medications to ease the symptoms and stayed over when she needed company.

Then followed the headaches and panic attacks. The debilitating dizziness along with nausea meant she did take some time off. Tim was supportive, which also helped her through some of the worst times. Without Joanne and Tim as well as her AA group, she may not have reached this milestone. During those first few weeks she understood how people prefer to keep drinking rather than go through withdrawal.

What kept her going as well, was the thought of Alexey possibly being released. Her lawyer was making progress. Their last meeting was positive. If Alexey is released and they are together again, she will confide in him. For now, his release is still a big if and she needs to concentrate on herself. She reminds herself every day she is a recovering alcoholic. She had kept her drinking problem away from Gee too, as well as James and Clara. They knew she drank but had no idea just how much. Now, with the support of her group, her two colleagues and a new perspective on looking after herself, she is determined not to wallow in self-pity again.

Chapter Forty-Five

The smell of success is all around Jonathan Talbert's rooms. His offices embody his lawyer status. Oil paintings adorn the walls, plush leather couches and chairs at the ready. This is where she is sitting. She watches as two stunning women answer phones as they sit behind a slick black reception desk. Nervously waiting to see him about any news of Alexey, she has sunken into one of the leather chairs, breathing in the smell.

James had called her asking what she is doing this weekend, he and Clara would like her to spend the weekend with them at their summer house in Tuscany. She is thinking about how pleasant this will be when Jonathan's secretary ushers her into his office.

They exchange pleasantries as she takes in the size of his office and the ridiculously huge mahogany desk dominating the whole room. Almost before she has a chance to sit down his secretary is placing a tray of tea and water on the desk and he asks what she would prefer.

"I'm fine thanks Jonathan, I really am stretched for time. I need to be back at the studio as soon as possible."

"Yes of course Larissa, let's get straight into this, shall we?" He proceeds to tell her his investigations have reached a stalemate with the Soviet authorities. He will need more time.

"Three months ago, you told me the investigations should take about a month, now you're telling me you want more time. Just how impossible is it going to be? Will I ever see Alexey again?"

Jonathan explains the situation is not an easy one, communist governments do not take lightly to defectors, especially those who are also accused of spying.

Exasperated she explains once again to Jonathan how Alexey was not spying, he was actually doing something to assist the Soviet people. The artefacts are back in Soviet hands. They were returned for all Soviet people to enjoy them again. "This is ridiculous. Maybe we should have kept the artefacts for ourselves? Can't the Soviets see Alexey did a good thing for the Soviet citizens. These treasures are back in their rightful place," says Larissa, her voice quivering.

He puts up his hand, understanding her plight. He tells her suspicion of spying is all that is needed, and the fact that he defected doesn't help Alexey's cause at all. He keeps talking about his ideas, but she is starting to think this is a waste of time. She has to come to terms with the fact she will never see Alexey again. Tears begin to well in her eyes and Jonathan stops talking about where they are at with investigations.

"Sorry to have upset you Larissa but I did warn you this was not going to be easy."

She nods telling him she will give him another month, if the situation is still impossible, she will give up her dream of being with Alexey. "I have to, I can't keep living in the past."

He stands and walks around to her side of the desk as she stands. Towering over her, he is an imposing man. Dressed in a designer suit, she can see how he has been successful in this business. She hopes his success works in her favour.

"I will do my best for you, I promise." He stoops down to kiss her cheek.

This is not a very professional thing to do but she appreciates his gesture. He has obviously noticed she is concerned with his ability to bring Alexey back to her.

Chapter Forty-Six

He fiddles. Nervous energy flows through his veins as he waits to be ushered into James' office. What will he think? Does James still hold a grudge about what happened with Larissa and Viktoriya? More importantly, will he help with convincing Larissa to see him?

He hears James' voice utter from the intercom on his secretary's desk. She nods to him.

Rubbing his sweaty palms onto his thighs, he enters the office.

"It is you… oh my, Alexey how in the world are you here?" James has one hand outstretched ready to greet him, his face alive with the quizzical eagerness of seeing his friend.

He gives James a huge bear hug with James slapping his back in return.

"It's so good to see you, my friend. You have no idea how much I've dreamed of the day to be back here. Do you have time? I have lots to tell you."

James nods, "Of course, please sit. I'm ah… you're here. Wow." He offers him a drink then buzzes his secretary to not disturb him unless it's absolutely necessary.

They sit on the lounge as James listens to Alexey's story of how he managed to escape Lubyanka Prison, and how this time he has no intention of ever returning to the Soviet Union. "I called in some favours and Vladimir's good deeds after the war paid off. Oleg, the son of his best friend, helped me hatch an escape plan. One of Oleg's friends is a guard at the prison, and he was happy to help." He continues explaining how he kept his head down in prison. The guard kept him informed of the progress of the plan. When the time was right, he was slipped a few pills to make him ill. "I'll admit it wasn't a pleasant experience, but it was the only way to have me taken out of the cell without raising suspicion. With his network of friends, Oleg managed to smuggle me out in an ambulance. He organised my papers. They were well paid, of course. All with my savings. I have nothing, except my camera and a few clothes."

"It's great to see you. I'm dumbfounded because I still can't believe you're here in my office."

"Well I'm definitely here and believe me, it's so good to see you too. How about another drink and I'll tell you more?"

"Sure, tell me everything," says James as he refills the glass.

Alexey finally has to the courage to ask about Larissa. "I went to her apartment but was told she moved to England. The supervisor mentioned she has tenants in there now."

James tells Alexey about Larissa and how depressed she was after what happened. How she needed to start afresh.

Alexey nods and understands why, the way it looked at the time he was guilty of having a fiancé and being a father. Even though he tried to convince Larissa he was set up. "Please James, will you help me to explain to her how it was all a cruel plan by Bruskev, who used Viktoriya to seek revenge against the Dubrovnik family. I would never hurt Larissa, she needs to know my feelings for her are as strong as ever, there is no one else for me. I love her with all my heart."

James explains how Larissa has moved on with her life. Also, how successful she is throughout Europe as an investigative journalist. "Alexey you must be absolutely sure you won't be deported again before I give you Larissa's details. Come over for dinner tonight and we can discuss this further. Where are you staying, I'll send a car for you?"

Telling James he is staying at the same hotel near the station, he shakes James' hand and assures him he will do everything in his power to stay in Italy, his papers are legitimate. Still, he will check with authorities. He too wants to be absolutely sure everything is above board this time.

Back at the hotel in another tiny room, this time the filthy window looks over a car park. It's freezing, so he fiddles with the thermostat. Nothing happens. Not even a hiss. He will call maintenance to have it looked at. For now, he keeps his overcoat, scarf and boots on to stay warm. He has important phone calls to make.

Dialling his agency number, he asks to be placed through to the Italian office. After hearing a few clicks, a receptionist answers, "Dusitrovii Agency, how may I connect your call?"

"Please place me through to extension 245, thank you. Alexey Dubrovnik calling."

"One moment please."

As he waits, he stares out of the window. The wind whips up snow depositing it on the few cars in the car park. The cold is sneaking in through the cracked timber frame. He wraps his coat further around himself and once he confirms an assignment, his next call will have to be to maintenance.

"Alexey, is that you? Where are you?" his agent, Stefano asks.

"I'm back in Rome, the same crap hotel you guys always use."

"We aim to please," he laughs, "I'm glad to hear you are back and safe. I assume you're here for good this time?"

"That is my aim. Thank you for helping out with my papers, Oleg was able to organise everything with precision. He assures me there are no loopholes this time, I cannot be deported again. However, I will do my own checks now I am back."

"I do hope it is the case. I am glad to hear I was of some help. Now, when would my best photojournalist like to come back to work?"

"As soon as possible, I have come back with nothing. Oleg and his mates helped me out with some money. It is only enough to last me maybe a week after I convert it into Italian Lire."

"No problem, I'll check our job books and be back to you in an hour."

He thanks him then presses down the hook switch, placing his finger in the number nine on the rotary dial face. Asking for maintenance he is told there is no one available today, they will send someone tomorrow. He slams the phone down. "Typical!" he exclaims as he looks for something to cover the crack in the window frame.

Chapter Forty-Seven

"What do you mean he escaped?" Viktoriya's voice booms towards Bruskev through the cell bars, "he was in a higher security section than mine and I'm still here!" She glares at him still screaming that she cannot stay in this place. It is dank and riddled with cockroaches. "You know I am innocent. How dare you, you have framed me."

Bruskev looks at her explaining he is close to having her released, the judge looked favourably on her case. Especially as Mikhail testified she knew nothing of Alexey's assignments, she was no more a spy than Bruskev himself. He told her to sit tight and behave herself.

She keeps yelling at him to use his many sources and have her freed now! She wants her freedom. Her hands grasp the cell bars in desperation, he must help her, or she will go mad in this place. She is not a spy; she was doing a job for him. He wanted revenge as well, why is he not doing any gaol time?

"As I have advised you Viktoriya, behave yourself and you will be out soon. Don't give me, or the judge for that matter, any reason to change our minds. If you rot in here it won't bother my conscience."

"I should not have been placed in here in the first place. You double-crossed me."

"Oh, you young people are so naïve. What makes you think I care about what happens to you. You have served your purpose. You are expendable." His snide face glares back at her.

Now she is scared. Fear wraps around her body like a snake, "Bruskev, please? You promised."

"Then behave and I will help you."

Should she trust him? Probably not, but she has no choice. Her dream to live in the West for the rest of her life is dwindling before her. What choice does she have but to trust him?

Chapter Forty-Eight

It's eight in the morning and she is driving from Milan airport down to Tuscany to meet James and Clara. It's lovely being back in Italy, she has missed home. Having settled in for the four-hour drive in the hired Fiat Bambino, she had decided to take in some of the scenery. But the unpredictable Tuscan weather had other ideas, rain was pelting down.

Even though she had been given assignments all over Europe since moving to England, she had opted out of any in Italy. It had taken some heavy persuasion from James to join them for this weekend.

"This isn't going to be work Larissa, it will be a whole three days of relaxation," James had pleaded with her.

The rain is still teeming as she drives along the Autostrada towards the rural roads of Tuscan farmland where their villa is situated. It is on the outskirts of Siena and this is going to be her first visit to this one, James and Clara only bought it recently. She consults the map on the passenger seat every half hour, James did give her detailed instructions on the best way to find the villa, but with this heavy rain she wants to be sure. Even if the rain keeps up over the next three days it doesn't bother her because she is ready for a quiet few days with her friends. Relaxation is what she is after.

She decides to take a break at Parma and instead of just stopping at one of the Autostrada cafés, she drives into Parma's town centre. The rain begins to ease as she enters the town and by the time she parks the car, it has eased to a sprinkle.

This picturesque, medieval town has character, which is a plus after her last stop along the Autostrada. Those cafes are all about convenience and nothing else. Besides, she knows of a local osteria where they serve the best homemade tortellini that rival any she has eaten, even her own mother's traditional version of this little *pillow* of pasta filled with meat. James and Clara are not expecting her until after lunch. She has time to explore. Her flight back to England is not until late Monday afternoon, so she is taking full advantage of this long weekend break.

Before going back to her car, she decides to do some shopping and buy a gift for little Matthew who is growing up fast. She finds a little boutique toy store that sells Ferrari merchandise. She buys two miniature cars. Both James and Matthew will enjoy them, she is sure of this. She wonders at times who is the bigger kid.

As she pulls up in front of the villa, James is already waiting for her. The driveway is wet but the rain, although still threatening, has stopped for now.

"Hi, how was your trip? Wet by the look of you."

She hugs him after getting out of the car. Stretching her arms and legs, she says, "It's been raining on and off since I left Milan. And when I stopped for a break in Parma, it was sprinkling. Visibility was bad at times, but I'm here in one piece."

James helps her with her luggage as Clara comes out to greet her. The three of them walk into the villa chatting. James takes her bags away as she remains in the kitchen with Clara.

"Then I had lunch at the osteria, you remember the one, it's famous for the homemade tortellini with different fillings?" She looks around, "Where's Matthew, I'd love a cuddle." "Yes, we've eaten there often. Matthew enjoys the meat filled ones they serve in broth. He's having a nap Larissa. He'll be awake soon," says Clara.

James comes back from placing her luggage in the bedroom and offers her a drink, or maybe a coffee? "Sit down Larissa, relax. We'll show you around after Matthew wakes up."

"This place is bigger than your other one," she says admiring the villa. It's not as rustic either, there are updated features. The kitchen has modern conveniences, including a dishwasher and a coffee machine.

"That one is our holiday villa. It's for our use only. We won't rent it like we do this one. The only reason we're here is because James booked this weekend especially for you to see it Larissa."

How could she have refused coming here after his special effort?

James is placing coffee in front of her as she hears rustling coming from behind her. "Matthew, come and give …" She stops mid-sentence.

"Hello Larissa." She looks back towards James and Clara and then looks behind her again.

"I'm home Larissa, permanently this time and I hope you will be part of my life again."

She is stunned. She just sits with her mouth agape. She is not able to move.

"Well, aren't you going to say anything?"

"Umm yes, but… I'm in shock. Alexey how are you here?"

"We haven't seen each other for three years and that's all you can say?" He moves towards her. "It's a long story, which took a lot of planning but I'm going to explain it all to you after I kiss you." He is holding his arms out towards her.

Without hesitation she is up running towards his familiar embrace. Alexey is assuring her he is here to stay. His papers are in order, he will not be deported again. "James has told me if I ever break your heart again, he will personally take me back to Leningrad."

Larissa looks over at James and Clara, both of them are smiling. Clara is wiping tears from her eyes. James nods with a sniffle, "It's true."

Chapter Forty-Nine

They are in the lounge talking and have been for hours. James and Clara took Matthew to bed and have not resurfaced. Alexey is grateful, they have so much to catch up on.

"Let me understand this. You didn't actually finish the court case, right? Judgement on whether you should be imprisoned didn't happen?"

"Yes, that's right. My judgement was meant to be on the day after I was taken away for medical reasons. I was violently ill. Believe me they could not dispute it. It felt like my insides came out from…"

"Ok, ok I understand. Spare me the gory details," she cringes. "You still look drawn and have lost a lot of weight. I can feel your bones lying here with you."

"I did. About fifteen kilos. Food in the prison is atrocious, best avoided where possible. I only ate if I was desperately hungry. I have already added a few kilos since being back in Italy." He is stroking her arm as they talk. Her head is warming his chest. How many times did he envisage this scene whilst locked up?

Continuing, he explains how he is confident all his papers are legitimate and names all the people involved in him being here.

"Are they safe Alexey? What if Bruskev finds out how you escaped and goes after them?"

"He would have no hesitation going after them. They knew the danger involved and have been compensated well. Oleg assured me they would all be safe. How? I'm not entirely sure. However, he did say all the names of the men who helped me, were fake. As for his friend who was the guard, he was moving away, as far away as possible with the money he earned."

She seemed reassured because she remains quiet for some time. Enjoying the silence, he thinks about her concerns for his accomplices. Having placed complete trust in Oleg, he assumed Oleg understood the consequences. He would not put it past Bruskev to keep going with his vendetta, he hopes Oleg foresaw any issues and will be able to handle them should Bruskev suspect him. He knows that if Bruskev or Viktoriya do try coming after him again, this time he will not be so accommodating.

She turns looking up at him, "As long as you are not taken from me again. It's my greatest fear."

"Larissa, it has been a long day. Some rest and a bright new morning will make everything seem a lot easier. Our bed awaits my darling."

"Fantastic idea," she yawns.

He has been awake since dawn. Larissa is sleeping soundly next to him. He brushes her cheek tenderly with his hand then quietly gets out of bed. The night before they had cherished each other's bodies before falling into an exhausted slumber. The feel of a woman you love, the one you have waited for, is an indelible experience. She is his one and only. Looking at her, she is peaceful in her slumber. His heart is elated, he is filled with love for her.

Heading towards the kitchen, he hears Matthew.

"No. Matthew not eat," he screams slamming his hand onto his highchair.

"Shhh, Matthew stop that. Larissa and Alexey are asleep."

"Larissa is sound asleep. Listen to your mother or Larissa will be angry with you for waking her," scolds Alexey as he ambles into the kitchen winking at Clara, "Good morning."

Matthew's little head drops in embarrassment.

"Thank you," mouths Clara. "Good morning Alexey, I hope you slept well. Help yourself to coffee."

"I sure did. It was an emotional day yesterday. You and James are wonderful for allowing me to do this. And in this lovely villa." He presses the button for an espresso and bites into a brioche, "How easy is this machine. I'll look into getting one of these. Is James around?" He pops his head out of the kitchen door, quickly closing it, "Brrr, it's freezing, but at least the rain has stopped."

"James went to pick up a few supplies that I ordered. He should be back soon. We thought you two would sleep in."

"I'm a bit of a morning person actually, Larissa is the one who enjoys staying in bed. Not that I'm telling you anything you don't know. Now, let me help you with something."

"Actually, would you mind watching Matthew until James returns? I have to run a few errands too."

"Not a problem. Come on little man, how about we go and play with your cars?" Taking him out of his high chair, Matthew giggles as Alexey tickles his tubby little tummy. There is a corner full of his toys, and the minute he is on the floor he runs over picking up a red Ferrari, "This one mine." He presents it to Alexey, his proud face beaming. "Which one is mine?" "No, all mine."

"Matthew, we have shown you how to share, now be nice and share with Alexey."

"Papa, come play."

"Only if you share," he says as he slaps Alexey on the shoulder.

They proceed to sit with Matthew who squeals with delight. He zooms the Ferrari around and around, whilst they talk and pretend to race the cars he decided to share with them.

"Good boy Matthew, now this is how you share."

Alexey is enjoying this. Seeing the joy on Matthew's cherubic face as well as James' is humbling. He feels the love between them and he knows he will revel in being a father. Just as he is thinking this, Larissa walks in.

"Oh look, one little kid and two big ones. Good morning boys." She bends down kissing Alexey then scoops Matthew up, "How's my favourite little boy?" She is holding him up and twisting him around.

"No! Not little, I big boy now."

The three of them laugh as Clara joins them.

Alexey is emotional. He takes in this scene and considers himself a lucky man to be here with the woman he loves and her good friends. This is the type of memories he wants for himself. His future will be with Larissa, he cannot see a future without her in it.

Chapter Fifty

"James and I have to go out later when Matthew has a nap, I don't suppose we can impose on you two to watch him again? We have to go and inspect the pipes at our other villa. A plumber is meeting us there. We will be as quick as we can," asks Clara.

"Yes, sorry about this. It is the only time the plumber had available. We will be as quick as we can then we can do something that is a bit more enjoyable." says James.

"Oh, what a pain, having to go out in this weather. Look out there, it's sleet, conditions will be horrendous. But of course, we're both fine with watching Matthew, especially if he is asleep," answers Larissa checking with Alexey who nods in agreement.

"Thanks. I hope he will stay asleep, but like I said, we should not be long. No more than an hour."

. . .

Later in the afternoon, James brings out one of his prized reds, bragging about how long it has been in his cellar. Larissa flinches. She is with people she loves with all her heart, but they don't know about her being an alcoholic. Panic flushes through her.

He proceeds to fill all their glasses. Her hands initiate the usual tingles and sweats. She has not touched a drop since being with AA, but some of the symptoms still haunt her.

The six-month token comes to mind. How does she handle this situation, there is no way she wants to regress? Alexey does not know yet, they have not had enough alone time for her to tell him. Nor has she had the courage to bring it up.

"Very smooth James," comments Alexey. "I know right? What do you think Larissa?"

"Umm, I'll let you know in a minute… just popping to the toilet. Umm, won't be long." Her chair screeches along the floor as she moves faster than necessary. She wants to be anywhere but with them right now.

The minute she is in the bathroom, the toilet bowl is smiling up at her pasty face. Her hands hold the bowl.

"Larissa, what's wrong? Can I come in?"

It' Alexey. Of course, she can't let him in. He cannot see her like this. Thinking fast she lies, "No darling, I'm fine. I'll be out soon," she gags, I have a bit of reflux. I've only recently developed this problem." Hopefully this will be enough of an excuse not to try James' wine.

· · ·

They are alone. She is cuddled into Alexey's arms. "Shh, I'm here for you now. So are James and Clara, we will support you through this."

The people in your life who really love you, cannot be fooled. Alexey knew it was something more than reflux the minute she was back at the table. Even though he did not mention anything, she felt his concern, it bore through her. It was the same with James and Clara. These three people know her better than anyone else, how could she keep something as serious as being a recovering alcoholic from them? Now they know. And it is a relief. She has their support, which will keep her going in her gaol of staying away from alcohol.

Chapter Fifty-One

The smell of espresso wafts into the bathroom as she is placing their towels in the drawer. It must be time for a break.

They had moved back into her apartment in Prato and were settling in again. When she moved to England, she often dreamed of moving back in with Alexey. Now it has happened, they are together again, and all the turmoil is behind them. In the first few weeks, it was surreal having him back, she kept worrying he would be deported again.

Delight fills her body as she heads towards the kitchen. It's only been a couple of months, but it already feels as if the last two years had not kept them apart at all. They are back as a couple, and each day he is with her, she feels more secure that he is here to stay.

She returned to Hebden Bridge for a month, mainly to sort out the apartment and organise a replacement anchor. The latter did take longer than she hoped because Tim was being extremely fussy about who to hire.

"No one is up to your standard," he had said.

Considering he almost fired her, this made her feel valued. Joanne promised to visit. She was welcome anytime; their friendship had blossomed, and it was Joanne who was at the airport seeing her off. She was a special someone. As she waved Larissa off with a tear-stained face, she yelled "I'll be over as soon as Tim approves my holidays."

James gave her a job as a special correspondent on Roma Tonight and Alexey is working as a freelance photojournalist for a few magazines. His agency came through with work when he returned, quickly cementing him back in the European circuit.

Life is good, and all the drama has settled with Alexey's papers approved. They are recognised by the Italian government. The fear of him being deported has finally been put to rest.

With all the support she has received from Alexey as well as her English and Italian friends, she has managed to think less and less about her need for alcohol. She is now able to be around people who are drinking without feeling ashamed or having too many of those hideous symptoms.

"Philip is going to be a dad. That's great news, right?" Alexey asks as she appears in the kitchen.

"I think Gee would have preferred that he and Rochelle were married first, but yes, it is great news." Larissa knows her mother is not pleased about his decision to live in Cape Town permanently, but she wants to discuss more pressing matters with Alexey right now.

She accepts the espresso he offers her. "Alexey now we are both back in Italy, I need to sort out this rift in my family. I want my grandmother and my great-aunt at our wedding."

He had proposed a few weeks after they returned from Tuscany. It was sweet to see him down on bended knee. He had surprised her with a lunch date that went into dinner. A string quartet played whilst he bent his knee. This time she said yes without any hesitation. Everyone in the restaurant exploded with applause when she said yes. Their photo was in the tabloids the next day. The headline was not as scathing as the last two, 'Rome's Favourite Reporter says YES to her Blonde Beau'.

"Our wedding is in a year; do you really think you can heal forty years of hurt in such a short time?"

"If I don't try, I won't forgive myself. They love each other, I know they do. When I met with my great-aunt, she told me her wish is to spend time in Italy with Simona every year. How will she be able to do that if Simona remains so obstinate? It's Simona we need to win over."

"Hmmm, it's not going to be easy. But of course, I will support you. What does Gee think?"

Gee had taken some convincing as well. However, Larissa felt deep down Gee wanted to meet her aunt, but she didn't want to go against her mother's wishes. Their relationship was strained already.

"Like me, she thinks it will be good for Simona, she spends too much time wallowing in self-pity. So, with both her support and yours, we won't fail right? Simona will have to come around."

He gives her a sceptical look. She chooses to ignore it. Her brain is already churning with plans on how to convince her grandmother. "I know exactly what to say to her. I'm going to call her right now."

She walks towards the bedroom, sits on the bed and dials Simona's number. She hears the click and says, "Nonna, how are you?" Her grandmother answers with a 'I'm fine and you?' She can hear the smile behind her words. She is in a good mood so choosing her words carefully, Larissa asks her about Amelia.

This time it is her grandmother's screaming voice attacking her ear. She moves the handset away, cocking her head sideways to speak into the mouthpiece, "Nonna, please calm down. Be reasonable about this. How about thinking about it this way - no one can change the past but don't let an awful past ruin your future happiness. The three of us, Gee, Alexey and I, want to see you reunited with your sister. I especially would like both of you at our wedding."

There is a pause. She can hear her grandmother sniffing. More crying. There have been so many tears shed over this rift, Larissa wants it over. She is determined to make it happen.

Simona answers telling her there is too much to forgive, and she is not sure she wants to. However, she will think about it because of their wedding.

This is a little win as far as Larissa is concerned, she is making progress. Wishing her grandmother well, she replaces the receiver and heads out to tell Alexey the (almost) good news.

"Ok I guess it's progress as you say. At least she is thinking about it. Well done."

"Now are you fine to keep going here on your own? I have to go out with Gee for a couple of hours."

"Sure. We're nearly done anyway."

Dropping Gee at her apartment after a successful afternoon of shopping, she drives home and finds Alexey in the kitchen again. "Yum, something smells good," she says as she cuddles up behind him placing her head on his back.

"I'm making a veal dish my grandfather used to make. The butcher cut up the veal in cubes for me and the other ingredients were all at the supermarket. I felt like enjoying a meal from my youth. I hope you like it as much as I do."

"I like it already. It smells divine, and I'm famished."

They continue chatting about her afternoon and he's happy to hear she didn't argue with Gee. Gee is now definitely keen to cure the rift, especially after Larissa's phone conversation with Simona. "She told me that Simona has always been difficult, but she has become more so now. I do remember many good times when we were younger, she hasn't always been like this. We both want her to start living again."

"She has healed well since the accident. What excuse does she have for remaining angry and cooped up in that apartment?"

"According to Gee she still needs physio occasionally. Not enough to keep her indoors all the time though. I guess in her current mood, she likes being stubborn."

"If you ask me, you are all stubborn. Each worse than the other."

She laughs, "You may be right. Anyway, let's leave the rift for a minute because Gee and I also discussed booking the church and the restaurant as well. With Papa not being around, I think it will be nice for her to be involved in some of our wedding plans."

He is serving her a taste of the veal on a wooden spoon, "Here try this... look I'm ok with her helping us out but I don't want her taking over. You know how forceful she can be about her ideas. And I especially don't want you two fighting."

"Haw, that's hot." She places her hand to her mouth breathing in cool air. Once she chews into the meat, she exclaims, "Yum! Alexey you are one talented cook." She sucks on the spoon, then, turning it upside down playfully slaps his bum.

He laughs and starts chasing her around the apartment, "Do you know what happens to naughty girls who can't keep their hands to themselves?"

She lets him catch her.

He takes the spoon off her and taps her bum as they both fall onto their bed laughing. "I won't let her take over our plans, I promise. And I've had enough of fighting with both Gee and Simona… oh Alexey. You're, oh yes… you're not listening to me, are you?"

He is kissing her neck and manages a muffled, "No."

Chapter Fifty-Two

She places her key in the post box as she hears the elevator doors opening. "Hold the lift please Alfio."

"For my favourite tenant, anything."

Running into the lift she gives him a sardonic smile, "Alfio, I've heard you say that to all of us."

"No, you are special. Honestly," he winks with a cheeky grin. "By the way, have you had a chance to try the wine I suggested?"

She winces. He doesn't notice, his back to her as she lies, "Actually, I'm going to open it tonight. Alexey is back from assignment." The bottle of Montepulciano is now part of James' collection, at least he will enjoy it one day. A distressed breath escapes her.

"Oh yes, I saw Alexey this afternoon. He dropped off his suitcase then went out again. I'm happy for you both, I see you worked things out. Now, you can both enjoy the vino and then I'm sure you'll enjoy what comes after." He gives a large guffaw at his lame joke.

"Oh, you're hilarious, Alfio," she says with a sarcastic grin as she walks out onto her floor, "and thanks, things are good between us again." He might be overly familiar at times, but overall Alfio was handy to have around. He had kept an eye on her apartment when it was rented and let her know if there were problems with her tenants.

"Enjoy your night Larissa," he says giving her his cheeky wink again.

Only minutes after entering the apartment, she hears the front door. Alexey is home. His new agency had given him an assignment to photograph the British Royals during their holiday in the Italian Alps. He had been away for ten days.

"It's good to be home, how are you darling?" he asks sighing.

"I'm glad to be home too, it's been a hell of a day." She places their mail on the mantle and falls into his buff, ever loving arms. Her nerves calm. She breathes in his smell; this is all she needs to feel assured. Being busy has been the key to keeping symptoms at bay. Since moving back home, joining a new AA group and the support she has received from Alexey, James and Clara, she is confident of staying sober. Conversations like the one she just had with Alfio, people who knew she enjoyed a drink, throw her confidence into a spin. This is when Alexey's hugs become imperative, his arms are her safe place.

Brushing aside her frazzled nerves, she fills him in on the events of her day, "The Minister for the Environment was an hour late for his interview, it threw out our whole schedule… but I don't want to bore you with my work problems, tell me about the Royals."

"I was only assisting the appointed royal photographer. The security surrounding the royal couple is tight, of course. When we were introduced, we shook their hands and that was it. There was no informal conversation and we had to work fast as Her Majesty had another appointment. It was all very proper and different to any other assignment I have done. We were scheduled to take one photo per day in various locations. Everything worked, we had no dramas."

"Assistant or not, you met Queen Elizabeth and her family, Alexey. It will be a memory you will remember all your life."

"True. The security guys were great to go out with, and did they have some stories to tell."

"Oh really, like what?"

"Sorry darling, I signed a confidentiality clause. But I will tell you this, they are a family with everyday problems, no different to any of us."

"Yes, I suppose they are. Speaking of family, I want to discuss my ideas on how to convince Simona to make peace with Amelia."

"Oh, that again! Ok, but first let's organise dinner. I'm going to feel better discussing it on a full stomach."

After dinner, she is on the lounge watching him trying to fix the reception on the TV. "Do you think I have a chance of fixing the rift before our wedding?"

He is flicking stations and fiddling with the antenna. He isn't really listening to her, "Alexey, did you hear me?"

"I did. Give me a minute to fix this, we keep getting static." She sits patiently and waits. Next to her are examples of wedding invitations, she will discuss these with him as well.

Her thoughts turn to Simona and Amelia. Amelia had told Larissa that when she and Simona were young, Simona was her shadow. Frail and easily frightened, Simona had inherited their mother's shy character. She relied on Amelia for protection, and up until they both married, this is what Amelia did.

The war was the beginning of their relationship changing. Simona became more reclusive where Amelia wanted to help and assist those in need. The day Vladimir arrived on her stoop, she hadn't been frightened of him because she had already helped others.

When Simona walked past the basement one morning, she saw Amelia with him. Closing the basement door behind her she implored Simona not to say anything. Although horrified at Amelia placing them in danger, Simona agreed but told Amelia how stupid she was to be harbouring a fugitive.

Ever since that day, Amelia and Simona have clashed. The loss of Simona being her compliant little sister has had a profound effect on Amelia.

Holding the TV antenna, he asks, "Does the picture look better from where you are?"

"No, it's still a bit blurry."

Fiddling with the antenna, then jiggling something around the back of the TV, he says, "What about now?"

"Yes, that looks better. Could we please discuss more important issues than the quality of the picture?"

"How dare you!" he mocks, "how am I supposed to watch the football if the picture is blurred?"

"You've dealt with it now, dummy. The picture is fine. Now sit here, I need you to focus." She knows he is avoiding the discussion. "Please help with me this. I'd like your opinion on getting Amelia and Simona talking and being sisters again."

"Didn't Simona agree the last time you spoke to her?"

"After I mentioned not letting the past get in the way of a happier future, she did mellow and said she would consider it. I haven't heard anything since. Not even Gee has heard from her." This is not unusual. Simona is notorious for not keeping in touch, even though both she and Gee have asked her to call, especially when important issues need to be discussed. Frustration at her grandmother's insistence of remaining angry with her sister is causing Larissa to have a conniption. In her mind it is ridiculous. If she and Philip had not seen each other for forty years she would be ecstatic at having the chance of seeing him again.

"Honestly Larissa, I'm not sure I will be of any help. You know your grandmother better than I do."

"This has nothing to do with knowing her. It's about us using our conflict resolution skills. We have both had to deal with argumentative people in our jobs, surely between us we can come up with a plan to whittle down her stubbornness?"

"I tell you what. I'll go and organise a hot tea for both of us, you grab a notepad and we'll come back and knuckle something out."

"Now this is better. You are already sounding like a good husband, one who looks after his wife when she really needs it." She chuckles, she is positive between the two of them, they will find a solution. Failing is not an option. Simona has been angry with Amelia for far too long.

Chapter Fifty-Three

She is stoking the fire. Embers float, flickering towards the flue. Simona is still arguing with her, but she is tiring of hearing her excuses.

"You met her once, why should she be at your wedding?"

Without turning from the fire Larissa speaks through gritted teeth. "Isn't it enough I would like her to be at our wedding? Up until a few months ago, Gee and I still thought she was dead. You changed all that Nonna. Why did you bother telling us if you are keeping this grudge? She is my great-aunt after all."

Gee interjects, "Your attitude is impossible. She is your sister and things went wrong a long time ago. Can't you let go of all your anger?" Gee is sitting next to Simona, frustration seeping through her voice.

Larissa turns away from the fire to see Simona, seated in her chair, looking Gee straight in the eye.

"There is so much more neither of you know about. Things you do not need to know, and I want to leave those things in the past. It is between Amelia and I; we bear the brunt of what happened to us."

"Nonna, whatever it is that happened, we cannot change. And it is exactly what I have said to you before, let them go. Leave them in the past. Don't let the awful memories get in the way of a better future with Amelia." Larissa is hiding her frustration by keeping her voice calm. She isn't having a lot of success as both she and Gee have pushed this point. They believe Simona, deep down, wants to be reunited with her sister. When this does happen and they are speaking again, their future will eclipse their past.

Tense silence descends between the three of them. Larissa moves towards Simona. Bending down, she takes her hand, "Nonna, it will make me very happy to see both you and Aunt Amelia at my wedding. Please call her. Don't you miss the conversations you both had last year?"

Closing her eyes, a tear drops onto Simona's lap. Her shoulders droop, "Let me think about it. I will decide if and when I will call her. It will be in my own time. Stop pressuring me. Now, don't you two need to leave? Alexey is waiting for you, isn't he Larissa?"

Gee and Larissa eye each other and nod.

"Yes Nonna, we are leaving now. Thank you for at least thinking about it." Larissa moves forward giving her a kiss on each cheek, "we will talk soon." She then collects her coat and bag walking towards the door. Gee follows her after saying goodbye to her mother.

They don't say anything to each other until Gee speaks as they reach the car.

"I think we made progress today, Larissa. If she doesn't make the call for herself, she will make it for you. She loves you too much to hurt you."

Larissa starts the engine without answering. She is not as confident as Gee.

Chapter Fifty-Four

Picking up the kitchen phone, she hears the international beeps. Could it be? Is Simona calling her?

"Hello" she answers tentatively.

"Amelia, it's me Simona. Umm…" There is a moment of silence then, "Err I guess we need to talk about Larissa's wedding. She wants you there, it is for her I am calling."

Amelia is so surprised to hear her voice again that she doesn't answer immediately. She hears Simona sniffling through the line. "Does that mean we can be on good terms, or am I just going to see you at the wedding and then you are out of my life again?"

Simona is crying now. "This… this is so hard Amelia. You want them to know about the past because of the love you had for Vladimir. I see no reason for them to know. If you agree not to reveal our secret, then, yes, we can phone each other. We can heal this rift."

Pulling up a chair closer to the phone, Amelia sits down. She too starts to cry. "They are getting married. How wonderful, I am happy for them," she says through sniffles, "When Larissa came to visit she asked me questions, some of which I answered. If she wants me at her wedding, then of course I'll be there. Simona, if it means you and I will be speaking again, then I will leave the past in the past, just as you wish." She shuffles in her chair and brushes down her apron, "I don't think I could come to the wedding and then never see you again. Please, no more anger between us Simona, we've suffered enough!"

"Oh Amelia, you have no idea how much I wanted to hear you agree to leave things in the past. Do you really mean it?"

"Yes, I do. All I want is for us to be sisters again."

"This is wonderful. Now we will be able to call each other again, as well as see each other."

William walks in, Amelia places her hand on the mouthpiece and whispers, "It's Simona."

He raises his eyebrows and places his hand on her shoulder as he walks past, giving her a smile.

Focusing back on the phone call she says, "I look forward to receiving the invitation. When is the date?" She sniffs and wipes some remaining tears from her eyes.

"I don't remember the exact date, but it is in October this year. We'll talk again before then but I have to go now. Take care of yourself."

"Yes, you too, thanks Simona, it was lovely to hear your voice again." She hangs up the phone, pulling her handkerchief out of her apron pocket. She blows her nose then sniffs and sighs with bewildering force. Exhaustion comes over her.

William, who is sitting in the lounge room says, "I knew as soon as I saw your eyes it was Simona. Your face was glowing." He looks up at her as she is walking over to him, "Oh not so much now, come and sit down." He pats the seat next to him beckoning her over.

At times she is amazed at how observant he is of how she is feeling. Her first husband never acknowledged her feelings, although his depression was probably the cause. How do you care about someone else when you don't care for yourself? She pushes these awful memories aside, she just promised Simona she will keep them in the past.

"Thanks, you really are observant and very sweet. But you know that already," she says as she cuddles into him, "Simona called because Larissa is getting married and she wants us there. We are invited to the wedding."

"So, the rift between you two is all over?"

She nods, "I hope so. Simona said we can phone each other again. The wedding is in October, she will let me know the date when she calls next time."

"Well I guess we had better start saving for another trip to Europe." He places a light kiss on her lips. "I'll go and make us a cup of tea."

As he walks away, she smiles after him. She and Simona made a decision long ago that has caused them to be apart and angry for so long. This has made her intolerable to live with, especially this last year. But having a tolerant and loving person like William in her life has made things more bearable.

Chapter Fifty-Five

They arrive at Tessutti Romana ready for their final fitting. Gee is beyond excited and has shed many a tear already. Larissa wonders whether her mother will be able to keep herself together on the day. Actually, she wonders whether she will too. When she sees Simona and Amelia together will she be able to hold her tears back?

"Good morning ladies. Larissa, your dress is in fitting room one. Clara, yours is fitting room two, and Gee, I will organise your dress to take with you today. Would you like a water before the fittings?" They are greeted by the elegant, Marisa, the owner. Coifed hair, perfect make up, fitted black shift dress with red pumps, this ex-model is ageless.

At the first fitting, Gee was a little intimidated by her, but Marisa had been professional and comforted her. Her dress selections for Gee were on point. The dress Gee finally selected, a soft pink lace gown, suited her and showed off her generous curves. Clara had chosen a green flowing dress in satin. Raglan sleeves split at the shoulder drop down softly along her arms. The sweeping V-neckline hugs her bust, which even after having Matthew, is still full and sexy. Clara is ageless as well.

Larissa remembers clearly how Gee had gasped at her beauty

when she first met Clara. One of the things she admires about her friend is she doesn't flaunt her beauty. Clara believes her intelligence to be the beautiful part of her body. This is her most endearing quality.

Larissa's dress is simple and elegant. The fabric is Thai silk in a soft green. The off-the-shoulder design has a full skirt and long sleeves. Both the neckline and sleeves are decorated with leaf shapes formed from the Thai silk, as well as being edged with delicate diamanté drops.

She had already decided to wear her hair full and long with the mid-length veil topped by the same leaf shapes. The veil compliments the shape and style of the dress, it forms a leaf shape with a large diamanté drop at the end.

Gee had expressed her concern when she saw the colour of the wedding dress. The arguments she has had with her mother about this wedding have been numerous, some she has conceded to please Gee. This argument, however, Larissa won. She was not going to wear a white dress just because of tradition.

Marisa had interpreted Larissa's ideas well, much to her pleasure. Her dress is feminine without being too *pretty and frilly*. She has never been one for full and flouncy dresses, preferring comfort over latest fashion. She loves good clothes that have a great line and cut, but comfort is her main priority.

She walks out of the fitting room to gasps from both Gee and Clara. Gee places her hand to her mouth and tears spill silently down her face.

"Come on Gee, my wedding is going to be a day of happiness, right?"

"Yes of course," she sniffs, "I was thinking of your father. He would be in tears too."

Larissa doesn't answer, knowing she is right. Her wedding day is going to be an emotional day. Alexey has no one, her father won't be there, and Simona will be reunited with Amelia.

"Ok Larissa, I have placed the last pin on the back. Please return to the fitting room and take the dress off carefully. Gee and Clara, let me organise your outfits ready to be taken today."

Marisa struts towards the back room, her runway model-walk still evident.

Larissa and Clara are sitting at an osteria having lunch after dropping Gee home.

"Well, the big day is only weeks away Larissa, are you nervous?"

"Not really. We have both been busy, so I don't think Alexey and I have time to be nervous. Sometimes I look at him and know he is sad, he has no one." Even though he has not mentioned anything, she knows he misses his grandfather. Also, he is a migrant, Italy is not his home like it is hers. This is all familiar territory to her and has been all her life.

"He chose you Larissa. He fell in love with you. He didn't leave his home for no reason. Yes, obviously it would be nice for him to have someone, but no one can change the situation. Worrying about this won't help him."

The waitress places their panini in front of them. Larissa nods and taking a bite she realises she is hungry. Clara is right, she will concentrate on the things she can control.

Chapter Fifty-Six

Placing his suitcase in their bedroom, he walks towards Larissa sitting on the lounge. "Hi," he says kissing her forehead gently.

"Hi darling, you look drained. Tough assignment?"

"They wanted a lot of shots with different scenery at different times of the day. We crammed a lot in."

"I've just made coffee. Do you want one?"

"Yes please," he says looking at the coffee table, "what are you working on?"

As she heads into the kitchen, she answers him, "Seating arrangements. I know you're tired, but we need to discuss a few things. This coffee will help." She hands it to him. Their wedding date is sneaking up fast.

He takes the cup from her. "Fire away, I'm listening."

"We have to finalise the menu. You are happy with Socristia aren't you?"

"Why wouldn't I be? It's one of the best restaurants in Rome."

It's also the first restaurant they went to soon after they met. A smile widens on his face as he remembers the awards night, the first time he saw her in person. She was even more beautiful than the photo Vladimir had placed in the folder. Another plus is, the restaurant is on Via Giovanni da Castel Bolognese, a short walk from the church.

They chat about the guest list, who has replied to the invitation so far, and their honeymoon. "Sounds like you have things under control. All I need to do is turn up." He laughs as he throws off his shirt and heads towards the kitchen. "I'm hungry. What's in our fridge?" Hmm, nothing too appetising but I'm sure I can rustle up something tasty.

He places a platter of antipasti in front of them.

"Yum. You amaze me at what you can find in an empty fridge," laughs Larissa popping an olive in her mouth. As they share their snack, she continues to fill him in on what else needs to be done. Once he has had his fill – of food and information – he takes her in his arms. Kissing her, he leads her to the bedroom.

Falling onto the bed, he looks on as she peels off her dress. Stripped naked she dances seductively towards him. He cups her breasts gently bringing one to his mouth. At this moment, her body is his. He breathes in her scent, the scent of a woman he loves with all his heart. Larissa moans with pleasure as he relishes every inch of her. They rhythmically move towards a mutual climax, both moaning with desire.

Breathing heavily, he lies next to her spent, enjoying their togetherness. Soon he will marry this delectable woman. Looking deep into Larissa's eyes he knew they had been destined to meet. He has no regrets; this is where he is meant to be.

Chapter Fifty-Seven

They are both standing in the arrivals area of Fiumicino airport. She stands looking out for Simona as William looks after their luggage.

She sees her heading towards them… time stops.

This is finally happening. They will be together again, be sisters again. The weight of all those awful years they were apart lifts. Simona is in her arms once more. This time she is not letting go.

"I'm sorry."

"Shh, there's no need to apologise. Let's move on and enjoy being together again." Amelia calms her sister. Looking over to where she left William standing, she notices their luggage has gone, "Have Larissa and Alexey taken our luggage?"

"Yes, they introduced themselves. Larissa said she couldn't bear to watch you two."

Amelia introduces Simona. "I'm happy to finally meet you William. Amelia has told me a lot about you."

Amelia translates for him. "Hmm, she kept you secret for a long time."

"William! Not now."

Simona is startled, why is her sister yelling.

Seeing the concern on Simona's face, she explains. Simona's face reddens asking Amelia not to start a fight here.

She acknowledges Simona's concern telling her she has no intention of causing a scene.

"Alright then. Let's acknowledge we made mistakes and move on from this shall we?" Amelia is not prepared to fight with William in front of Simona. She will speak to him later.

Taking Simona's arm, they walk towards the car. William is in tow, silent.

Amelia is commenting that Simona's health has improved since their last meeting and then she stops as they reach the cars. Time is suddenly suspended once more as Simona introduces them to Alexey. His resemblance to Vladimir is uncanny. The same blue eyes. The same thick, blonde hair. Even his dimple chin… exactly the same. History is repeating itself, this time with her granddaughter. Is it right for her granddaughter to be dating Vladimir's grandson?

"Amelia are you getting in?" yells William.

Walking into Simona's apartment, William stops and looks at her photo on the mantle. "You are still my Italian beauty," he says giving her a peck on the cheek.

Amelia knows he is apologising for his behaviour at the airport. He never holds grudges, so it is hard to stay angry with him. She is with her family again, it's time to concentrate on them.

Larissa is placing drinks on the coffee table as William is given the tour of the apartment after being introduced.

Amelia says, "This is it. Not as much room as our place is there?"

"It is compact. I guess you get on well with your neighbours Simona?"

Amelia translates his question with Simona laughing, "Most of them William. There isn't much choice when you live on top of each other like this. Sometimes we do annoy each other. But the advantage is the security of having people close when needed."

• • •

After chatting and getting to know each other, Larissa and Alexey decide to leave the three of them. "Thanks for coming Aunt Amelia and Uncle William. I appreciate you being here for our wedding."

Amelia gives them both a hug and whispers to Larissa, "Thank you for doing this. I will always appreciate what you have done to help me."

Simona sees them to the door, "See you soon. It was wonderful to see you both. Drive safely."

As Simona sits back down, Amelia continues explaining to William what is happening at the wedding. "So, the arrangements for Friday are easy. The car collecting Simona will pick us up as well. The only downside is we have to be up by six am."

"Great, another early start! You know what? I'm totally whacked. Let's go to our motel, the long flight is taking its toll."

"Oh William, Simona and I have a lot to discuss. Why don't you go? I'll meet you later."

He gives her a shrug, "Sure. Is there anything you want me to take? Alexey and I dropped off our bags earlier, so I'll make sure they're in our room."

"Well yes, take this overnight bag. I won't be needing it until the morning." She walks him to the door.

"I'm sorry for being short with Simona at the airport. I blurted it out without thinking."

She kisses him saying, "We've had a long few months. I haven't been the easiest person to live with." Watching him leave she promises herself to make it up to him. William doesn't deserve to be treated this way. He agreed to accompany her to meet people he didn't even know existed until recently.

"I can see how much he loves you Amelia. He seems to be a gentle soul," says Simona as Amelia sits down next to her again.

"He is, and up until I started missing you terribly, when I became moody and irrational, we rarely argued. Now, everything will settle, I hope. You are willing for us to visit again? Or, you visit us in Australia?"

"How about we take this one step at a time? We have a wedding to enjoy, let's concentrate on making Larissa and Alexey's day memorable."

Amelia is finding Simona's obstinance unnerving. Why does she want to place barriers in front of them? This is the time they can speak without distance between them. There is still three days before the wedding. "The wedding is not the only reason I have come all this way. Now I have met Alexey, I know we have to resolve this issue. When I saw him at the airport, I thought I was seeing Vladimir. He is a young version of him."

"And what good will it do? Do you want to break Larissa and Alexey up now, right before their wedding?

"No!" she exclaims, "that's not it. What I want is for them to at least know the truth. Gee is Vladimir's child."

"I don't believe you want to start all this again," Simona is yelling, "Have you thought about the effect on William and your two children? We agreed to forget about what happened. We have discussed this so many times."

"That was before I met Alexey. Now, meeting him and seeing how much he resembles Vladimir… this is a real problem for me. As for William and our children, they will support me. I know it in my heart."

Simona pleads quietly, "Amelia, let's enjoy the wedding. You and William are here for three weeks, there will be time to discuss what we tell Gee. Now is not the right time. Not before the wedding."

Amelia places her hand on Simona's knee, "There will never be a right time, but for my sanity, something has to be said. It is time for us to heal our wounds Simona."

Chapter Fifty-Eight

Their wedding ceremony is at the Sacro Cuore del Suffragio Church. Tucked away from the religious hub of The Vatican, many of Rome's churches have their own intimacy and style.

Larissa arrives at the neo-gothic church with Philip by her side on this glorious autumn morning. A slight hint of chill is in the air with the sun streaming down on them as they walk towards the entrance. The leaves of the bushes in front of the church sway in the light breeze.

"I guess there is no turning back now," he jokes. Stopping in front, he looks up, "wow, this church is a mini-Duomo. Those spires and turrets belong in Milan not Rome." This was the first time Philip had seen the church, only arriving two days before. He missed the rehearsal.

"Gee wanted us to marry in a church and we both liked this one. And you're right, the priest told us it was modelled on the Duomo when it was built. Now, do you think we should go? Alexey might be waiting," she laughs. Philip has lifted her spirits all morning. Keeping her from missing their dad, but she knows he is feeling the same. "This is your day," he had told her, "And Joseph is watching over us."

As they walk in through the Gothic arches, she feels their father's presence in amongst the congregation of their family and friends. The full-bodied tones of the imposing pipe organ play *La Vita e Bella* as they stride towards Alexey. It was her idea to break from the traditional *Ave Maria* for her entrance. Alexey's break from tradition was coming later. No matter how many times she tried to find out what he had planned, he remained unruffled.

Taking his hand in hers, they both turn to face the priest.

"My dear friends, we are gathered here today…"

Her smile doesn't wane as she looks into his eyes. This man has given so much of himself. He risked his life to be with her and left his home forever. She is grateful of his love as she peers deep into his eyes.

Voices of the local choir resonate throughout the church as they sing *Panis Angelicus*. Their sublime voices bring tears to her eyes. Her father hummed this hymn often.

"… by the power vested in me I now pronounce you man and wife."

Alexey and Larissa kiss each other to raucous applause. Turning to face everyone, Alexey scoops her up and carries her down the aisle to the strains of *The First Time I Ever Saw Your Face*. She can hear someone singing and it's not Roberta Flack. Alexey is singing! He is serenading her to the cheers and applause of their guests. Their bridal entourage follow suit, then everyone is singing along.

Cameras click and video cameras whir. Confetti and rice rain down on them as Alexey places her on the sandstone step. She kisses him with fervour and pride. Looking out towards all her loved ones she beams, "You all knew about this. Everyone knew the words except me."

"It was Alexey's idea, we were all sworn to secrecy," James tells her with a congratulatory kiss.

"Congratulations."

"Good Luck."

"May God protect you."

These calls from the large crowd gathered outside the church.

Larissa is shocked to see so many people. She had tried to keep their wedding date a secret.

"All your fans, Mrs Dubrovnik." She finds herself blushing despite her experience with crowds. She drinks in the atmosphere and is thankful for this beautiful autumn day as sun pours over them. Everyone she loves is with her today.

Alexey calls over Simona, Amelia and Gee. He then moves away, "This is a photo I need to take. You are all together at last."

Clara runs up to the four of them, adjusting Larissa's dress, touching up their make-up and asking them, "We want smiles now, no more tears. This photo will be a testament to your love for each other." Thanking her, Larissa turns to look towards Alexey behind his camera. The camera clicks. He then hands his camera to their wedding photographer, making his way back to her side.

"You brought your camera especially. You are so thoughtful, thank you. And now I can add singing to your talents."

"It is because of you we are all together, I wanted to capture the moment. My camera will be well looked after. Besides, I want to take photos later as well. Natural, unintentional ones. I'll leave the formal ones to these guys," he points to the photographer and videographer in front of them. "Now smile Mrs Dubrovnik, there are many more photos to be taken."

Her face aches from smiling, the photos keep coming as others come onto the steps to join them. She notices a few paparazzi and mentions this to James.

"Oh Larissa, this time you don't have to worry about them. This is your day, a happy day that should be shared. Now, let's head to the restaurant. It's time to party."

Alexey takes her hand and threads it through his arm. They walk along with their friends and family as more confetti and rice is sprayed over them by her fans.

"Let the wedding feast begin," announces Alexey.

Everyone indulges in the Mediterranean dishes expertly served by the wait staff. Larissa's face beams with happiness. To be sitting with Alexey in front of her family and friends is… beyond believable. But they have achieved what many were sceptical about – a successful relationship between someone from the communist East and one from the decadent West. She smiles, miracles do happen.

The speeches are kept short. James and Alexey amuse the guests with anecdotes about how their friendship has developed into one of mutual respect both professionally and personally. Alexey concludes his speech by mentioning his late father-in-law, bringing tears to everyone's eyes.

When it's Larissa's turn to say something, she finds herself choking up. Her hands sweat and she is tongue-tied. For someone who makes a living out of talking, without a script in front of her and with an audience instead of a camera lens, she is suddenly out of her comfort zone. Tears slip silently down her face, her cheeks wet as she looks towards Gee who is walking towards her. She hugs her telling her to continue.

She and Gee talk about their happiness at being here with the people they love. Their tears subside as Gee talks about Joseph and her special memories of her life with him. Of when Philip and Larissa were toddlers, how he protected them. Gee explains how both her children were shy, timid little things who held onto her or Joseph for dear life whenever someone asked them a question. "Two toddlers who have made my life full of beautiful surprises, and I'll admit, the occasional shock. Larissa, today you join with the man of your dreams, cherish every moment together. It's your turn for special memories."

Larissa hugs her mother who remains by her side. With more silent tears, she also talks of her father. Gee squeezes her hand each time she needs reassurance. Then she turns to Simona and thanks her for giving her the love of a good story. "All the stories you have recounted over the years inspired me to become a journalist and for this I thank you."

Simona tears up and smiling weakly places her hand on her heart and mouths, 'thank you'.

Turning to Alexey she says, "I will never forget what you did to be with me. Ours is a love that has endured many obstacles already. I know we will be prepared for anything in the future because we're going to be by each other's side."

Beaming, Alexey stands and hands her a champagne flute. Interlocking arms they drink to their union. Larissa has perfected the art of pretending to sip alcohol, no one suspects, no one notices. Only Alexey notices her slight tremor, which he soothes by whispering "you're doing great".

Their guests cheer him on as he swoops her down with a flourish, kissing her playfully, his left arm in the air. Then he twirls her towards the dance area. He sings, *How Deep is Your Love* to her as the Bee Gees hit song begins. "It's all over Larissa, no need for any more tears. We won't be apart ever again," he whispers in her ear.

At this moment there is no one else around them. It is only the two of them. This is all she wants from now on, the two of them always together.

Amelia and William are the first to join them when an Italian love song plays next. Larissa's eyes sting with tears as she sees Amelia who is openly crying.

William winks at Alexey, "Get used to this. They cry all the time."

James is up next as the tempo changes and taps Alexey's shoulder, "May I?" he asks taking Larissa's hand. He twists her around placing his hand on her waist.

"Wow look at you, when did you learn to dance?"

"You were away a long time Larissa. I have learned many new skills. Little Matthew enjoys listening to music, so he's teaching me how to dance."

Clara, who is dancing with Alexey next to them scoffs. She laughs telling Larissa he took a few lessons so he could impress her. This will probably be the first of two times he will ever dance, the next time will be at their wedding.

"You two are getting married!" she screeches, "oh that's wonderful news."

"Yes, Clara and I are getting married. We couldn't allow the two of you to steal all the limelight," confirms James.

Alexey asks, "That's great news. When?"

"It's a winter wedding on December 5," announces Clara, "I guess we should make ourselves respectable, especially as Matthew is going to be a big brother."

Again, Larissa shrieks with happiness. Gathering up Matthew who had sidled up to James wanting to be picked up, she coos, "Your mummy is pregnant. How wonderful, you're going to be a big brother." Her kisses smother his face. Matthew wipes his face furiously and urges to be put back down.

"Nahhah, where are you?" He is looking for Hannah, wanting to play with her.

Running towards Philip and Rochelle, he finds his playmate, still wiping his face.

"Wow," says Alexey, "we have even more celebrating to do. Congratulations to both of you."

Her feet ache and her face aches from smiling, but she has never been happier. As Alexey takes the garter off and throws it, there is a whoop from everyone as James grabs it. Clara had already caught the bouquet. How appropriate.

With everyone on the dance floor, ready to say goodbye to the newlyweds, Gee is hugging Larissa, "I missed you terribly when you lived in England. It means so much to me to have you back home. And you too Alexey, I'm so happy for both of you."

"Thanks Gee. Thank you for everything you have done, you made this all so easy for us. I love you, Mamma. You know how special you are to me." Larissa and Gee fold into each other. As Larissa is cherishing the moment, Simona joins them enveloping herself around the two of them.

"Larissa, take care of that man of yours. What you have together is exceptional."

"Thank you, Simona. I promise to take care of her too," interjects

Alexey. Then turning to Larissa, he says, "We have to go, or we'll miss our flight."

She turns waving to everyone and takes his hand as they walk to the car waiting for them.

Stopping by their apartment to change and collect their suitcases they check their tickets, grab their passports and head off to the airport. They will board an Olympic Airlines flight that will whisk them away to a honeymoon in the Greek Islands.

As they are walking through customs, she is stopped a couple of times by people wanting her autograph. Exhausted after their day, she obliges.

Their wedding day has whizzed by, all those months of planning and now she is Mrs Larissa Dubrovnik. Gratified and blissfully happy, she walks hand in hand with her husband.

Chapter Fifty-Nine

He will make sure the medals are returned. By order of the KGB, the name Vladimir Dubrovnik is to be struck off the honourary medals list. Yegor Bruskev will receive an honorary mention and promoted to Major General for the Engineering division of the Leningrad office of the KGB. He will achieve this dream and his broad smile says it all. But before this can happen there is one final mission. Revenge is sweet; and it will be even sweeter once this is done.

He reflects on his past remembering how many comrades he lost. As well as the many members of his family. The world was an unsafe place to live in during the war years, too many innocent people lost their lives. And for what? The generations of people born after the end of WWII are the benefactors. In the end it doesn't matter who won, it is up to the individual to fight for what is right, to undo the wrongs done to them. Those wrongs Dubrovnik caused will be righted, he has ensured this will happen.

Pressing the buzzer on his desk, "Ask her to come in now, thank you." There is one more thing left to do, and he will be able to happily retire with all the accolades he is meant to have. The Dubrovnik name will be fully destroyed.

• • •

He can see she is mulling over his proposal as he stands at the window. Walking back towards where she sits, he stands over her noticing she has had some cosmetic work done.

Her breasts heave as she breathes a sigh, "This time I will not be deported?"

"I have told you many times Viktoriya, you behaved while in prison. You listened to me and so I have honoured my promise to free you. Do this last assignment and you will never hear from me again."

She remains silent looking up towards him. He is dangling the promise of her living in Italy for the rest of her life. Or anywhere else in the West she wants to go. Now she has been cleared of any spying charges, he said she would receive safe asylum no matter where she wants to live. "You promised me a life in the West before? What is different this time?"

He is becoming impatient. "Young lady, I warned you last time about doing such an assignment on your own. Do you remember I wanted to send an accomplished agent with you? You refused and look what happened. The authorities embroiled you in with Dubrovnik's mess of a life."

"So now I have enough experience? I have completed one assignment, and this qualifies me as an *accomplished* agent."

He strides to the other side of his desk. Pulling up his sleeves he places his hands flat on the cold timber. Leaning forward with a menacing look he says, "I am trying to help you." He pauses. "Do you want this assignment, or shall I throw you back in prison?" This is not a threat she will take lightly.

Viktoriya knows he is able to send her back to Lubyanka for the smallest reason. These things happen regularly. With her head bent she utters, "Yes, I want the assignment." Then she breathes in and with a more determined voice she says, "Give me all the details."

"I am glad I have earned your trust," he says handing her a folder. He waits as she scans the contents.

"Who is Amelia Lillostra?" she asks.

"She is Larissa's grandmother, now living in Australia. This is a scandal about her and Vladimir. And it is waiting to be heard.

Giovanna, Amelia's daughter, could be Vladimir's child. This means Larissa and Alexey are related."

Viktoriya holds up a death certificate towards him, "And this? Who is he?"

"That certificate is Teodoro's. He was Amelia's father found dead outside the basement with a crowbar in his hand. The basement that housed the artefacts Vladimir stole from all his comrades, all his countrymen. Did Vladimir have something to do with his death? If so, he was a murderer as well as a thief."

He keeps talking explaining how he wants her to tackle this assignment, "I want you to leak the documents to the tabloids, slowly. Build up the story. Did the sisters' father stumble in on their plot or was he a scapegoat? How many traitors did Vladimir recruit? Once this expose happens, our revenge against the Dubrovnik name is assured. The satisfaction I will have in ruining Vladimir's reputation and taking my rightful place as a leader within the KGB, will be my reward." He can taste the success; he is so close to it now.

"I wasted enough time in the hell-hole of Lubyanka prison. Until you contacted me to meet you again, I had not realised my anger was still so raw. I too am ready for revenge. I confirm I will take on this assignment and do it with pleasure."

As he knew she would. His name will not be connected to the scandal. The authorities will bestow everything he wants, everything they owe him. He continues discussing how and when to leak this information, "You will see information in the folder of journalists to contact. They are trusted hacks who do not reveal their sources. You will be safe, and once this assignment is complete, you are free to live wherever you wish."

She stands and walks around to his side of the desk holding the folder. As he turns towards her, she kisses him, biting his lips.

Then she turns away from him saying, "Comrade Bruskev, you have been good to me. But if you cross me this time, I will return, hunt you down and kill you."

He tastes blood. The little minx had pierced his lip, but, as she sashays out of his office, he knows she will succeed. She wants this revenge as much as he does.

Chapter Sixty

Looking out at the turquoise Mediterranean Sea, she sips her fruity Tequila Sunrise, a mock one. Alexey is gazing at her from the next sun lounge. "What?" she asks. His blue eyes are even more striking in the sunlight. She will never tire of looking into them.

"Let's stay here. I could live this life, just you and me away from everyone and everything."

She smiles. The past two weeks have been blissful. Doing whatever they want, whenever they wanted. With nobody bothering them, they have slept in, swum, eaten whenever they felt hungry, and partied whole nights away. It would be nice to stow away in Greece for the rest of their lives, Alexey has a point. "With this view and unending sunshine, believe me I'm tempted Alexey. I could get used to life on an island. By the way, what time is our flight home tomorrow? It has been the furthest thing from my mind," she says breathing in the warm salty air.

"Oh, it's been the furthest thing from mine too. We can check when we return to our suite, but I think you should really consider my idea."

Leaning towards him she kisses him gently, "maybe one day we will retire here but tomorrow we have to return to reality."

. . .

They walk out of customs to a swarm of paparazzi and journalists throwing questions at them.

"Is it true. Are you married to a defector and traitor Larissa?"

"Are you two really related?"

"Are you still a spy Alexey?"

James runs up to them, "Don't say anything, don't answer any of them. Just follow me."

In shock, they follow James to a car he has waiting. He bundles them into the back seat, sprints to the front seat and orders the driver to go as the swarm of journalists surround them.

"What's going on?" asks Alexey.

James explains a trashy tabloid has run a story about the two of them and their family history. "Larissa there are some accusations about your family background, and Alexey, your grandfather's reputation has also been tarnished. Do you have any idea who is behind this?" he asks handing them both a copy of the magazine.

As they scan the story Larissa gasps and Alexey, sitting next to her, fumes.

"This is rubbish. James, you don't believe all of this do you?"

"Larissa, it doesn't matter whether it's true or not. The fact is the story is out there and questions are being asked again about Alexey being a spy. People also want to know why your great aunt harboured a fugitive."

Alexey is quiet while reading the story. Then he says, "Viktoriya. She is behind this. Bruskev has recruited her again and has assisted her, I'm sure. They both want revenge. She warned me about 'watching my back' when we were in the holding cell." He looks at Larissa with tears welling behind his eyes, "I'm sorry, this is all my fault."

Larissa rests her hand on his, "In this story they are talking about my great aunt Amelia and fake birth certificates. Don't be sorry yet Alexey, we need to speak to my grandmother first. There is a lot more to this and Simona needs to talk whether she likes it or not."

James knows Larissa's journalistic mind is going into overdrive. "One thing at a time Larissa. Here is the plan for now, I'm taking you both back to my place. I thought about taking you to Gee's apartment, but the paparazzi are already there. Larissa your apartment is surrounded by media as well. You two need to keep quiet until we find out all the facts, so my place is probably the safest bet for now."

He was almost right, there is one lone paparazzo waiting for them as they arrive.

"I'll divert him, you two run up to the front door, Clara is expecting you. The driver and I will worry about your luggage."

Even before they reach the top of the stairs, Clara has the door open. Matthew runs into her arms, "Larissa, did you bring me a present?"

"Matthew, say hello first, where are your manners? You do not ask for presents. Go to your room now."

"But I want…"

"No buts… to your room please. Larissa and Alexey are here to have a rest."

"You can both come and rest in my room," yells Matthew as he heads for his room.

"I'm sorry Larissa," says Clara giving her a hug, "Alexey, you too. Quick, come inside. Matthew was not meant to be down here. I had told him to stay upstairs."

"The innocence of children, what I would give to have some now," says Larissa.

"He's cheeky and doesn't obey us at the moment. He needs to learn how to behave."

Looking at her friend with her bump showing, her beauty enhanced by the growing child, she asks how she is feeling. "I'm fine. This pregnancy is going well. I'm not feeling ill like I was with Matthew. Enough about me, both of you come and sit…"

She is stopped mid-sentence by James running inside with their bags, the driver right behind him. After placing the bags in the hall, he thanks the driver and goes into the dining room to join them. "You two ok?" He is puffing.

They both nod yes, "I don't think the paparazzo was able to get any close photos, so that is a good thing."

"It depends on the quality of his camera James, but let's not worry about photos now. We have other things to discuss," says Alexey, his face drawn.

Larissa thanks them, "You are both putting yourselves out for us. We will head home once we decide how to handle this. I will make a statement to the media about respecting our privacy."

Clara brings them tea. As they begin discussing things, Matthew calls out from his bedroom.

"I'll go," says Clara, "I sent him to his room when he was rude to Larissa."

"What did he do?" asks James, "he is naughty sometimes. Actually, quite a lot lately."

"Clara told us he can be, but honestly it was so innocent. He asked whether we had brought him a present, nothing too naughty."

"Hmm, he keeps forgetting his manners. Sorry about that."

Larissa doesn't argue. She has to let her friends discipline their child as they see fit. Her thoughts turn to her own problems and this awful article. Unfortunately, some of what has been written about her family is true. Amelia did harbour a fugitive in the family basement, she is an accomplice to Vladimir hiding the artefacts. The other accusations may or may not be true. Until she speaks to Simona all she can do is make a statement. Their privacy has to be respected. The good thing is both James and Alexey agree with her. She will draft something when she returns to work. She will deliver the statement at the end of her first night back on-air.

For the first time in a long time she wishes she could have a drink.

Chapter Sixty-One

Amelia is reading the articles Simona posted to her. What have they done? The decision she and Simona made all those years ago has caused these problems. Larissa's love life is splashed in this trashy magazine for everyone to see. None of this is Larissa's fault.

'Vladimir Dubrovnik and Amelia Lillostra were lovers during WWII, and she became pregnant by him. They tried to cover it up because they were both married to others at the time. But this baby was born. We were shown two copies of birth certificates; Amelia Lillostra is listed as the mother with the father listed as unknown on one certificate. The other shows the mother as Simona Pittola, Amelia's younger sister. What were they covering up? Were they all spies? Vladimir Dubrovnik is Alexey's grandfather. Is our beloved TV personality related to her husband? Is he still a spy?'

The phone next to her rings. She picks it up automatically, she has been waiting for the call. "Hello Simona. Yes, I'm reading the stories now. We should have sorted this out between ourselves."

She hears Simona crying on the other end. It's a bit late crying now, this mess needed to be cleared up as soon as Larissa and Alexey's relationship became serious. Keeping such a secret has caused nothing but hurt for themselves and everyone they love. All this because they were embarrassed to talk about the abuse. The abuse that was not their fault.

They discuss the second article that mentions their father and how he was found dead outside the basement with a bloodied crowbar in his hand.

"Amelia, our father snapped when he found out about Vladimir. He had every intention of killing you both with that crowbar. Vladimir's actions were in self-defence."

Amelia remembers the day with such clarity it frightens her. Chills crack through her body. If Vladimir had not been there that day, neither she nor Simona would be alive. Having protected Simona from their father's abuse for so long she was grateful someone had finally stood up to him. Vladimir was given no choice. This is when Vladimir fled back to the Soviet Union. According to the police he was the murderer of the Mayor but both Amelia and Simona considered him their hero. Closing her eyes, she is right back to when it happened...

He is ranting again. Amelia is hiding from him with the crowbar in her hands. Since the day her husband had died, the abuse had started again. There was no one to protect her again, she was on her own. She had warned Vladimir to stay out of this even though he had vowed to protect her. She tried to keep her problems away from him. But her father was such a despicable tyrant, it did not take Vladimir long to work out what was happening, her bruises and injuries were too obvious.

"That bruise on your arm and your swollen eye could not have come from you hitting into a door jamb, Amelia. Tell me the truth, who is attacking you?" he asked many times as their relationship grew deeper.

When she told him the truth, he was ready to take on Teodoro right away. She calmed him, letting him know she could handle her father. Losing Vladimir was not an option for her. Reluctantly, he promised to stay low, but did warn her if he ever sees Teodoro abusing her, nothing will stop him.

While she is hiding, she hears venomous words spurt out from Teodoro, "Where are you? This is my home you are living in.

Without me you would not have a roof over your head. And your lousy husband was just as bad as you, living off me and my charity. You owe me, you are mine to do with as I please." He is yelling, stomping his feet and swigging at the bottle he is holding. She can hear the alcohol sloshing around as the smell abuses her nose. He is too close to her hiding spot. She has to escape.

"I'll find you my little darling and then I will give you what you deserve." He keeps ranting but his voice is becoming muted. He's heading further away, hopefully in the direction of the bedrooms. He has definitely moved out of the kitchen.

Stealthily she crawls out of the cupboard. The glass on the bench above her shatters as the crowbar she is holding hits it. She runs.

The key is in the basement door. She unlocks it. He is behind her. She blacks out.

"Amelia are you listening to me?"

"Yes… yes Simona, I'm listening."

"You had better get on a flight over here. You have to help me sort this out. Gee wants to know everything. Quite frankly, I don't blame her, she needs to know because right now she is furious with both of us and totally confused about her past."

"*You* don't blame her? You're the one who wouldn't listen to me. How many times did I ask you to talk about our past? About the abuse. You were the one who wanted to sweep everything under the carpet." Amelia had been worried the secret would come back to haunt them. She had almost told Larissa the whole sordid mess when they had met. Why didn't she tell her that day at the beach? They could have dealt with it as a family. Not like this, their private lives splashed all over a tabloid magazine. "Simona, let me organise myself. I will let you know once I have flight details. For now, try and keep everyone calm." She replaces the receiver after saying goodbye.

· · ·

As she prepares dinner, her memory takes her back to London, probably because her life was as turbulent then as it is now…

After running from Stefano, who was no better than her father, and stowing away on the ship, she ended up in Tripoli. Then she found herself heading to England. What she should have been doing was making her way back to Naples. Instead she made her way to London, the escalating war preventing her from returning safely back home.

Once in England, not being able to speak English became a hindrance. Also, there was the problem of having no money. Amelia had spent all her money bribing her way to anywhere she thought may be safe. Living with others who had fled, trying to survive each day by begging or stealing. Their home was a bombed-out building on the streets of London's docks.

One wet summer morning in 1947, she woke to people yelling and waving their hands. "I have my papers, I'm willing to work, take me." She went to investigate and overheard people discussing the 'Displaced Persons Scheme'. She had noticed posters, reading them and understanding with her limited knowledge of English, that Australia had work available.

I can work and make money to return to Italy.

Hunger wracked her body; she was merely existing with other wretches who fled just as she had. Desperately wanting to return home, she pushed through the crowd staying close to a group who were soon shunted aboard. Her days etching out an existence in the slums of London sailed away with this vessel.

What she didn't understand at the time, was how far away Australia was from Europe.

Chapter Sixty-Two

They are both sitting on Gee's lounge. Larissa's head rests on her shoulder. There has been no conversation between them for some time, each of them trying to come to terms with the situation.

Gee is numb. Who is she? She has no sense of identity. And did her daughter marry a man who could be her cousin? These questions keep going around in her mind driving her insane. How did Amelia leave her when she was a baby? She would not think of abandoning a six-month-old baby? Ever! The thought of leaving her two children has never crossed her mind. The hurt churns her insides into mush, the nausea ruining her appetite. Until the results of the DNA test come through both her and Larissa's lives are in limbo. Beside herself with anger towards Amelia and Simona, it has subsided, but ever so slightly.

After hearing how they were abused, she felt sympathetic towards them. They are victims too. Every woman in her family is a victim, a victim of an abusive man whose power kept him safe.

"Are you sure you want me to go?" asks Larissa, "I'm happy to stay the night if you feel like some company."

Gee knows Larissa is worried about her. Since coming home from England, forgiveness from both sides has helped them rekindle their special bond. With Joseph gone, this is more important than ever.

Oh, Joseph, how I wish you were here with me. She desperately needs him. Unfortunately, God had other plans for her Joseph. With this crazy situation she finds herself in, she is asking why God has abandoned her? Why is this happening to her family? How is she supposed to deal with the lies; the secret, the hurt, and most of all, her lack of identity?

"Thanks for offering Larissa, but no. You go home to Alexey. He needs you too." Gee drops her eyes. She does want Larissa to stay but what do they achieve from them both wallowing in self-pity. Soon they will all meet at Simona's apartment, things will be dealt with as a family unit. Maybe they will seek professional help. They will move on from this once the DNA tests answers their questions.

Until then they have to remain strong. The issues Larissa has had to deal with professionally since the story broke have been more than enough for her. Both she and Alexey have had their lives turned upside down. They are now followed by pesky photographers, who seem to pop up everywhere they go. For Larissa, being somewhat used to fame, she has taken this intrusion only slightly better than Alexey. He has taken a few swipes in anger, which has just inflamed the tabloid writers into spinning more lies about them. Each time he has lashed out, Larissa has been there to stop him causing further harm. The last thing they need is a photographer taking them to court for abuse.

She sees Larissa out and waits on the stoop as her car pulls away. Then she walks back closing the door behind her. Standing with her back on the door, her hands cover her face. Silent tears flow down her cheeks as she mourns Giovanna Mina. Who is she?

Chapter Sixty-Three

"How could you keep something like this from us for all these years?" Larissa is pacing in the lounge room of Simona's apartment. Furiously waving her arms about she continues spitting out words of scorn towards Simona, "And you had the opportunity to open up and tell us everything when Alexey and I found the artefacts."

Alexey is sitting opposite Simona trying to appease Larissa, "Why don't you sit down. All this anger, along with the accusations and finger-pointing, is not helping anyone.

He is right, but she doesn't sit down immediately. They have to know how angry she is about all this. She wants to drive her point across before she sits down. Besides, he has not exactly helped their situation with his outbursts towards paparazzi.

Their abuse was unforgivable, she has tried to come to terms with having a great-grandfather who would do such things. But keeping quiet, harbouring guilt and staying away from each other has not done any good either.

Simona sits in uncomfortable silence. She is staring blankly towards Larissa. Opening her mouth about to speak, she closes it without uttering any words.

Larissa is standing at the mantle waiting for her grandmother to say something. A deep breath of frustration gushes from her mouth. With nothing forthcoming, she moves towards Alexey and Simona.

Sitting on the edge of the lounge, she stares at the floor. If she looks up, they will see her tears. Fierce tears that will not help the situation. Her exhale is loud, resentment riddles her body. More for her mother than for herself.

Bringing her head up and wiping her eyes, she says, "Ok, I'm ready to listen to why you both made such a decision."

Alexey squeezes her hand.

"Larissa and Alexey, both of you are lucky you have not had to witness the atrocities of war. Please remember this as I recount my version of the story. The next time we meet to discuss this situation both Gee and Amelia will be in the same room. This will be the first time they will be together since the truth has come out."

They both listen as Simona talks. Larissa can see how remembering is taking its toll on her. She moves closer and holds onto her hand, remorse replacing her anger. She cannot fathom the pain the two sisters went through.

Alexey stands up excusing himself, "Larissa, I'll be in the car when you're ready to go. Take as much time as you need." He bends to kiss Simona, "it is not necessary for me to be here, you two need to speak privately."

Simona nods meekly, thanking him for his consideration, and continues recounting the sordid mess to Larissa once he has left.

Later as Larissa opens the passenger door, she wakes Alexey from his short nap. Her eyes are red-rimmed. She is exhausted. They have not had a lot of rest since returning from their honeymoon. They are both jaded.

"Let's go home. Simona is organising a visit by Amelia. Once her arrival date is confirmed, she will contact us, and a family meeting will be organised."

He starts the car without saying a word.

She closes her eyes to rest trying not to think about this nightmare they have found themselves in. But sleep alludes her because thoughts of everything that has happened since meeting Alexey race through her mind.

They have had the highs of meeting each other and of returning the artefacts. The lows of breaking up when he was thrown into prison, and the even worse low of when she thought she would never see him again. This is when being an alcoholic hit her the hardest. There is never a day where she does not struggle with some element of this addiction.

Then the highs of finding each other again and being married. Now this. Both the Dubrovnik and Mina names trashed in the tabloids. What an awful way to find out this family secret. A decision made between two sisters with catastrophic consequences, all because they were too embarrassed to talk. What this family secret means for their marriage is not clear to yet, but Larissa's fear of possibly losing Alexey again is too much to bear.

Chapter Sixty-Four

She places her suitcase in front of the mantel as Simona walks into the kitchen. They have been arguing all the way from the airport. Her relentless attitude of not wanting to discuss the past is now beyond stupid. What was the point of Amelia flying all this way? This situation has to be discussed if they are going to resolve anything. "Honestly Simona, as awful as the stories in the tabloids are, part of what they say is true. Why do you want to hide from the truth? Gee and Larissa deserve to know everything." She hears cutlery being bashed about.

Simona swears under her breath and comes out sucking her finger, "Damn well cut myself didn't I. All this pent-up anger and I can't even make us some lunch. Look, I'm sorry. You are welcome here Amelia, I didn't mean what I said at the airport."

Simona had told her to take a flight back home right away. This was after Amelia had begun their conversation by saying, "I told you something like this might happen, the secret was going to come out one way or another." Now Amelia realises how tactless her words were, her timing was way off. She should have kept her mouth shut.

"Let me see. How bad is the cut?"

"Oh, it's a little nick. There's plasters in the bathroom," says Simona as she shuffles off.

"I'll put my bag in the bedroom. Then let's sit down and talk about how to handle this situation like adults." She perches herself on the end of Simona's bed. Rubbing her face with both hands, weariness takes over.

"Why don't you rest for a bit? We can talk later."

Simona startled her; she had not heard her come into the room.

"I think I will. Is your finger ok?"

"I'll live," she says holding up her middle finger to show her, "now make yourself comfortable, we'll have plenty of time to talk. Gee won't be arriving until tomorrow midday."

She wakes with a start. It takes her a minute to realise where she is. Stretching her limbs, she puts on a jumper before heading out to find Simona.

"Feeling better?" asks Simona her knitting needles clacking together without her looking at them.

"Hmmm, I needed that sleep. How long was I out for?"

"Three hours. Now, I managed to make us some food." With that she puts her knitting on the table, stands up and places her arm through Amelia's, "let's eat before we talk. I hate arguing on an empty stomach."

"Oh, you're hilarious," mocks Amelia realising how hungry she is, "I don't know about you but I'm going to discuss things rationally from now on."

"Sure, whatever you say. But what has happened is not a rational thing to deal with."

Deciding not to answer, Amelia sits down to enjoy the panini Simona prepared. Watching her as she flits around this small kitchen, she reflects on what might have been had she not left Italy when she did. She would have been Gee's mother, and Simona… well Simona had two miscarriages. She would never have been a mother. This had been her gift to Simona. The chance to be a mother.

It was unintentional; however, the fact remains, Simona is Gee's mother.

Oh my, that's it! This is the reason why she didn't want to discuss our past. She was worried about losing Gee. Why have I not realised this earlier?

No matter what happens over the next few days, in Amelia's mind, Simona is Gee's mother. She has no intention of taking this away from her sister. It was Simona who took on the responsibility of adopting Gee and bring her up to be the person she is today. Amelia had yearned to meet her, to see who she had become, not to take her away from Simona. This is something Simona needs to understand if they are to move on and heal their wounds.

"Come on, we'll have coffee in the lounge room. Did you have enough to eat Amelia?"

"I sure did. The panini were delicious. Here, I'll wash those whilst you make the coffee."

They're both sitting in the lounge room, musing over their ideas. Simona had confirmed her concerns about losing Gee. This had been her fear since Amelia first contacted her.

Finally, both of them are agreeing on something. Amelia wishes she had worked this out before this debacle with the tabloids. She would have tackled this situation with more discretion.

"I guess we can get started on sorting this mess. You're right, they deserve the truth. I cannot protect them from our horrible past any longer." Simona fiddles with her apron, rolling the end of it backwards and forwards.

"You do worry more than you need to, Simona. Gee and Larissa love you; they will not disown you now that the truth is out."

"I'm more embarrassed than worried. Ever since Larissa started digging around the basement, I have been paranoid of them finding out. My behaviour towards them at times has been inexcusable."

"We were teenagers at the time, young girls in a world of hate masquerading as love. We have nothing to be embarrassed about.

What happened to us is not our fault. It's Gee who is going to need looking after."

They continue discussing how to handle Gee tomorrow. This is a delicate situation neither of them could have fathomed. How Amelia wishes she could turn back time and take all this pain away.

Chapter Sixty-Five

The apartment bears the same resemblance as when she lived here. But it feels very different. In light of the allegations in those trashy publications, everything is different. Who is she now? Everything she has known all her life is a lie.

Gee peers blankly into the space she grew up in. The rosewood mantle topped with what was once a white marble slab is now yellowed and ageing from the fires burnt in the fireplace for some 100 years. The family photos on top of the marble, the copper pots shining over the antique cooker Simona refuses to part with. The old clock in the kitchen near the window. All this now feels so foreign to her. Is this going to be her new life? One without familiar things to comfort her. What is her reality now?

She and Simona are sitting at the kitchen table waiting for Amelia. Simona holds a photo frame on her lap. Gee knows it's a photo of Amelia. Who is this woman? Simona has been her mother for forty-seven years. And what about her beloved father, Marco. Did he know of this secret? Even if he did, it does not matter. Her reality now is very different to when they brought her up.

As all these thoughts swirl through her mind she looks over to Simona wanting to ask so many questions. The uncertainty of what is happening is torture. However, she has been ordered to wait. All will be revealed once Amelia and Simona are together in this room with her. Amelia will return from the hairdresser soon.

The clock in the kitchen strikes twelve. It ticks incessantly as she waits. There is food on the table. Simona has set the table for guests. The good crockery is out, the polished coffee percolator is on the cooker. It has a platinum shine just as the copper pots do. The apartment is ready to receive guests. This is the norm, when guests are coming the home is prepared to receive them, but this situation they are in is not normal. Nothing is normal for Gee anymore. She is detached and feels desperately alone.

Gee watches on as Simona hugs her sister. Both their tears are raw, falling freely as they whisper to each other. They walk towards Gee holding each other's hands.

"Gee … I umm, we did what we did out of love," whispers Amelia. Her voice raspy with the emotion of the circumstances, "there are no winners in war. Our decision may not have been right, but it was right for the turmoil we both went through at the time. I was so pleased to be able to finally meet you at the wedding." She stops clearing her throat. "We didn't want this secret to come out, but it has. So, we will now attempt to explain to you…"

Gee watches on as they both break down again. Sitting on the same chair she has been seated on for hours, she is not sure what to do. Her instinct is to console her mother, but which one? They are both her mother now, as weird as that is. But it is the truth.

Once they compose themselves, Simona asks Amelia to sit down opposite Gee. She then moves over to where Gee is seated, resting her hand on her shoulder. Keeping her hand on Gee's shoulder she looks towards Amelia giving her a comforting smile, "It's time to set things right Amelia."

Amelia nods then clears her throat, looks towards the floor and fidgets before she speaks.

Gee knows she is nervous, Simona is too. Simona has been distant with Gee since all this blew up in everyone's faces. Neither of them knows how to be in this new reality.

"I want to start by saying you are loved Gee. I wanted you from the moment I found out I was pregnant. Vladimir was the man I wanted to be with for the rest of my life but we both became fugitives." Amelia continues explaining how the day Gee's grandfather, Teodoro, died with a blow to his head was the day Vladimir became a murderer. He knew what Teodoro was capable of because as the mayor of Naples he wielded power beyond his position. Teodoro mistreated his wife and two daughters. This resulted in the death of his wife from internal bleeding after a drunken rampage. There was no investigation.

He continued the same abuse, usually with Amelia but at times with Simona, telling both his daughters if they told anyone they would suffer the same fate as their mother. The war meant women were used and abused. They had no one to turn to. Who would believe them? Their father, Teodoro Lillostra, was a man of status, his friends were high-profile politicians and shady businessmen.

To escape the tyranny of their father both she and Simona married young. As married women, Teodoro left them alone, he did not want the husbands to find out his dirty secret. "We despised Teodoro. I especially wanted to be rid of him, but unfortunately my husband was a poor farmer and a depressed war veteran, he didn't have much to offer me. So we lived in my father's home. This was Teodoro's *generous* offer to us. My husband accepted the offer without consulting with me first. He had no reason to refuse such an offer," continues Amelia.

Simona adds, "It was his way of keeping power over the two of us. He gave your father and I this apartment and made sure we were always indebted to him. On the surface he was a grieving widower being generous to his two daughters."

Gee sits listening in horror as Amelia continues recounting the events of the morning of their father's death.

Amelia had gone out in the morning as she always did, to buy what meagre supplies were available for the day's meals. With Teodoro's status came some advantages, there was always something extra given to her from the butcher or the baker.

"For your grieving father who works hard keeping us all safe," they would say.

Amelia wipes her eyes, then sighing, continues. She explains how she hid any extra food for Vladimir. Their father had no idea because if he did, she would not be here today.

This particular morning, he was still home when she returned from shopping. She walked in with the food in her arms and was startled by his presence. He was drinking the coffee she had prepared and asked if they had any headache tablets. She placed the food on the table and took a box of pain killers out of the cupboard handing them to him. His hand brushed hers as she attempted to walk towards the bedrooms. He grabbed her by the hair and holding her from behind whispered in her ear he had been hearing rumours his eldest daughter was seeing a man. She remained calm asking him to let her go, she had chores to do. He turned her around and slapped her face. She dropped to the floor and grabbed the crowbar from under the sink telling him she would kill him if he came near her. As she crept back towards the door, he came closer and she hit him hard at his ankles. He stumbled in agony. She stood up and grabbed the basement key. She ran frantically towards the lane. Her hand is on the basement door as she unlocks it, but Teodoro is behind her. She screamed, and Vladimir ran out of the basement rescuing her. Their father was dead on the cobbled street and her guttural wail had drawn a crowd.

Vladimir ran down the lane, yelling that he will contact her, he will come back for her. A spy, and now a murderer, it was no longer safe for either of them if he stayed. This was the last time she saw the man she loved.

Her neighbours, although in shock, gathered together to help. This was their esteemed mayor dead on the street. They were asking her questions about the man from the basement, "Who was he?"

"Why was he in her basement?" "Should they send someone to alert the police?"

"No," she screamed stopping them, "call an ambulance. There is still a heartbeat," she lied wanting Vladimir to be as far away as possible from the scene of the crime.

Their father was given a state funeral due to his services to the greater Naples community. The monster was laid to rest next to his wife. Amelia and Simona were now free from his abuse and could live without fear. All Amelia wanted now was to hear from Vladimir. During the month after their father's funeral both Amelia and Simona were subjected to many visits from authorities, both police and colleagues of their father, asking who the mystery man was? Their neighbours had all given their versions of what they saw, now these authorities wanted answers, especially the police. Both she and Simona considered telling the police how they had been tormented by their father, but they were too scared. Would they believe them?

It was at this time Amelia found out she was pregnant. She had not heard from Vladimir and desperately wanted to find out where he was. She wanted to be with him.

Simona starts talking before Amelia has a chance to explain, "This is when I convinced her to stay until you were born. We were at war, where was she going while pregnant?" She nods to her sister to keep going. Amelia continues.

The police threatened to send her to gaol as an accessory to murder. Her fingerprints were found on the crowbar. They asked whether she planned this murder with the mystery man? This was when she blurted out the whole sordid mess about how their father abused them, and how he killed their mother. The police, some of who were friends of Teodoro, were shocked. After this the sisters were never bothered by anyone again.

"We kept to ourselves after this last meeting with the police. I would go and check on Amelia and make sure she was eating enough and take her to the midwife when required. We trusted no one, and Amelia especially, was angry the police did not pursue our accusations against Teodoro," Simona interrupts again then glances over to Amelia who, exhausted, asks her to continue.

Clearing her throat, Simona says, "Amelia went into a deep depression. She wanted to find Vladimir and tell him about the pregnancy. It took all my energy to stop her. It was a reversal of our roles. This time the little sister had to rescue the older one.

The day her waters broke, the midwife came to deliver you. We both fell in love with you, but Amelia's depression meant she didn't have enough milk, so it was up to me to feed you. That winter Amelia became weak with fever and almost died. As you grew Amelia became more despondent about Vladimir. She needed to find him, and I couldn't stop her. By this time, I too was exhausted making sure you would survive. All my energy was reserved for you.

You were six months old when Amelia left for Rome to try and find details of where he might be. One of our father's colleagues was helping her in her search, he told us he felt obligated to help after Amelia told him about the abuse."

Simona pauses looking over to Amelia. A small nod given by her sister and she reluctantly continues telling the story. "One day she came home to tell me about her plans to go to the Soviet Union, she had found out where Vladimir lived. She would go to him and then they would organise to be reunited with you. The Partisan army and Vladimir's comrades were assisting in making this happen. However, with the war raging, if for some reason they didn't contact me within six months, I was to adopt you and never speak of this to anyone.

Gee gazes towards Amelia, "How did you end up in Australia?"

"Our father's colleague was not as honourable as he seemed. On our second trip to Rome he tried to abuse me just as our father did. This was my payment for him protecting me all the way to Rome." She continues, explaining how she once again defended herself and as he was writhing on the floor of the motel room, she grabbed her few belongings and ran. She stowed away on a ship having no idea where she was headed.

The three of them now remain quiet. The ticking of the clock pulsates through her head. Turning towards it, she sees it is four o'clock. Time seems to have stood still while the story was being recounted to her. She has even more questions now than she did before. "So, because Simona did not hear from you…"

"Yes, your father and I adopted you," interrupts Simona, "it was seven years before I heard from Amelia again. We had a disagreement that led us to not speaking for all these years. By then I had had the miscarriages and Amelia had married William. You have two Australian cousins."

Then Gee asks the question she wasn't even sure she wanted to know the answer to, "So, is Vladimir my father?"

Amelia answers. "As far as I know yes, he is, but …" Amelia starts to tear up, so Simona walks over to her hugging her by the shoulders.

"You can do this," she whispers, "we all need to know the whole truth for Gee's sake. Larissa and Alexey will deal with the fallout together and we all need to be here for Gee."

Amelia explains through wracking sobs that their father may also be Gee's father. The abuse had continued after her husband's death, and although Vladimir had wanted to do something about it, she had stopped him. She also explains how much she wants Vladimir to be Gee's father, in her heart this is what she has always felt.

Gee breaks down. Holding both hands to her face, she rocks back and forth in the chair as Simona and Amelia run to hug her before she falls.

Chapter Sixty-Six

Larissa and Alexey arrive. Gee, having composed herself, asks Amelia and Simona to spare the young ones the gory details.

She walks over to the lounge. Larissa walks past her, gently placing her hand on her shoulder, "You ok?"

Gee nods, "Go and listen. I need to rest for a bit." She flops into Simona's rocking chair hearing their chairs scrape as they sit. Then the muted voices of Amelia and Simona retelling their story again. She closes her eyes trying to come to terms with what she has heard.

"Alexey and I may be related? Are you kidding us here? This is a huge reason for you and Amelia to have spoken up sooner about this secret you have both kept for forty years. Do you realise how selfish both of you have been?" Larissa is standing, her voice booming throughout the apartment.

Gee forces herself up from the comfortable rocker and walks into the kitchen. Alexey has his hand on Larissa's arm squeezing gently.

He whispers, "Calm down, don't make this worse."

"Worse? What could be worse than what is happening here? They kept something from my mother that has changed her whole life. You and I may be related," she barks at him, her face hot with fury.

"We cannot change what has happened Larissa," says Gee as they turn to look at her, "I have the love of two amazing women to be thankful for being alive today. What they did was for me, to save me. This is a selfless act. Please remember this." She pauses. Taking a long breath, she says, "We have discussed doing DNA tests. Aunt Amelia and I want to find out the truth. Until then, I am going to get to know my aunt. All this hurt and anger, it's ruining us. Larissa, you sent your great aunt a letter. Had you not gone to Sydney all this may still be a secret."

"Me? You are accusing me of causing this mess? Gee have you gone mad?" yells Larissa still standing, her face stern.

Alexey, disagreeing with Gee defends Larissa, "Gee that's unfair. Larissa going to Australia to meet Amelia helped this situation. She was the instigator in healing the rift. She is not the cause of this current mess. Do DNA tests if you wish, however, my feelings for Larissa will not change. I am not giving up the woman I love after everything I've been through to be with her."

Gee sits next to Alexey and kisses him, "You are an admirable young man. My daughter is lucky to have you. Larissa, sit down and calm yourself. This is a lot to take in and I'm still processing the consequences. The secret is out and we will deal with it together. Until the results of the DNA tests are produced, we should rejoice in Amelia being alive and the fact we have a new family in Australia to get to know."

Simona has her hand on Amelia's arm, both have their heads down.

Larissa, sitting on Alexey's lap, has her arm around his neck. Their heads are touching. "I'm sorry for my outburst," says Larissa calmly, "Gee go ahead with the DNA test if you wish. If this is what you need to be able to deal with this, then fine. I feel the same as Alexey, no matter what the result is, it won't change my love for him."

Gee nods without answering. They will all have their own way of dealing with this. Amelia and Simona have suffered enough, she does not want them to suffer any longer. The important thing is the sisters are together again. Whatever the results of the DNA test, she will have to accept them. Her life has already been turned upside down, whatever is coming her way cannot be much worse. She hopes.

Chapter Sixty-Seven

Driving home from her AA group, she feels relieved to have released some of her anger within this safe environment. Without revealing the reason for her anger, she was able to discuss her feelings. If anything was going to drive her back to drinking, this latest family revelation was it. Her anger towards Simona and Amelia was unpalatable. If only they had opened up earlier, let their secret out and shared the burden. It is all so sickening and could drive her back to drinking.

But no, she would not do such a thing. It would add more fuel to an already unbearable situation.

The elevator opens with Alfio's smiling face greeting her, "Did you have a nice evening Larissa?"

"Yes, thank you Alfio. I hope you did too."

"It was sunny today, so I spent some time in my garden. But now I'm glad to be inside. Is it snowing again?"

"No, not yet. It feels like there will be some later tonight." This inane chit chat is therapeutic after the drama of tonight's meeting. As she steps out onto her floor, he wishes her good night.

"You enjoy your night too, Alfio," she says placing her key in the door. She amazes herself how light and flippant her voice is, her body tells a very different story. She is tense, her muscles tight with the anxiety of everything happening to her family.

She wakes with a pounding headache. Turning towards where Alexey should be, she remembers he had an early assignment this morning. Damn, I really need to talk to someone!

Picking up the receiver, she dials Clara's number. "I feel like a drink…"

Before she can finish her sentence, Clara begs her to wait, "I'm on my way. James will look after the children until I return. Don't do anything stupid."

Replacing the receiver, she is thankful to have a good friend like her. Clara picked up the anxiety in her voice. She must sound as bad as she feels. Clara knows her too well.

They are both standing in the kitchen. Clara is warming her hands on the teacup. "I had a shower, a good long cry and I'm fine. You didn't have to rush over, I just needed to talk." "With the morning chaos at my place, believe me, it's better I came over here. Besides, only Matthew is up, Elena is still asleep after waking up at five this morning. Look, this is an awful rough patch, you will survive. Was last night's meeting a tough one?"

"You were up at five? Now I feel terrible about calling you."

"It's all part of being a parent Larissa. James can handle things if she wakes. Now, about the meeting?"

Thinking about how much to reveal about her anger towards Simona and Amelia, she gulps down the guilt. She finds it easier to confide with the strangers at the group than with someone as close as Clara. "Umm, yes. One of the toughest since I started with this group. It's hard to explain, sometimes I hit a wall of exhaustion. And now with everything that is happening, I feel helpless. How do I cope and how will Gee cope? I need my strength to help her if she collapses in a heap. Although, I think she is coping with this whole debacle better than me."

"Larissa, you have discovered an awful secret. This happened a long time ago, it was out of your control. Don't try and control it now. Between the four of you, and Alexey, there will be enough strength and support to get through this. Sure, it is going to take time, but you are family, a family who look after each other."

She has always been close to Gee and Simona, but this may change everything. She is finding it difficult to accept that Amelia is her grandmother, how is Gee supposed to feel? She has found out Amelia is her real mother and now there is doubt about whether Vladimir is her father? Isn't it enough to deal with finding out Simona is not her mother? Everything she and Gee have known all their lives has changed. They have to wait twelve weeks for the DNA results. What a wait! For Alexey and herself it is a wait that will not impact on their relationship. For Gee, if the result shows Vladimir is not her father, it means… it means something so horrible she doesn't want to even contemplate such a thing.

The fury within her heats up again. One man's actions have caused so much heartache. She clears her throat, keeping tears at bay. Patience is what is needed and Larissa has little of it. She hopes Clara is right and once (or if) they survive all this they can be a family again. At the moment, the immense degree of anger and hurt seems insurmountable. She has to focus on channelling her anger to think positive. To help support her mother, and above all, take one day at a time.

Clara places the teacup in the sink and prepares to leave.

Larissa, embracing her says, "Thank you for coming, you are so good to me. What did I do to deserve a friend like you?"

"The pendulum swings both ways Larissa. I'm here for you just like you are for me when I need you. Now, I had better go, James has to go to work… and so do you," says Clara kissing her cheek.

Seeing her friend leave, she is glad to have had her company. Clara being here and listening to her did stop her wanting a drink. The demons are always there, ready to pounce when she lets down your guard.

Closing the door, she places her forehead on it for a moment. Taking a huge gulp of air she recites the words to 'The Serenity

Prayer', just as her group always recites at the meetings… "God grant me the wisdom to accept the things I cannot change; the Courage to change the things I can, and the Wisdom to know the difference."

She is strong, her family is strong. They will survive. She has to believe this.

<h1 style="text-align: center;">Chapter Sixty-Eight</h1>

As she is saying goodbye to Alexey, Gee arrives. They are going to spend the day together. After the day at Simona's when all the awful truth came out, Gee had wanted to be alone. Unfortunately, she was in danger of becoming a recluse like Simona. Larissa didn't want this to happen, and when Gee's friends called her asking why Gee was avoiding them, Larissa took action.

"Hello Gee."

"Off to process more photos Alexey?"

"Yes, on my way to the studio now. I'll be back soon."

Larissa welcomes her with kisses on both cheeks, "Alexey will be away for a few hours, we have the afternoon to ourselves. We'll do whatever you feel like – a walk maybe? You've rugged up against the cold."

"If you don't mind, I'd like to stay in. There is something I need to ask you. It's been on my mind since you returned from England," she says taking off her coat, gloves and hat.

"Sure," answers Larissa knowing what Gee is going to ask. Deciding it is time to divulge her struggles with alcohol, she says, "I've anticipated this moment."

"I know you haven't been yourself for the last couple of years. A mother knows when her child is suffering. Exactly what are you dealing with?"

"You have so much to deal with Gee and you're worried about me?"

"No matter what is happening in my life, yours and Philip's well-being is my priority. And until the results come through, what is the point of me worrying myself sick? Now, talk to me please. I don't want any more secrets."

Gee is worrying herself sick. This is the reason Larissa called her to come over. Gee is not the type to stay home on her own, to not socialise and be with her friends. Until the results come out, Larissa is keeping a close eye on her.

Making themselves comfortable on the lounge, Larissa begins explaining her struggles with alcohol. How things unravelled after Joseph's death, then losing Alexey and moving to Hebden Bridge. Keeping her demons under control became harder, especially once she moved from everyone she loved.

"Remember how angry I was with you? This anger stopped me from helping you even though I knew something was bothering you. That was my mistake. I was selfish."

"We both made mistakes. I was guilt-ridden for leaving you, I missed Alexey terribly. And Papa too. The alcohol drowned every-thing I felt. At my lowest, I loathed myself." When she thinks back, she doesn't remember functioning. Her memory is clogged with blackouts. Days, even weeks, lost in the fog of alcoholism. She had sought help just in time. Her recovery is ongoing and with help from her close friends, she is coping.

Now, recounting her struggles with her mother is cathartic, and she knows Gee will support her.

"It's wonderful you're opening up to me, I just wish you had done this earlier."

"Had I realised I had a problem, I would have spoken sooner. The descent is gradual, and it is not until you hit rock bottom you start to seek help. The struggle is not so crucial now I have been sober for this long, but I will always be aware of my limits. The group has taught me many strategies to help me survive every day."

Her heartbeat quickens. She has lifted a weight by talking to Gee. Together they can concentrate on dealing with whatever happens once the DNA test results come through. Her struggles will take a back step, especially if the test shows what neither of them wants to think, let alone talk about.

Hearing the door, they both turn to see Alexey.

He smiles, "How are my two best girls? All talked out?" Larissa's lips meet his as he bends towards her.

"This was a talk that was more than necessary. Maybe I should be angry with you Alexey?"

"Me? What did I do this time Gee?"

"Larissa needed me, and you didn't tell me. Neither of you did."

"There are times we have to work things out for ourselves. Besides, Larissa asked me to support her, which is what I did. She has told you now, so you can support her now. The important thing is she stays well, we can all help her with this gaol."

Tension seethes into the room. Alexey and Gee continue sparring with each other as Larissa escapes into the kitchen. Neither of them will admit they are wrong, the best thing she can do is let them argue it out. Loving them both equally, she will not be the pawn in their game.

Joining them again and placing some snacks on the coffee table, she finally intervenes. "Will two of you stop arguing please. What is the point of all this? Gee, you know now, and it is my decision if and when I tell anyone else. I would appreciate you not discussing this with anyone, especially not Simona or Amelia."

Alexey excuses himself, "I need a shower." Grabbing a handful of nuts, he stomps towards the bathroom.

Larissa decides she will deal with him later. "He'll calm down Gee, let him be. Now, how are you? All I have done since you arrived is talk about myself."

"Well you certainly had a lot to tell me," she says with a disgruntled tone.

Choosing not to comment, Larissa listens to her mother. She is coping as best she can without thinking too much about the results. Maintaining her stance that the sisters made their decision in her best interest keeps her positive. She is a believer in not judging unless you have walked the same path. Only Simona and Amelia know how hard things were during those awful years. She is angry Teodoro inflicted horrible pain on his own children, pain that has never been resolved.

They both agree maybe the time has come for all of them to heal. This horrible secret will be put to rest.

Chapter Sixty-Nine

They are sitting in Simona's apartment. Amelia is holding the test results in her hands. Both she and Simona are distraught with the findings of the DNA test.

Gee asks them to hand her the findings. When they hesitate, Gee exclaims, "Hand them over now!"

"Gee, we… this is the hardest thing to… please forgive us," Amelia apologises as she hands the papers to her.

Gee's hands shake. Reading the results, she is numb. Walking back and forth flicking the papers through her hands, anger surges through her. These past months have taken a toll on her mental health. Her identity has been tarnished, who the hell is she? What is she supposed to feel other than distraught?

Simona and Amelia are staring at her. Their faces full of pity.

Stammering she says, "The good news is Larissa and Alexey are not related. But now I'm more confused than ever. Your father Teodoro is also my father. How… how do I deal with this? Who am I now?"

Simona walks over to her enveloping her in a hug. Gee breaks down again just as she has done many times since their awful secret came out.

"You are still the same person Giovanna. This doesn't change who you are, you are still Larissa's mother. Don't allow the awful things that happened to Amelia and I ruin your future. We have to move on from this, we have to support each other."

Gee howls in anguish with her hands covering her eyes. When she removes them, she looks towards Amelia who is also distraught. There is so much hurt to deal with, and this test result has made the issue even harder for all of them. She is sure this is not what Amelia had wanted by reuniting with her sister.

She stares at the results again reading them out loud, "Restriction Fragment Length Polymorphism (RFLP) analysis of DNA shows Giovanna Mina has 50% DNA from Amelia Lillostra and 50% DNA from Teodoro Lillostra."

She was the one who insisted on having this DNA test. She wanted it for Larissa and Alexey's sake as well as her own. Amelia had argued even if they were related, it was distant. Gee wouldn't listen, she became obsessed with wanting to know who her father was. Both Larissa and Alexey said the result would not change their love for each other. They are married and will deal with whatever is thrown at them together.

"This is entirely my fault," says Amelia, "I was a selfish young person, self-centred and full of my own self-interest. It is the nature of young people to be like this. Nothing was going to stop me finding Vladimir. Now I know why I ran. Deep down I knew that Teodoro was Gee's father. Simona, I'm sorry for not trying hard enough to come back. I buried my shame away where I thought it could not hurt either of us. But look what I caused. I created where we are now."

"No. Stop right now!" Gee's scream reverberates around the room. Her anger seeps into the silence.

Amelia stares at her stunned. Simona is also alarmed.

"You're wrong." She is whispering now. "The circumstances you were both placed in motivated your actions. No one in this room is at fault. And it no longer matters whose fault it is anyway. The result won't change. So, we will move forward and heal. This is how I choose to cope."

Simona coaxes Gee to sit down and heads to the kitchen to organise food for the three of them. Looking back towards them she says, "We will organise professional help for the three of us. This whole situation is something we are going to need help with for some time, maybe years."

Gee is staring into space as Amelia follows Simona to the kitchen. They are both busying themselves doing normal, domestic duties. Normal everyday things like preparing food. Will I ever feel normal again? Is this my reality now?

She knows she needs help to deal with her overwhelming emotions. And it may take years just as Simona mentioned. The three of them have much to come to terms with. Larissa has too, but she has Alexey for support. They will be good for each other. Alexey has already dealt with his grandfather's past; he has suffered the loss of his parents, leaving his birth country, and is now dealing with his family name being destroyed. They will help each other to deal with their sordid family histories. Histories so intertwined there was no possible way of knowing how much hurt one man's actions could invoke.

This long emotional road is ahead of them, but with support they will overcome all the trauma. She is determined not to let her family suffer any more than they already have.

Chapter Seventy

He is asking the three of them how they have been since the last session with him. This is their fourth group session.

Gee stares around his rooms. A bland space with cheap timber furniture, a too soft lounge and two armchairs that have seen better days. He came highly recommended by the Ministry of Health as their top psychiatrist in family matters. A matter she wishes would go away. This decision made by two sisters so many years ago has impacted her whole being. Now she has to share all this with a stranger. Finding it hard enough to speak with the two women in her life who placed her in this situation, where are the words to tell this stranger what this is doing to her?

She sits opposite Simona and Amelia in this drab office, on this drab couch. Even his voice is drab.

"Giovanna, you may not feel it, but you are making progress. The fact you have come to every session means you want to heal. You want to move on from this. Now Simona and Amelia…"

She tunes out again. The three of them need time to work this out he is saying. Sure. But all Gee wants to do is escape this mess, she is sick of talking about something too horrible to think about.

Four sessions? He thinks she can come to terms with what has happened in such a short time. Her grandfather is also her father, she will never be used to this. They, Simona and Amelia, as well as the Ministry, had forced her to come to this group therapy. She had agreed on the proviso that if she did not want to talk, they could not force her. Mostly, she listens to their stories and wonders how they survived, how they dealt with the abuse. They were children! Wasn't it enough to be living through a war?

What sort of person does this? A person like Teodoro who had more power than he should have had. This power combined with problems with alcohol made him an abuser. He was an abusive monster who had no right being a parent.

Looking towards the clock, the session will end soon. It ticks over to five. Another ten minutes and they will leave. Larissa is picking them up, dropping Simona and Amelia back at her villa, then she is going out with her daughter. She is looking forward to spending time with Larissa, alone. She and Alexey had been relieved the results did not affect their marriage, although they had said all along, it did not matter. Alexey had apologised to Gee, he felt responsible for things coming to a head like this. Vladimir's dream had turned into this nightmare. She did not blame him. She did not blame anyone she loves. She blames Teodoro. She hopes he is rotting in hell.

"Thank you so much, Larissa."

"You're welcome." She smiles as the lady walks back to her spot at the bar.

"Your fame follows you everywhere, even in this little place."

They are sitting at a tiny pizzeria, tucked away in a lane not far from her home. The lady had recognised Larissa and asked for her autograph. "It doesn't bother me Gee, you know that. It only takes a minute to sign."

She has taken fame in her stride and has never let it go to her head. This is something Gee loves about Larissa, the fact that she keeps things real. People see this, which is why she has been successful in her career. Her natural ability comes through in her work.

"Everything ok with the session?" Larissa asks after their pizza is placed in front of them.

"Same as the others. Look, could we talk about something else? I'm tired of talking about all this rubbish. Talking about it isn't going to change anything."

"Gee, we're all worried. You are the one this has impacted the most. We're all trying to help. Please don't shut us out, least of all me."

Worry etches over her face. This is the last thing she wants, she needs everyone to get on with their lives, so she can move on too. She wants to be far away from this mess.

"But sure, let's talk about something else," continues Larissa, "I've been thinking, why don't you go and visit Philip and Rochelle? I'm sure Hannah would love to see you. A change of scene, what do you think?"

Picking up a slice of pizza, she thinks about it. The thought of seeing her daughter-in-law does not thrill her but seeing Philip and Hannah would be a real treat.

"I can help you with the arrangements. Come on Gee, it will do you good to get away. You haven't been anywhere since Papa passed away. You need to do something for yourself. A holiday would be great, don't you think?"

Gee smiles, "Well, we have been kind of busy with a certain wedding you know? Look, I'm not saying yes or no. I promise I will think about it." Larissa's suggestion has lifted her mood. Not a whole lot but enough to give her something else to think about other than who she is meant to be. Also, a holiday is a good excuse not to attend those awful sessions. Yes, a short overseas trip will do her good.

Chapter Seventy-One

Finding her car, she leaves Fiumicino airport. She had helped Gee organise her trip to Cape Town, and now she is driving home after seeing her off. Once she had convinced Philip it was a good idea, Gee agreed to taking a short break. Three months after she first mentioned it, Gee was on her way. Philip had agreed with her that a change of scenery would do Gee good when she had called him. He promised to take some time off work and spend some much-needed time with his mother.

"Please don't leave her with Rochelle for too long, she does not need more arguments in her life," she had pleaded with him. It was no secret Rochelle was not fond of Gee, and vice-versa.

"Don't worry sis, Hannah and I will keep Gee out of Rochelle's hair. I will take her sight-seeing, that will keep her busy and tire her out. She won't have any energy to fight with Rochelle."

She hoped he was right. Energy is something Gee has lacked. Her spark has gone, even the therapy hasn't helped. They were all struggling to come to terms with the decision Simona and Amelia made. The consequences of their secret had affected all of them in negative ways. But placing blame doesn't solve the issue. The struggles with their abusive father was not their fault. Making life changing decisions when you're young will impact your life in the future. The problem is, no one can predict whether what is going to happen will be good or bad. In this case, the decision led to something that was so much more than bad.

"Hi, obviously the plane left on time." Alexey is on the balcony.

She falls into his arms, "I hope I've done the right thing. She was nervous about flying." This was Gee's first overseas trip.

"She is a big girl and I'm sure Philip will look after her. Don't forget how excited she was about seeing Hannah again?"

Looking up into his eyes she hopes he is right. "Well, she's on her way now. Philip will have to deal with things. There isn't much I can do from here anyway." She remains in his arms, his warmth enveloping her. Looking forward to them being together for the whole weekend with no one around to disturb them, she closes her eyes and relaxes.

"Yes, Gee, I'll be there to pick you up. Remember, I was the one who booked your flights," Larissa is calming her mother down. She had called earlier that morning, and this was Larissa's first chance to return the call. Meetings had filled her day.

Gee is telling her how Hannah has grown, "Wait until you see the photos Philip has taken, you won't recognise her. She has grown taller since your wedding."

"I look forward to seeing them, I'll see you at the airport on Sunday. Put Philip on now, please?"

Her brother comes on the line. They have spoken several times since Gee arrived in Cape Town and he has assured her Gee was enjoying herself. Hannah has loved being spoiled by her grandmother, and Gee, although not herself at first, settled in and handled things well. "Stop worrying about her Larissa. You can't change what has happened, everyone has to deal with this in their own way."

"I know, but you're all the way over there. Amelia is on the other side of the world. I'm the one who is dealing with Gee and Simona."

"Sure sis, but don't forget you have Alexey. He is a burly Soviet who can handle anything the two of them throw at both of you."

In spite of herself she laughs. Philip has always had a way of looking at life from a different, if somewhat overly positive, perspective.

Epilogue

1987 - KIAMA

AMELIA

She surveys the scene. Almost everyone she loves is with her. Her two lives have finally come together. This is happiness. Something she thought she wasn't going to feel again.

Larissa and Alexey arrived during the week with their daughter, Sirenia; Gee and Simona arrived yesterday, Jacqueline and Todd are on their way. This family reunion is something she thought would never have been possible.

Philip and Rochelle are visiting later in the year. Unfortunately, they were not able to arrange their holidays at this time. This is their excuse. The more likely reason is the issues between Gee and Rochelle are keeping them away, but there is nothing she can do about this now. Most of the family is together, this is the important thing she will focus on. When they do visit they will enjoy another celebration, with many more to come. This is her hope for a better future for all of them.

Her current life is very different to how she would ever have imagined. Out of trauma has come togetherness and love. The healing process required for such a family reunion has taken three years. This healing is ongoing. For all of them.

After the harrowing results of the DNA test; she, Simona and Gee needed an enormous amount of support to be able to come to terms with the final result. She had convinced herself Vladimir was Gee's father. This was the reason she went looking for him. She wanted the three of them to be a family. This was her dream, a dream so skewed in the love of a man it changed her life forever. Along with the lives of her daughter and sister. Will the shame and guilt ever leave her? For a long time, she totally blocked out the thought Teodoro was Gee's father. She blocked it out for years. In fact, with William coming into her life soon after arriving in Australia, that horrible thought all but disappeared. She had a new life and a new family. She was too busy to think about the past. It was not until she and Simona connected again that she started doubting herself, doubting Vladimir was Gee's father. She tried to keep this horrible niggle down, but in the end the secret came out.

Both she and Simona were placed in a situation by their father's abuse where their trust in men was minimal. He frightened them into submission. This was the power he had over them. Amelia craved the gentle love Vladimir had shown her, she needed it, and this clouded her judgement.

When she left Italy, the war was only just gaining traction. Too many families were fractured, split apart or obliterated altogether. William was her saviour in Freemantle. This is where the ship carrying 'Displaced Persons' docked. He, along with a couple who befriended her on the ship, kept her safe. As a senior officer for the Australian Border Force, William risked everything to save her. He said he fell instantly in love, "with this gorgeous continental woman with full dark locks and huge brown eyes". She will be forever grateful to him and her friends, Jack and Mary Dorsett. They restored her faith in the human race.

As fate would have it, Jack and Mary live in Kiama, which was one of the reasons she and William decided to settle in this quaint, beachside suburb.

There are many awful memories from her past, but Gee is the victim in all this. Amelia has to keep strong for her sake.

William walks into the kitchen carrying chairs, "Do you want these in the dining room? Or are we going to eat on the balcony?"

Admiring her husband, his once red locks are now grey and sparse. His paunch arrives before him now, but it was his masculinity that caught her eye back in Freemantle. He was gallant in every way, always making sure she felt safe, even though his stature is the same as hers. The uniform he wore was enough to make people take notice, everyone listened to a man in uniform during the 1940s.

"Amelia, are you listening? Where am I putting these chairs?"

"Oh yes, balcony thanks. Let's make the most of these last days of summer." She smiles as he walks past her. He has been supportive through all of this. He listened, accepted and has embraced the decisions she and Simona have made to ensure Gee's happiness. The three of them will always need to watch out for each other. With the help of everyone here, they will survive.

Jacqueline and Todd walk into their family home with their partners. Amelia introduces them to their Italian family. Once all the introductions have been made, William asks everyone to grab some plates and begin eating. This is a day for celebration he tells them, "Come on, mangia, mangia."

Everyone laughs at his attempt at speaking Italian asking them to eat. Amelia kisses him on the cheek. He smiles, takes her hand and together they walk over to the banquet they have prepared.

LARISSA and GEE

Sirenia pulls at Larissa's dress as she is filling a plate for her. "Mamma look." She is pointing towards the waves crashing and backwashing over the golden sand. "Can we go for a swim? Please Mamma, can we go?"

Gee, who is standing next to Larissa answers her granddaughter before Larissa can speak. "How about we all have something to eat first. Look at this wonderful food Aunt Amelia and Uncle William have prepared for us? You be a good girl and eat your lunch, then we can go down to the beach."

Sirenia huffs, "Oh ok, but let's hurry. And can we collect shells?"

Both Gee and Larissa smile and nod, "Sure," they say in unison.

Sirenia is telling her dad about going to the beach. "You come too Papa. Mamma and Nonna Gee are coming with me, please come?"

Alexey looks at Larissa who smiles saying, "Of course he'll come with us Sirenia. He will even help with finding shells."

"Well then, let's eat up. And Sirenia, how about we have a race down to the beach?"

"Yes, Papa and I'll beat you like I always do. Come on, hurry and eat. I'm finished," she says showing Alexey her empty plate.

Alexey laughs taking Larissa's hand in his. He kisses her hand saying, "She is bossy just like her mamma."

"Come on Papa, I'm ready and waiting. It's time for the race."

Larissa looks at Alexey, "You were the one who suggested a race. Off you go with your bossy daughter, we'll be right behind you."

With that Alexey grabs Sirenia's hand, "Let's go, we're going to beat everyone."

"I'm going to be first," yells Sirena letting go of her father's hand and running ahead.

"You had better move Alexey, she'll be way ahead of you," says Larissa laughing.

"See you down there," Alexey says as he runs to catch their daughter.

"She certainly keeps you two on your toes," says Gee, "and she has her papa right where she wants him – at her beck and call. Now, we had better get a move on, those shells won't be found by themselves."

"I'm right behind you Gee. As for Alexey, he can't get enough of playing with Sirenia. But yes, she is a four-year-old with heaps of energy."

AMELIA and SIMONA

With the afternoon breeze coming from the beach behind them, and their family playing on the shore, Amelia and Simona leave them to it. They amble back to the house hand in hand. Quiet lives comfortably between them. Amelia notices people frowning at them. Two women holding hands in public. This is just not done. Do I care? Not in the least. This is the new me who does not give a hoot what others think.

"You live in paradise Amelia, but the people here are small minded. Look at those stares! This is normal behaviour back home. We all go on walks hand in hand." Simona playfully swings their arms backwards and forwards, "Anyway, who cares? We are together."

"Exactly, Simona. I was thinking the same thing. What others think of us no longer matters." She is pleased with her new attitude of not being afraid and living her truth. She has suffered enough, from now on she will lead her life with a more leisurely and carefree approach. The seriousness of what has happened in her past will take a backward step.

They stroll along the path both quiet again until Simona stops short, turning an austere face towards Amelia, "Deep down you knew, didn't you? I never wanted to think the worst, but it was there. I always wondered."

"I did know Simona. I always knew but it was too horrific to bear at the time. Running away to find Vladimir was my way of coping. I buried the thought of Teodoro being Gee's father as deep as I could. This is not an excuse because I have paid for my decision ever since. We both have."

"We can't change anything that happened back then now. Our decision placed us where we are today. Look at what we have: a beautiful granddaughter and two families who support and love us despite everything. And distance will no longer keep us apart."

A comfortable silence descends between them again as they reach the hill that meanders towards Amelia's home. Her little sister is right, they have come through the worst of times and now have their own loving families to cherish. This is something their father ruined by his actions, he had no idea how to treat his family and he paid for this. Simona and Amelia have risen above his actions.

She has forgiven him. Forgiveness has not been easy, but she had to forgive Teodoro. If she didn't, she would have ended up as disturbed and bitter as he had been.

Each member of her family has their own way of coping with the actions of this one man, forgiveness is her way. The decision they made has caused hurt, anxiety and at times, hate between her and Simona but now the secret is out, they no longer have to hide.

- The End -

Acknowledgments

Writing a novel is a collaboration. Sure, the writer has the idea, but without the assistance of others, professional and otherwise, the story remains only an idea.

As a child of Italian migrants, I was not particularly fond of school. My parents would not hear of this. They taught me that education is the backbone of success. Taking this advice onboard has given me the tools to arrive where I am today, a published author. I am grateful for parents who encouraged a love of learning no matter your age.

To my colleague and friend, Mark Drolc, for my cover design and sticking by me all these years. You kept up the encouragement when I became overwhelmed and discouraged. Thanks for reading, commenting and giving feedback (it wasn't always positive but always constructive).

To both my editors, whose editing skills and knowledge of publishing steered my writing in the right direction. Thank you for taking on a novice novel writer when I first started reworking this story and believing in my ability.

To my amazing friends who support me every day. Your encouragement has never wavered. You can now read this story you have heard me talk about all these years.

To my writing group, *Write on Water*, thanks for your knowledge and camaraderie. Our meetings are always full of facts, fun and food. We encourage each other and together we can achieve anything in this writing and publishing gig.

To Tony, my patient husband and our two children, Sebastian and Alessia: this is the book I kept hidden for years and it's now a reality. Your love, support and optimism kept me going; especially when doors were slammed in my face, the rejections kept coming, and when writer's block took over. Without the three of you keeping me on track, this book would never have been completed. I promise the next books will be easier on all of us.

Happy reading,
    Maria P Frino

About the Author

Maria has made a career of using words to communicate. Working at a TV station, her first paid job nurtured Maria's love of words. A move to Sydney to study Communications gave her the opportunity to work with advertising & public relations agencies, corporate companies and newspapers. She has written PR, ads and newsletters for products from food to jewellery, fashion and interiors as well as garden and building products. For both traditional print media and digital. When she is not writing website content or as a Senior Reviewer for the online site, Weekend Notes, she works on her short stories and novels.

Her first published story, *The Studio* and is a crime short story. *Xenure Station: A Billion Light Years* is Maria's second short story. Both are available on Amazon Kindle.

The Decision They Made and *Xenure Station: A Billion Light Years* are now available in print on Amazon Kindle and selected bookstores.

9 780648 894636